Everything
I Promised
You

ALSO BY KATY UPPERMAN

The Impossibility of Us
How the Light Gets In
Kissing Max Holden

Everything I Promised You

KATY UPPERMAN

sourcebooks
fire

Copyright © 2025 by Katy Upperman
Cover and internal design © 2025 by Sourcebooks
Cover design by Kerri Resnick
Cover images © Ruth Black/Stocksy, Yurlick/Shutterstock.com
Internal design by Tara Jaggers/Sourcebooks

Published by Sourcebooks Fire, an imprint of Sourcebooks
P.O. Box 4410, Naperville, Illinois 60567-4410
(630) 961-3900
sourcebooks.com

Congress Cataloging-in-Publication Data is on file with the Library of Congress.

Printed and bound in the United States of America.
KP 10 9 8 7 6 5 4 3 2 1

For Mom und Dad,
the inspiration behind my books' very best fictional parents.

GOOD FORTUNE

Prologue

When my mom was seventeen, she caved to a dare and paid a traveling carnival's clairvoyant twenty dollars to reveal her fate.

Leaving her friends on a dusty footpath beneath a string of glowing bulbs, Mom was led into a candlelit tent. Tapestries embroidered with constellations adorned the walls. The table in the center of the space was blanketed in an ebony cloth. Scattered atop were crystals, celestial charts, seashells, and bones. Cinnamon incense burned in a wooden tray. As Mom got settled, the clairvoyant, who was a cliché in chiffon scarves and silver jewelry, began to sort the items, combining shells and crystals and bones into cryptic groups. She regarded the celestial charts before moving on to Mom's palms.

Once, I asked her if she'd felt uncomfortable.

"The opposite," she told me. "I went into that tent a skeptic, but after I sat down… The fortune teller was a stranger, and she was certainly strange, but I was at peace."

Speaking quietly, in an accent crisper than Mom's Mississippi drawl, the clairvoyant shared what she'd perceived from the seashells, the stars, the crystals, and the palmistry.

"For you," she said, "education is essential. Continue to learn well."

Mom, an insatiable reader with a memory just short of photographic, nodded.

"You seek deep friendships; they're your life's blood," the clairvoyant went on. "Family, too, is important. Your mother acts as your scaffold. You will remain close, though not always physically."

Then she fell into a trancelike quiet, eyes darkening.

Mom leaned forward, confused but intrigued.

The clairvoyant delivered a blow: "Your father will pass before you leave his home."

Mom planned to leave her parents' home the following year; Ole Miss waited. Shaken, she fell back in her seat. She wanted to raise questions, to protest: her daddy was robust, a live oak of a man.

Why was she in a medium's tent when there was a whole carnival just outside? She ought to be with her friends. She could get up and go—she *should* get up and go.

The clairvoyant's somber expression left her heavy in her seat.

She blinked back tears and braced for more.

"You'll meet your soulmate after your father's passing," the clairvoyant said. "In her, you'll mine the strength to carry on. Romantic love will find you soon after. Your first impression will be less than favorable, but be open to possibility—open to him." Reaching across the cluttered table, she rested her fingers against Mom's wrist, where her pulse surged. Tingles scattered through her, sparks and shivers alighting her skin. "A nurturer's heart beats within you. You were born to love."

This is the part where Mom always gets misty eyed.

Next, the clairvoyant spoke of me.

"You will bear one child, a flaxen-haired girl with eyes like her father's, blue as the ocean's depths. She will be your greatest joy, and she will walk a path similar to the one you blaze. The woman I spoke of—your soul's mirror—will mother your daughter's fated."

The reading ended, and Mom left the tent.

Outside, the carnival persisted. Bells rang and lights flashed neon. The aromas of hot dogs and funnel cake mingled in the hazy air. She tracked down her friends, who begged her to tell them about her future.

She refused.

She held it close…

…awed as it unfurled before her.

My mom is an educator with a tightly knit circle of friends. She and Grandma talk every day. Prostate cancer took her daddy two weeks after she graduated high school. She met Bernadette—Bernie—on her first day at Ole Miss. They shared a dorm room, and to this day swear that one cannot exist without the other. At

3

a fraternity party a month later, an azure-eyed pledge dropped a watermelon Jolly Rancher into Mom's Zima. They danced two songs before he declared her the love of his life, then puked up Trash Can Punch all over her Steve Maddens.

She forgave him.

They were college sweethearts, and she pinned his rank when the Army commissioned him. A few weeks later, beneath a fragrant magnolia tree, they married. At the reception, to Grandma's chagrin, they ladled Trash Can Punch into Solo cups. They moved, weathered a deployment, and moved again. Bernie married Dad's ROTC battle buddy, Connor Byrne. Not long after, they had a baby boy who weighed a whopping eleven pounds. Connor fainted, slumping into a heap on the delivery room floor. Mom cut the umbilical cord.

Beckett Byrne.

Hair: rusty red.

Eyes: army green.

Heart: promised to me.

Eighteen months later, I was born, as slight as Beck was strapping, with wispy flaxen hair and eyes blue like the sea.

Holding me in her arms that very first time, Mom didn't cry—but not because she wasn't moved, and not because she wasn't happy.

"Because, my sweet Lia," she says, laying her hand against my cheek as she finishes the story she's told me countless times. "I've known you since I was seventeen."

4

ARMY BRATS

Seventeen Years Old, Virginia

When I was in eighth grade, my dad deployed to Afghanistan for a year. On one of the many nights I couldn't sleep, I opened my ever-present journal and did some calculating: Of my thirteen years, Dad had been away for six. For nearly half my life, he'd had boots on the ground in various foreign countries.

Every time he deploys, I cry rivers. Mom does too. But before long, we settle into a routine. We carry on. We survive.

God willing, Dad will too.

Six months, eight months, twelve months later, he redeploys. Mom and I meet him with posters that boast my bubbly handwriting in red and blue: *Welcome home, Daddy!* He hugs me, smelling of elsewhere, and murmurs, "I missed you, Millie."

Onlookers blot tears, thanking him for his service. He smiles, humble. He's third-generation military. It's not as simple as service; patriotism pumps through his veins.

Tradition dictates that, post-deployment, we swing by Burger King for Double Whoppers and sodas. Then we head home, to whichever house we're renting, in whichever Army-post-adjacent town we're living. Dad drags his dusty duffels into the garage. After a hot shower and a couple IPAs, he passes out in the recliner, jet-lagged and in desperate need of uninterrupted sleep.

I've always been close with my parents. That's the way of most Army brats, I think. We're transient, a family of caribou traversing the land as Dad's orders dictate, our only constants being each other. I've made friends along the way, but when I think of them, I think of fun, blowing off steam, filling time. I don't think *lifelong*.

With the exception of Beck.

Beck was an Army brat too. He knew what it was like to move every few years, to pack up a room and wave goodbye to buddies. He knew how it felt to be the new kid. His dad deployed as often as mine. He'd pulled construction paper links from plenty of countdown chains. He leaned on Bernie in all the ways I've leaned on Mom.

Beck understood.

I grew up vacationing with the Byrnes. FaceTiming Bernie to dish about the angsty TV series we streamed in tandem. I attended Connor's promotion ceremonies, just as I attend my dad's. When I was three-four-five (Beck was five-six-seven), our

6

dads were assigned to the same unit at Fort Bragg. We lived in the same development. When I was eight-nine-ten (Beck was ten-eleven-twelve), it happened again. Fort Lewis. We lived on the same street. When I was fourteen (Beck had just turned sixteen), Dad was given a stint at the Pentagon. Connor was assigned to Fort Belvoir, also in Northern Virginia.

Together again.

Bernie and Mom were ecstatic.

Beck and I fell in love.

PERMANENT CHANGE OF STATION

Seventeen Years Old, En Route to Tennessee

A senior-year move is many an Army brat's worst nightmare.

But not mine.

Leaving Virginia.

Leaving Connor, Bernie, and the twins.

Leaving Rosebell High School.

Our July departure date can't come fast enough.

Escape, flee, withdraw.

These are the words that loop through my head as I tuck my life into boxes. As we embark on our trip to Tennessee. As I watch summer raindrops race across our Explorer's windows. As I fill Moleskine pages with meaningless lists and verbose musings and swirling doodles. As I pet Major, our sixty-pound Pointer pup, who's stretched out on the backseat beside me. As I consume the gas station snacks my parents push into my hands because I'm "not eating enough" and "we're worried, Lia."

It's been one hundred ninety-nine days.

Four thousand seven hundred eighty hours spent navigating a world without Beck.

As Mom and Dad put it: I'm not myself.

How infinitely fucking stupid to suppose I would be.

On the road, my parents fill silences with falsely cheerful chatter. They order peanut butter milkshakes from fast-food drive-throughs. They stretch what should be a ten-hour drive into a three-day trip because "a vacation might make Lia feel better."

Just east of Knoxville, Mom turns to look at me, eyes doleful. "Oh, lovey. Daddy and I miss him too."

I hate when she equates her sadness to mine.

"It's true, Millie," Dad puts in, his gaze trained on the endless highway. While everyone else in my life shortens my given name, Amelia, to Lia, he likes Millie. "Mom and I loved that kid like our own. It's bullshit what happened."

What happened.

No one ever says it like it is: Beck died.

Dad's still talking. "I wish there was something we could do to help you through this. Make it easier for you somehow."

"For Bernie and Connor and the twins too," Mom says.

There's no fixing death, for it is permanent and perpetual.

Those are the words the reverend used at Beck's funeral. He was speaking of the community's love for Beck, but staring at

9

my boyfriend's mahogany casket, surrounded by a veritable field of flowers, with my teary-eyed parents beside me, Bernie and Connor weeping in the pew in front of us, each holding one of the twins, preschoolers who desperately wanted their brother back, it was hard to think about love.

Loss is permanent and perpetual.

While Mom and Dad and Bernie and Connor cried showers, I'd used up my tears. That past summer, they were a drizzle while I helped Beck pack for college. They became a downpour when he left for Charlottesville—for Commonwealth of Virginia University, his dream school and mine—to begin training with the track and field team. I made a rainy season of that autumn. In November, my tears became sleet, icy and dangerous.

And then, that word again: permanent.

A permanent change of station—military speak for "pack your shit and hit the road."

We're off to Fort Campbell, where Dad will serve as Commander of the 3rd Brigade Combat Team.

A fresh start. That's what he proclaims, swinging open the door to our just-acquired rental in River Hollow, Tennessee.

A new beginning. That's what Mom preaches, stacking dishes on shelves she covered with fresh liner.

I don't want either, I tell Beck, retreating to my room-for-now, where boxes stand like mountains in a crowded range.

Dad's already been in here. He hung my bulletin board over my desk, a collage of my life before: ticket stubs, CVU stickers, photos of friends from Virginia and before that, Colorado

Springs. Photos of Beck. Seeing him in full color, smiling, *alive*, is like opening a scabbed-over wound, again and again and again.

I shut my bedroom door quietly, with restraint.

That's my grief these days: quiet, restrained.

I, too, am closed off.

Permanently and perpetually, it seems.

MEANT TO BE

Five Years Old, North Carolina

One of my earliest memories is set against the backdrop of a popular park in Spring Lake, North Carolina. I was getting ready to start kindergarten, which means Beck was about to turn seven. Dad and Connor, captains back then, were deployed to Iraq, and Mom and Bernie were constantly looking to fill our days. The park, with its wading pool and climbing toys and green spaces, kept Beck and me busy. We arrived early, before the sun got too hot, and staked out a spot from where Mom and Bernie could keep an eye on us while working on their tans.

Beck and I'd been playing in the water, setting up battles waged between his aquatic GI Joes and my rainbow-coiffed mermaid Barbies, when a pair of boys who'd been in his class at school showed up.

He left a wake in his haste to ditch me.

Dolls in hand, I climbed out of the pool and flopped down on a towel beside Mom and Bernie. Mom reapplied my sunscreen. Bernie handed over bunches of grapes, which I ate until I was practically bursting with pent-up indignation. I blurted out that Beck was mean, I hated him, and I'd *never* play with him again.

Bernie said, "Sometimes he's a real stinker. You do you, girlie."

"I think Beck will be sad, though," Mom reasoned, "if you never play together again."

"He's not sad right now," I said, glaring toward the far side of the pool, where he was playing Keep Away with his friends.

"Boys can be rotten sometimes," Bernie said.

"I know!" I crowed, happy to be understood. "Beck always ignores me when his friends come around."

"But *you're* his friend," she pointed out. "His oldest friend. His most special friend."

"You're more than friends, lovey," Mom said. "You're soulmates."

I frowned, circling my arms around my knobby knees. "What does that mean?"

She reached over to tuck a tendril of hair back into my ponytail. "There's a bond between you and Beck unlike any other. A bond that'll last forever."

I squinted up at her. "The same way you and Daddy will be together forever?"

"Daddy and I are married. Who knows—maybe you and Beck will marry one day." I made a show of retching, and Mom paused to laugh with Bernie. "Or maybe you'll stay friends, but

13

best friends, like Bernie and me. No matter what, you're a part of each other's lives. You always will be."

"But how do you know?"

"Your mama's been informed of the future," Bernie said, giving Mom's hand an affectionate squeeze. "She knew we'd meet and become forever friends. She knew she'd fall in love with your daddy. She knew I'd have a son, and she'd have a daughter. She knows that you and Beck are meant to be. Like...Mickey and Minnie."

"Or Han and Chewbacca," Mom put in, and I giggled.

"Socks and shoes," Bernie said.

"Campfire and s'mores," Mom countered.

"Peanut butter and jelly," I said, grinning.

Bernie slapped me a high five and Mom kissed my cheek, and I felt okay enough to look over at Beck. I watched him, the monkey in the middle, nick the ball from the air, while I thought of other celebrated pairs: bees and honey; Barbie and Ken; cookies and milk; sidewalks and chalk.

As he was switching spots with one of the other boys, Beck glanced toward where I sat on the lawn. Our eyes caught. "Lia!" he called. "Come play!"

I looked to Mom and Bernie.

"Only if you want to," Bernie reminded me.

"Though it looks like you could show 'em how it's done," Mom said.

I pretended to consider for as long as it took to count to five, then hopped up and ran to join the boys, leaving my towel rumpled on the grass.

14

INHOSPITABLE

Seventeen Years Old, Tennessee

Millie," Dad says, removing his earbuds to pause one of the many history podcasts he streams on his phone. "Let's take Major on a walk."

It's the evening before the first day of my senior year. We finished dinner an hour ago, and we're all in the living room. A trio of *Jeopardy* contestants duke it out on TV. I'm penning my schedule, which was emailed this morning by my new guidance counselor, into my current journal, alongside sketches of rulers and apples and fountain pens. Mom absentmindedly murmurs *Jeopardy* answers—questions, I guess—while ironing. She's vacillating over what she'll wear tomorrow for her first day of teaching at East River Elementary. Like a bunch of little kids are going to give a rip about whether she pairs her chambray blazer with charcoal slacks or a black skirt.

"I'll get the leash," I say, leaving my journal on the coffee table.

Outside, it's humid and buggy. The August air smells of barbecue and honeysuckle. Dad's sporting a Rakkasans T-shirt and running shorts with dorky flip-flops, and I'm wearing a knit cardigan over a tank, with denim cutoffs and Converse that've seen better days.

We set off down the block. Dad holds Major's leash, quiet until we get to our development's community area: a play structure, a grove of picnic tables, a few charcoal grills, and a basketball court set along the southern end of a retention pond.

Nudging me with an elbow, he says, "Ready for tomorrow?"

"If I tell you I'm not, will you let me ditch?"

He gives me a side-eye smile. "You wish."

"Then I'm ready as I'll ever be."

He hooks an arm over my shoulders like he used to, back when things were better. "You should spend some time with Mom later. Maybe take a crack at the new puzzle."

For as long as I can remember, no matter where we're living, we've had a puzzle-in-progress spread across the trestle table in our formal dining room. Florals, landscapes, cats sporting hats, hamburgers with all the fixings, Sleeping Beauty's Disneyland castle, all jigsawed into a thousand pieces. The three of us work one when there's a family matter to talk over, or independently when the mood strikes, until it's complete. Then we start all over again, with a new thousand-piece puzzle.

How pointless. How Sisyphean.

I sigh and tell Dad, "I'm tired. Tomorrow's going to be a lot."

"You could give her an hour."

16

"What if I don't want to?"

He tugs Major to a stop. The sun is on its way to setting, but there's enough light to show me the full scope of his sorrow-filled face. "What's going on between you two?"

I think, *You wouldn't understand.*

I say, "Nothing."

He shakes his head. "It's brought me a lot of peace over the years, knowing you and Mom have each other, especially when I'm away. Lately, though, the two of you hardly speak. I can't remember the last time you gave her a hug."

I can't either.

"I'm growing up," I say, flippant enough that his brows pull together. "I don't need my mom for every little thing anymore."

"Maybe not, but you should work to maintain relationships with the important people in your life. You haven't been doing the best job of that lately."

"Yeah, well, I've been out of sorts," I say, crossing my arms, as if my father, an Army officer of more than two decades, won't recognize my defensive posture.

A couple months after Beck was laid to rest, Dad went on a mysterious errand.

"He has a meeting in Virginia Beach," Mom told me when I'd come downstairs and asked where he was. She was sitting on a stool at the kitchen counter, writing lesson plans for the long-term substitute who'd taken over her class for what remained of the school year. "He'll be home for dinner."

17

Back then, I'd wondered why she hadn't gone to Virginia Beach with him.

Now I know she stayed home because she didn't trust me to be alone. I was depressed, and not in the romanticized way of movies and novels. I survived as if under a wool blanket: my senses muffled, thoughts muddled, emotions intense and erratic. I was too anxious to sit still, too agitated to sleep, angry as often as I was sad, and fixated, suddenly, on my own mortality. I couldn't stop thinking about how healthy Beck had been. How vivacious. If his heart could fail, who was to say mine wouldn't malfunction while attempting to repair its horrific break?

"Have some tea with me?" Mom had asked, pushing her lesson plans aside.

I shook my head and ended up dizzy, swaying on my feet.

Thick with concern, she said, "What did you eat for breakfast?"

I couldn't remember eating, drinking water, or exercising. I couldn't remember the last time I'd slept for longer than a couple hours or felt the sun on my skin. It'd been weeks since I'd opened my journal, or put on makeup, or spoken to Macy, my closest friend in Rosebell. Even longer since I'd texted Andi and Anika, the friends I'd made in Colorado Springs. My parents insisted I attend sessions with one of the best grief counselors in Northern Virginia, and they were as supportive as they could be while navigating their own sorrow, but my boyfriend was dead, and I was a ghost.

"Cereal," I lied.

Mom got up to rummage in the pantry. "I'll make soup."

"I don't want soup."

"A smoothie, then," she said, and the blender came out. I watched, detached, as she sliced a banana and then retrieved coconut milk from the fridge. She opened the freezer next, reaching for the bag of frozen strawberries that sat next to six pints of artisan ice cream. That's when she inhaled sharply, slamming the freezer door shut, strawberries forgotten.

Slowly, she turned to face me, to discern whether I'd seen the offending ice cream, to assess whether I'd be okay.

I had, and I wasn't.

The day that ice cream arrived, Beck—who'd sent it—ceased to exist.

I crumpled to the floor.

Mom rushed to my side. She pulled me into her arms, and I let her, even though we hadn't touched since the obligatory hug we shared at Beck's wake.

I blame her.

Not for his death—

—no, not that.

I blame her for the shock, for the upheaval, for the gut-wrenching agony.

All my life, my mom has spun stories about soulmates, about Beck and me and our happily ever after. I never questioned my destiny. Never doubted my fate. Beck was mine and I was his, and *how dare she* let me believe forever would be ours?

On the kitchen floor, I wept.

When at last I composed myself, Mom made brownies

19

instead of a smoothie. We ate them out of the pan. They were rich and slightly underbaked, exactly the way I like. She matched me brownie for brownie, and I wondered if someday I might stop holding her decades-old fortune against her.

That night, Dad came home with a twelve-week-old Pointer puppy, who had a stub of a tail, a wet nose, and too-big paws.

I named him Major.

He's been a glimmer of light through a run of very dark months.

Now, Dad reaches down to scratch the top of his head. Major flicks his tail back and forth. He's so sweet, so loving. I've a feeling Dad thinks the opposite of me lately. His frown lines are pronounced. Silver dapples the hair at his temples—not quite camouflaged by sandy blond. His forehead is lined with concern. As if he doesn't have enough going on with work, with Mom, and with Connor and Bernie, I'm causing him all sorts of worry.

"You need people, Millie," he says. "You need community. Beck's life is over and that's terrible—just *terrible*—but you've got to go on. He'd want that. You know he would."

I blink away the threat of tears.

Dad gives Major's leash a tug, then reaches for my hand and urges me forward. We're moving again, a slow march down the darkening sidewalk.

My dad has two temperaments: peacetime and wartime. At home, with Mom and me, he's almost always in peacetime. Relaxed, receptive, funny. During disagreements or times of stress, *tonight*, he adopts his wartime persona. Serious. Contemplative. Take no shit.

20

"Tomorrow at school," he says as we near home, "I want you to try."

"I always try."

That's the truth. I've been an Honor Roll student since middle school. Last semester, I flung my whole self into studying and earned my first 4.0.

"I mean socially," he says. "Smile. Converse. Make a friend."

"But that feels—"

Like starting over is what I almost say, but starting over is what Dad wants. He'd like me to emerge from the cocoon I've been hiding in since November, to test my wings in this new, inhospitable world.

He doesn't understand that starting over is the same as leaving Beck behind.

"Feels like what?" he asks.

"Just...really hard."

"Hard isn't impossible," he says, giving my shoulder an affectionate jostle. "You're better for conquering the tough stuff."

Our house comes into view. Mom's there, sitting in one of two rocking chairs on the front porch, sipping from a stemless wineglass. She waves when she sees us.

Dad grins and waves back.

Major wags his docked tail.

Look at my family, I tell Beck. *Surviving. Thriving, even.*

Gaze trained on the sidewalk, I tell Dad, "I'll try. Tomorrow, I'll try to make a friend."

21

Grief

<u>Shock:</u> A balloon, stuck with a pin. Shallow
 breath, fuzzy vision. Heart-halting.

<u>Denial:</u> Irrational, immature.
 Fists clenched. Jaw set.

<u>Pain:</u> A tinny flavor. Split skin, cracked
 ribs. Gasping, clenching, begging.

<u>Guilt:</u> A last petal, plucked.
 Retrospect and regret.

<u>Anger:</u> Dynamite, lit. Sizzling,
 scorching, searing.

<u>Bargaining:</u> This for that. Smells
 bitter. Tastes spoiled.

<u>Depression:</u> Rain-dark clouds, oily hair, empty
 belly, forlorn nights. I n f i n i t e.

<u>Reconstruction:</u> A clean bandage. Level ground.
 A stutter step forward, then another.

<u>Acceptance:</u> Inconceivable.

NEW GIRL

Seventeen Years Old, Tennessee

First day of senior year.

First day at a new school.

In a new town, in a new state.

Since I started kindergarten, my mom's photographed me on the front porch holding a blackboard with my grade written in white chalk. She texts the picture to Grandma and Bernie, and Dad if he's overseas. The older I've become, the sillier I've found the tradition, but I never complain because it takes two seconds and I used to genuinely like first days.

Today she brings out the blackboard: *Senior Year!*

I get up from the table, dumping my plate of toast crusts in the sink. Dad left for post a few minutes ago, looking sharp in ACUs and tactical boots. He pressed a kiss to the top of my head and said, "Good luck, Millie," before slipping out the door. Now he's on his way to Fort Campbell, but I'd like to think that if he were here, he'd defend me against Mom's dumb photo.

She holds out the board. "Quick picture?"

She went with the chambray blazer and black skirt, with her hair styled in soft waves. She took a leave of absence after Beck's death to be present for his family, as well as for Dad and me. I don't envy her the impossible task of comforting the comfortless, but as I suffered through the second half of junior year grief stricken and lonely, I often wished I could've taken a leave of absence too.

Now, she's been hired as our neighborhood elementary school's literacy specialist. It's the perfect job for her and I don't want to ruin her morning, but I'm not about to smile for a picture.

I stand, smoothing the floral minidress I plucked thoughtlessly from my closet after showering, and grab my backpack. "I'm running late."

She lowers the board, then follows me out the door. My car, a recently purchased, pre-owned Jetta, sits next to hers, a recently purchased, brand-new Volvo. Dad's content to cruise around in the Explorer we've had since I was thirteen.

I'm halfway to freedom when Mom calls, "Lovey, please?"

I don't stop.

I don't tell her to have a good day.

I wave without turning back, then shut myself into the Jetta.

It's not until I'm backing down the driveway that I allow myself a glance toward the porch. She's still there, wilted. The blackboard hangs at her side. She brushes a tear from her cheek and watches me go.

24

I'm a monster, I tell Beck.

He doesn't disagree.

Driving to East River High School, I'm a ball of nerves. It'll be the sixth school I've attended in my seventeen years, which isn't a terribly high number for a military kid, but I haven't started at a new school alone since sixth grade, when I was a transplant to Colorado Springs. It's terrifying to walk into an alien building, to face hundreds of unfamiliar faces, to internalize new policies, and to convince a slew of unknown teachers of my merit. But in North Carolina, I had Beck. In Washington, I had Beck. In Virginia, I had Beck.

In Tennessee, today…I have no one.

The parking lot is chaos. Cars idle or cruise haphazardly. Groups of people weave in and out of traffic, making their way to campus like flocks of oblivious pigeons. Spots are assigned— mine is 132—though the paint marking them is faded. It takes me forever to find the right section. I sigh, relieved. It's a small victory.

Cranking the Jetta's wheel, I make a sharp left into 132—just as a raven-haired girl toting a messenger bag steps into my waiting spot.

A half second becomes an eternity as my car careens toward her, allowing me to observe her hair, which fans out as she whirls toward the sound of approaching doom. Her mouth, an oval of shock. Her hands, thrown up like they might protect her from the impact of a three-thousand-pound vehicle.

I think, with terrifying clarity, *I'm going to kill her.*

And then another thought, another voice, deep and desperate: *Fuck, Amelia—brake!*

I shriek, slamming my foot down on the pedal.

The Jetta lurches to a stop.

The girl's chest heaves as she stands in front of its hood. Its bumper can't be more than an inch from her knees.

Through the windshield, our eyes meet.

I shift into park, then fumble with my seat belt. Nearly face-planting in my hurry to bail out, I manage to get my feet beneath me as I say, "I'm so sorry! Are you okay?"

She lowers her hands, gold bangles tinkling. Tossing her hair, she squares up, jaw clenched, brows narrowed. She's beautiful in that airbrushed, flawlessly contoured way that feels unattainable to mascara-and-lip-balm types, like me.

She looks pissed.

But then, like snow sliding from a pitched roof, her imposing demeanor falls away. She takes a hurried couple of steps in my direction. "I'm good. Are you okay?"

"Yeah, totally." I pull in a breath, hoping to slow my racing pulse. My brain fog nearly resulted in calamity, and I'm not sure how to wrap my head around the miracle that, somehow, this girl was spared my ineptitude. "God. Seriously, I'm so sorry."

She laughs—*laughs.* "No worries. Happens all the time."

I blink. "Uh—does it?"

"This parking lot's madness on a good day. You're not the first to nearly run a person down, and you won't be the last."

I'm not sure if she's bullshitting to make me feel better, or if I should wear a crash helmet while walking to and from my car.

"You're just starting at ERHS?" she guesses.

"Is it that obvious?"

She laughs again, a sunny sound. "What year are you?"

"Senior."

"Oof—a senior-year transfer? Shitty."

"It's not so bad," I say with a shrug, resisting the urge to pull out my phone and call up my schedule, then beg her to show me the way to my first class: AP Government.

"I'm a senior too." She gestures at the Jetta, its engine quietly humming, its butt hanging out of space 132. "How about you finish parking—I'll stay clear—then we can compare schedules before the bell."

I want to drop to my knees and thank this gracious girl.

I'll try, I told Dad last night. *I'll try to make a friend.*

"Yeah," I say, "that would be amazing, thank you. I'm Lia."

"Paloma. And don't sweat it. I was the new girl last year. We've gotta stick together."

ROOTS

Tennessee, Seventeen Years Old

Serendipitously, Paloma and I have first period together. As we walk to class, she talks about Advisory, the thirty-minute free period between third and fourth. "Most of us use it like a study hall or a social break," she says, "but it's also when clubs meet. Come to the library. I'll introduce you to the girls."

AP Government is okay because I have Paloma to sit beside. Through our whispered conversation, I learn that she moved to Tennessee from California, because her tío and tía and a wealth of cousins live here. The South is growing on her, she says, but she misses Glendale and Liam, the boyfriend she left behind.

"I mean, *sometimes* I miss him," she clarifies, rolling her eyes like, *You know how it is.*

I don't. For me, the missing is incessant.

Physics and French are a drag. Syllabi are read and rules are recited. I spend the better part of two hours slow-cooking in guilt, remembering the defeat on my mom's face as she held that stupid blackboard and watched me drive away.

I send up a silent wish: *Let Mom have a nice day.*

By the time Advisory rolls around, I'm itching for a break. I find Paloma in the back of the library, where groups of upholstered chairs look out over the southern end of campus. There's a baseball field in the distance, and a football field in the foreground, ringed by a red track, a lot like the one at Rosebell High.

Out past one of the end zones, there's a dedicated shot-put circle. I imagine Beck there, hurtling shot after shot, watching the iron balls arc through the air as if they weigh nothing more than hens' eggs. He used to beat himself up over lackluster puts, and he refused to celebrate spectacular efforts. He was always pushing, always chasing excellence.

Paloma's with a couple of girls, who she introduces as Sophia and Meagan. They're Southern hospitality personified, all welcoming smiles and cheerful banter, and they spend the next few minutes filling me in on the essentials. Sophia, the youngest of five, is the product of a Tennessee senator and an accountant. She plays varsity volleyball and has brown curls that cascade down her back. Meagan's blond like me, though her hair is pixie short and streaked with pink. She has two sisters: a freshman at ERHS and a fifth grader at East River Elementary, Mom's new school. Meagan's mother died three years ago, breast cancer, so her dad's doing all the parenting while working at Bridgestone's

29

corporate headquarters in Nashville. She and Sophia—Soph, as Paloma keeps calling her—began as next-door neighbors, became besties in fourth grade, and in tenth grade, realized they cared about each other in a way more intense than friendship. After weathering a storm of disapproval on the part of Soph's initially unaccepting parents, they got together and have been a happy couple ever since.

When Paloma moved to town last year, she landed in gym with the both of them, which included a unit in the on-campus pool.

"Torture," she says.

"Utterly sadistic," Meagan confirms.

"It was Paloma's idea to fight the prerequisite that juniors swim a mile to meet promotion requirements," Sophia tells me.

"We marched on the courtyard with signs," Meagan says. "Hell no, H2O!"

Sophia hushes her, giggling. "We launched a protest on social media, too, and Paloma raised hell at a school board meeting. A splashing success."

Paloma grins and singsongs, "No more mile."

And that was it: Meagan and Sophia's duo turned into a trio.

I hope they're open to the idea of a quartet.

"Lia moved here from Virginia," Paloma tells her friends. "We met in the parking lot this morning. She drives a Jetta, which almost turned me into a pancake."

I grimace. "I'm still mortified."

I give them the basics of my dad's time with the Army, and

my mom's new job at East River Elementary. "We have a house in The Glens," I say, naming our development. "At least, for the next few years."

Meagan and Sophia give me pity eyes, a reaction that's not uncommon from those who've spent their whole lives in the same town. They assume it must be awful, picking up and moving all the time. It's not though. At least it hasn't been for me. People have the wrong idea about what it means to put down roots. You can have ties to more than a location. Sometimes experiences serve. So do people.

"You must miss your friends back in Virginia," Meagan says, taking Sophia's hand.

I think, *What friends?*

My junior year at Rosebell High, Beck had graduated. So had Wyatt, Raj, and Stephen, his friends who'd become mine by default. I still had Macy, Wyatt's girlfriend, who was tons of fun and a trustworthy confidant, but I wasn't easy to be around. I spent most of first semester lamenting my aloneness. Second semester, following Beck's death, I plummeted into a chasm of sorrow. Everyone knew what had happened, of course. Counselors had been poached from nearby schools to aid us in our grief, but I was too far gone. And so, in an effort to save her from my pain, not to mention spare myself the countless reminders of Beck, I shoved Macy out of my lightless world, just as I'd done to my parents and the Byrnes.

I told myself—keep telling myself—it's for the best.

"Oh, we stay in touch," I say lightly.

31

"But still," Sophia says with sympathy. And then she brightens. "Let's go to The Shaggy Dog for dinner. Ring in senior year right."

"Twist my arm," Meagan says wryly.

Paloma nods, then looks to me. "You've got to come. It's a brewery downtown. They have the best bread pudding."

I consider. Dinner with my parents, tiptoeing over eggshells, Mom and Dad making gentle attempts at prying life out of their Very Sad Daughter, versus dinner with three girls who've got loads of friend potential?

I'm about to respond when movement by the study carrels snags my attention. A boy, lean and very tall, with a lock of dark hair swooping over his forehead. He has a mouth that lifts crookedly and eyes like chips of obsidian. They catch mine, and his smile widens. The connection lasts long enough to distract me from my conversation with the girls. Long enough to prod my heart into something like wakefulness.

"Lia?" Paloma says as the boy breaks eye contact to turn a corner, unnoticed by everyone but me. "The Shaggy Dog? Are you in?"

I extinguish the treacherous flicker of interest sparked by the boy, then mold my mouth into a smile that mimics hers. "You had me at bread pudding."

VIVID

Tennessee, Seventeen Years Old

Paloma drives a Civic with a University of Southern California sticker adhered to its back window. I'm out the front door and sliding into the passenger seat before my parents have a chance to ask questions.

"Go Trojans," I say, buckling up.

She pulls away from the curb and heads out of The Glens. "USC is the only school I'm applying to. My parents can't wrap their heads around the risk. They keep going on about eggs and my singular basket."

"Well, it's a very good basket."

She grins. "Where're you applying?"

"CVU. Probably William and Mary. Ole Miss because my parents are alums."

"No Tennessee schools?"

"Maybe UT. Maybe Austin Peay."

"Megs and Soph are aiming for Austin Peay. Together, of course."

"Of course," I echo without judgment. I, too, had grand plans to attend college with my significant other. Last year, higher education without Beck by my side was unfathomable. It's *still* unfathomable. I tell Paloma, "Commonwealth of Virginia University is where I really want to go."

So much so, I'm seriously considering applying early decision. Mom and Dad don't want me to go to CVU, but Beck and I had a plan. We'd attend college in Charlottesville, where he'd chase a civil engineering degree and I'd major in early childhood development. Then he'd get a job in city planning, and I'd work with kids. We'd be together, forever and always.

I will not abandon the plan.

"Happy to help you compare schools," Paloma says. "My brother ended up super stressed trying to decide on a university. That's when I stepped in with a level head and a Venn diagram app. I got pretty good at weighing the pros and the cons, which is how I know USC is where I want to be."

"Where does Liam want to go?"

She flashes a sheepish smile. "USC."

She swerves into the driveway of a tidy two-story in a neighborhood that looks a lot like The Glens. Sophia comes skipping out the door, with Meagan close behind. They buckle into the backseat, and then we're on our way to The Shaggy Dog. The girls chatter as Paloma drives. I try to listen, to participate, but my guilt-ridden brain keeps regurgitating those brief but bewildering seconds in the library earlier, when my heart stirred in response to a boy.

A *different* boy.

As Paloma turns into the parking lot of The Shaggy Dog, my phone, tucked into the pocket of my denim jacket, begins to ring. I slip it out to find Bernie's face lighting the screen.

It's as if she knows.

I silence the call and drop my phone in my lap.

Paloma's circling the lot, looking for an empty space. "Your mom?"

"No, her best friend."

Bernie's been calling since before my parents and I moved to River Hollow, though I hardly saw her in the months before we left Virginia. With Beck gone, I couldn't bear to go to the Byrnes' house. And when they'd come to ours, I'd hide out in my room. It's impossible to listen to Bernie's infectious laugh, or hear one of Connor's sardonic jokes, or see Norah and Mae's paint-spatter freckles without being knocked off my feet by a tsunami of missing.

"She's so pretty," Sophia says, leaning forward to peer at my phone. Bernie's call is still trying to connect.

"If she's your mom's friend," Meagan asks, "why's she calling you?"

Finally, Bernie gives up. The screen goes dark.

"Her son and I..." I start, but the words snag on one another like burrs.

I've gone nine months without speaking Beck's name aloud.

35

Paloma's scored a parking spot, but no one's made a move to leave the car. Instead, we sit in front of a brick building with a neon *The Shaggy Dog* sign, my preamble unfinished. The girls' attention feels like sandbags atop my shoulders. Paloma glances at me, brown eyes glinting with curiosity.

Beck whispers, *Don't bury my memory.*

"Bernie's son and I grew up together," I say, because I want Paloma and Meagan and Sophia as friends—I sincerely like them. And because I want Beck to be known. "He died suddenly, two hundred forty-six days ago."

It's the sort of announcement that sucks the air from a space. The car's interior is so quiet I can hear my hurried heartbeat, and I wonder if I should've kept Beck to myself. But then Paloma exhales, letting go of the steering wheel to take my hand.

"I'm so sorry," she says. "What was his name?"

"Beck. Beckett Byrne."

She gives me a sympathetic smile. "You must miss him so much."

"You've had a hell of a year, huh?" Meagan says.

I nod, not sure I can trust my voice to remain steady.

"But you're here now," Sophia points out.

"Yeah," Meagan says. "At The Shaggy Dog, where the bread pudding's to die for."

Sophia gasps.

Paloma's eyes go big with horror.

"What?" Meagan asks, looking between the two of them. "What'd I say?"

She reminds me of Bernie, the way she speaks with conviction, without contemplation. She knows loss. And so, to my surprise perhaps more than anyone's, I give in to a fit of hiccup-inciting giggles and, God, it feels good.

The girls laugh too, and I'm overcome by a rush of warmth.

In a day's time, they've reminded me how good it feels to be part of something.

FOREGONE CONCLUSIONS

Ten Years Old, Washington

As we were nearing the end of our time at Joint Base Lewis-McChord in Washington State, I spent the better part of the summer between fifth and sixth grade outdoors with Beck.

The Byrnes lived two houses from ours, in a neighborhood close to JBLM. Dad and I both loved Washington: its soaring evergreens, ample ski slopes, and cold, rocky beaches. Mom thought the Pacific Northwest was too gray, and too expensive. She missed the South's swampy summers and the snow-white beaches kissed by the cerulean waters of the Gulf of Mexico. Still, she had Bernie, and Dad had spent the last six months stateside, so she rarely complained.

Except, since school had let out in June, she hadn't been well. I exhausted the daylight hours with Beck using scrap lumber to build forts and bike jumps in the undeveloped lots in our neighborhood, but the oddness of coming home to find Mom on the couch, sipping lemon water, zoned out on whatever documentary she was streaming, didn't escape me.

When she wasn't on the couch, she was in the bathroom, preparing to vomit, vomiting, or brushing her teeth post-vomit. She rarely ate anything more than buttered toast. She hardly ever wore makeup. More than once, I'd woken up late at night to my parents' hushed conversations floating down the hall from their bedroom. They weren't arguing—they seldom do that—but they didn't sound happy either.

Something was wrong.

On a rare sunny day, while outdoors with Beck, I coughed up a confession. "My mom's dying."

He lowered the hammer he'd been using to nail a 2x4 to a piece of particleboard. His hair was windblown, and there was a smudge of dust on his freckled cheek. "Are you serious?"

"I think so. She's always tired. She hardly goes out. She throws up all the time."

He dropped the hammer, nicked from Connor's toolbox, and made himself comfortable on the ground, draping his arms over his bent knees, peering at me through the sun's glare. I'll always appreciate this about him: Beck played hard and acted tough, but when circumstances dictated, he transformed into this thoughtful, attentive boy who'd lay down his hammer to hear a friend out.

"I haven't seen a lot of her, now that I'm thinking about it," he said. "But my mom would've said something if your mom was sick. If she was *dying*."

I raised a shoulder, then let it drop. "Maybe she doesn't want you to worry, the same way my mom doesn't want me to worry."

"Have you talked to your dad?"

I huffed. "He acts like everything's fine. Like I'm a moron who doesn't notice that her mom suddenly lives on the couch."

"Hey now," Beck said with a gentle smile. "I'm the only one who gets to call you *moron*."

"I'm just—" To my dismay, my eyes flooded with tears. What I said next came out waterlogged and pitiful. "I'm worried about her."

He laid a hand on my knee, skinned the day before thanks to a bike wipeout. "She's fine, Lia. She's gotta be. I mean, what would my mom do without her?"

"What would *I* do without her?"

He sighed, a compassionate sound. "She'll be okay. And even if she isn't, *you* will be."

I sniffled. "How do you know?"

"You have me. No matter what, you'll always have me."

A few nights after I laid bare my worries to Beck, I was startled out of sleep by a crash.

A bellow followed, and my body went cold with fear.

I scrambled out of bed and sprinted down the hall to my parents' bedroom. Throwing open their door, I heard Dad curse, and curse again. The bed was rumpled but empty. The bathroom light was on, though, and I was across the room in a flash. Dad was crouching over Mom. Her face was pallid. Her eyes lolled. She was on the floor, tangled with a pair of terry cloth towels. Two holes yawned in the drywall, where the towel bar had been torn from its anchors. Her top was damp around the neckline, and her pajama bottoms...

There was blood—a lot of blood.

My head went chaotic with questions, but I lacked the composure to do more than release a shaky breath.

I whispered, "Daddy?"

He looked at me, eyes glassy. His voice was remarkably calm when he said, "Get my phone. Call Bernie. Tell her to come *now*. Then dial 911 and bring the phone to me."

I did as he asked. Panic pinballed through my body, but I functioned on autopilot because in my head and my heart, I knew Mom needed me.

As soon as I had a 911 dispatcher on the line, I shoved the phone into Dad's waiting hand, then hovered, listening as he described the scene. "She's thirty-four... Yes, bleeding... Just the last few minutes." And then, brusquely, "I don't know!"

Mom moaned, clutching her middle. Her mouth contorted, and her eyes pinched. I stooped down, afraid to touch her, but desperate to comfort her. Carefully, I set a trembling hand on her brow. My palm slip-slided on her clammy skin.

And then—

"She's pregnant," Dad told the 911 dispatcher.

I reared back, snatching my hand away. I saw white, that

41

word—*pregnant*—making me feel like I'd been swept up in an avalanche.

Dad's gaze collided with mine.

Mom was carrying a baby.

"Sixteen weeks, I think," Dad said into his phone.

To me, he mouthed, *I'm sorry.*

Distantly, the front door slammed. Footsteps clambered up the stairs. Bernie appeared in the doorway, hickory hair scooped into a sloppy ponytail, cheeks flushed. Her eyes fell to my mom, helpless on the cold travertine tile.

She breathed, "Oh, God, Cam."

"I know," Dad said. "Jesus, *I know.* Paramedics are on the way."

Bernie dragged her attention from Mom—her best friend, who lay delirious and bleeding—to me, curled practically fetal beside her. "Lia, baby. Come with me."

"But—Mom."

"Your daddy's got her. Let's go meet the ambulance."

I took Bernie's hand. We made a sluggish trip down the stairs and through the front door. Together, we stood on the driveway, listening for sirens. And then, a faraway *whee-ooh* that upsurged as an ambulance screeched to a halt at the end of our driveway.

The rest is a blur: paramedics racing into the house, then hurrying back out, jogging alongside Mom on a stretcher. Dad, climbing into the back of the ambulance with a rushed "No, Millie. Stay with Bernie." Bernie, holding me back as I flailed in a hopeless attempt to race down the street after my parents.

42

I collapsed onto the driveway, dropping my face into my hands, and sobbed.

Bernie cried too.

Eventually we went in the house. The clock above the mantel said it was nearing three and while I was drained, I wasn't tired. Bernie made me hot cocoa, the good kind, on the stove, with melted chocolate, then fixed us a nest of blankets on the couch.

I sipped my cocoa.

Bernie sat silently next to me.

When I couldn't stand the quiet another second, I asked, "She's really pregnant?"

Bernie nodded. "She didn't want you to know—not yet. There've been complications."

"I thought she was dying."

For all I knew, she *would* die. Was *already* dead.

Bernie reached over to take my mug. She set it on the coffee table, then took my hands in hers. "Tonight…what happened… We'll have to wait for your daddy to call, but, Lia. She'll be okay."

Beck had said the same thing, just a few days before.

As much as I wanted them both to be right, neither could say with certainty that Mom would pull through. That she'd come home.

"She's not supposed to have any more babies," I said.

Bernie lifted a brow. "She's not?"

"The fortune teller's reading? *You will bear one child.* That's me. Another baby…it doesn't make sense."

I studied Bernie's expression as she absorbed my words, as

43

she tried—and failed—to hold back an amused smile. She was looking at me like I was silly, naive, because I put stock in a carnival clairvoyant's prophecy, which was *so* hypocritical. Mom believed in that reading. Bernie did too. I knew, because she'd been referring to her son—*Beck*—as my soulmate for as long as I could remember. And now, because the prediction didn't serve the narrative, it was silly?

"Life is confusing," she said. "Things aren't as simple as a fortune teller's prediction."

I wrinkled my nose, deeply unsatisfied with her nonanswer. "Fine. Then I guess Beck and I *won't* be together forever."

She laughed, a straight pin to the bubble of anxiety I'd been trapped in.

"Oh, Lia. Be with Beck because you want to. Not because a clairvoyant told your mama you're supposed to. I'll always adore you, no matter what."

She pulled me in, tucking the blankets around us. Using the remote, she turned on the TV, then navigated through our streaming services, finally settling on the pilot episode of *Dawson's Creek*, a show my mom wouldn't let me watch because of its supposedly mature themes. It was like that, though—Bernie let me get away with more than Mom did, just like Mom laughed it off when Beck dunked Oreos into our peanut butter jar.

"I loved this show when I was a kid," Bernie said as Dawson and Joey argued about sleepovers. "This, and *Beverly Hills, 90210. Party of Five* and *Veronica Mars*...teen drama at its

44

juiciest. Girlie, it's high time you get to know Pacey, and Rory Gilmore, and Buffy, and Tim Riggins. Oh, God—Texas Forever. Swoon."

I giggled and, in Bernie's arms, drifted to sleep.

Sometime later, I woke groggily to her phone ringing. Bernie slipped her arm from beneath me and tiptoed out of the living room. I followed stealthily. She went into the kitchen, listening, and rooted around in our coffee cabinet. She knew our kitchen as well as Mom did. She selected a medium roast pod, then tucked it into the Keurig, murmuring *yes* and *no* and *I'm so sorry.*

It was Dad—I knew by her tone.

I also knew that Mom was all right. Otherwise Bernie wouldn't have been on her feet, choosing a mug, pulling hazelnut creamer from the fridge.

But why was she *so sorry*?

"Lia's okay," she said, puttering around as her coffee brewed. "She slept a few hours. I'm here, as long as you need me."

Dad said something—thanked her, probably, because she hummed an assent.

I pressed a hand to my heart. It was beating too fast for a body standing motionless.

"Give Hannah my love," Bernie told Dad, and then she ended the call.

When she turned around, she didn't seem surprised to see me

45

lurking. The aroma of coffee filled the kitchen, warm and rich, as we sized each other up. There was a heaviness to her expression, as if sadness was tugging her features down.

"Your mama's okay," she said finally.

"You knew she would be."

"I *hoped* she would be."

"And the baby?"

"The baby...is no more."

A gentler version of *dead*. That sort of delicacy is unnatural to Bernie and, while I appreciated her consideration, I was ten, not two. After what I'd witnessed the night before, I was in no mood for vague, flowery language. I wanted candor—I *needed* candor.

It bothered me, the certainty with which I'd known the pregnancy would end.

But there *had* been a baby.

Already, my heart suffered the loss.

Bernie moved toward me. "Lia, I'm sorry."

I nodded because I didn't have words. I had feelings. Big feelings, warring feelings, feelings that burned so hot, I was sure they were turning me feverish. I was frustrated at not having been told. Devastated at having been denied the chance to love my sibling. And most of all, furious with the clairvoyant for speaking the previous night's turmoil into truth.

Mom was to bear one child—not two.

"I don't feel well," I told Bernie.

"Lia—"

"Please," I said, shuffling toward the staircase. "I want to be alone."

In my room, I took to my bed, a phrase Grandma uses, meaning I lay down and cried dramatically into my soft blankets. I must've exhausted myself, because the next thing I knew, I was being jostled awake. I opened my eyes to find Beck roosting on the edge of my mattress, his warm hand on my shoulder.

"My mom sent me to get you. She made pancakes. She wants you to eat."

"I'm not hungry," I said, rubbing my bleary eyes.

"I know. But when I feel crappy, food helps."

I pulled my quilt up to my chin. "The thought of syrup makes me want to hurl."

He took the Magic 8 Ball, a stocking stuffer from a few Christmases before, from my nightstand. Closing his eyes, he said, "Should Lia eat pancakes?"

"Beck—"

He consulted the ball, then said sagely, "It is certain."

"Give me a break. That thing's just a toy."

"A smart toy. How 'bout this? I'll fix your pancakes with strawberry jam. Or Nutella."

My stomach rumbled.

"Nutella sounds good. And…you'll bring them up? So I can have them in bed?"

He nodded, offering a sweet smile.

I thought, then, of the time Bernie had quipped, "Aww, Lia, you're practically my daughter-in-law." Mom was fond of saying:

47

"Beckett Byrne and Amelia Graham: Certain as the setting sun."
And Beck himself, a few days before, had promised, "You'll always have me."

It wasn't until that moment, though—him in my bedroom on the worst day, promising pancakes and comfort—that our future felt like fact.

Beck and I were a foregone conclusion.

I gazed at him, trying to call up the love I'd someday feel, wanting to try it out, like a Costco sample or a movie trailer. My eyes fell to his mouth, quirked uncertainly, as I imagined my first kiss—with him.

Weird, I thought. *Kissing Beck would be so weird.*

He cleared his throat. "You good?"

"I think I will be."

He got to his feet. "I'll be back, okay?"

I nodded, then watched him cross my room, his overt boyness out of place among my mostly feminine things.

As he reached the door, I called his name. He stopped and turned, one hand coming up to rest on the jamb. He looked at me, eyes gray-green and inquisitive, and I suddenly couldn't remember what it was that I'd wanted to say.

Flustered, I settled on, "Thank you."

His mouth lifted in a smile. "You're welcome."

INTUITION

Seventeen Years Old, Tennessee

Thanks to Paloma, Meagan, and Sophia, the first few weeks of senior year aren't so bad.

But then, a day I've been dreading: Beck's birthday. It's the hardest I've had in months. I'm planning to bury myself in bed as soon as school's out, but my friends talk me into a trip to Buttercup Bakery. Once we've ordered drinks and a quartet of lavishly frosted cupcakes, we squeeze into a corner booth and Paloma toasts Beck's nineteenth, because even though I mentioned his birthday to her in passing just after we met, she remembers.

Last year, Beck spent his eighteenth birthday in Rosebell, his first trip home since he'd moved to Charlottesville the month before. His mom and I fixed a lunch of his favorites: brats in buns, homemade macaroni and cheese, caprese salad, and the peanut butter sheet cake Bernie makes for special occasions. We hung out in the Byrnes' backyard with his family and mine, then ducked out to spend the rest of afternoon, just the two of us.

Together, we went to the stables at Joint Base Myer-Henderson Hall to sneak apples to the horses that pull caissons for military funerals at Arlington National Cemetery, then walked The Mall, finishing at the Jefferson Memorial, where we watched the sun sink spectacularly below the horizon.

I miss him, and our easy assumption of forever.

I miss his family too. Our gatherings, the food, the laughter, the affinity.

"I'm thinking about reaching out to Beck's mom," I tell my friends, swirling the tines of a fork through my peanut butter cupcake's frosting.

"You should," Meagan says. She's beside me, so it's easy to catch the *take it easy* glower Paloma aims across the table. Meagan shrugs, unapologetic. "I'm just saying, today's probably been a bitch for her too."

Remorse hits me square in the chest. All my life, Bernie's been an ally, this cool bonus mother, a proxy on the rare occasions my mom's been out of commission. Yet I've abandoned her during the worst year of her life.

I must look every bit as guilty as I feel, because Soph swoops in with damage control. "What Megs is trying to say is that when your gut speaks, it's usually for a reason."

I look at Paloma, her kind eyes lined in black, lashes miles long. "What do you think?"

50

She smiles. "There's something to be said for honoring your intuition."

I set my fork down and make a shameful admission. "I've barely managed today, and I'm pretty sure talking to Bernie will break me. That's what's holding me back...fear. Is that the most selfish thing you've ever heard?"

"No," Paloma and Soph say in unison.

"Yes!" Meagan squawks. But in her brusqueness, she abandons her cupcake to squeeze my hand. "I've seen this shit play out, Lia. Like, after my mom passed, my gran started coming over all the time. She cooked our dinners and did our laundry. She cleaned our bathrooms. She got in my dad's way. Irritated the hell out of him. That first Christmas we spent without Mom, Gran insisted on doing all the cooking. She wouldn't even let Dad roast the turkey. When we sat down to eat, he looked at my mom's empty chair and lost it. Told Gran she was out-of-bounds, trying to take over. Gran stormed out, leaving my dad, my sisters, my pop, and me at the table. I thought Pop was going to blow a gasket, but he just started carving the bird, totally chill, talking about how Gran was super sad, and how trying to fill in for Mom was part of her grieving process."

"That makes a lot of sense," Paloma says.

Meagan sends her a smile before looking to me. "People cope with loss in different ways. You want to deal on your own, but maybe Beck's mom needs connection. It'll cost you, letting her in, but imagine what you'll be giving."

Soph reaches across the table to link hands with her. "Smart girl."

51

Megs *is* smart: Bernie's love language is quality time. She's a talker and a listener. She's bolstered by eye contact and shared laughter. Beck was the same.

He must be so disappointed by how I've shut his mom out of my life.

I spear a bite of cupcake and look at my friends. "I can do better."

Paloma gives me an encouraging grin. Soph nods, eyes bright.

"Hell yes, you can," Meagan says.

A PROMISE

Seventeen Years Old, Tennessee

My text thread with Bernie used to buzz with messages about soapy TV, plus check-ins about where Beck and I were, as well as reminders that he'd better have me home by curfew. For almost a year, though, the thread's been one-sided: Bernie saying hello, Bernie hoping I'm well, Bernie sharing pictures of Norah and Mae.

I feel awful, having left her on read for so long.

Am I heartbroken or heartless?

With the peanut butter cupcake I ate earlier churning in my stomach, I rally my courage and key in a simple Hi.

I tap send before doubt has its way with me.

It's late, so I'm not counting on a response, but one comes quick.

Girlie, hi. So good to hear from you.

Struggling to breathe through the heaviness in my chest, I

scroll back, looking at the dozens of photos of the twins Bernie's sent. It slays me, knowing I've missed out on so much of their growing up.

Can't believe how big Norah and Mae are getting, I text.

A new photo arrives: two strawberry blonds, rosy-cheeked and grinning, in identical sundresses. I'm so thankful Bernie and Connor have them. They're tiny sunbursts.

They're loving kindergarten, she tells me. And then: How are you?

I go with unsparing honesty. Terrible. You?

Dreadful, she messages. But this helps.

Meagan was right.

What's stunning, though, is that reconnecting is helping me too.

We miss you, Bernie texts.

I promised myself I wouldn't spend today crying. Beck's birthday should be joyful; it was in the past. I blot my eyes with my sleeve and ask, What are you watching these days?

Nothing. Teen dramas don't feel right without you.

Nothing feels right anymore.

I think of the boy I noticed in the library on my first day of school. He and I don't share classes, but I've seen him around campus, sometimes with buddies, sometimes on his own, backpack slung over his shoulder, expression thoughtful. His bottomless eyes and self-assured stride appeal to me in a way that's as exciting as it is reprehensible.

No, nothing at all feels right.

I cross the room to my desk, where I flip through a drawer filled with completed journals. When I find the one I'm looking for, I turn to a page I created just after I turned eleven: *Lia and Bernie's Marathon List*. Running my finger down TV show titles inked in purple—*My So-Called Life, The OC, Gossip Girl*, among many others—I find where we left off, then send Bernie another message: I'll start Friday Night Lights if you will.

Done, she replies. And then, Love you, Lia. We all do. Beck especially. He loved you so much.

This I will never doubt.

Beck made me feel cherished every day, in little ways and big ways and ways in between. Scanning the bulletin board over my desk, I find one of my favorite photos, taken at Rehoboth Beach a couple months before he left for CVU. His hair is windblown, his freckles multiplied by the sun. His smile is wide and bright. I'm beside him, sporting a banana-yellow bikini and a messy ponytail, laughing so hard my eyes pinch shut.

He's looking at me like I'm made of stardust.

My phone buzzes again.

Tonight, Bernie texts, do something special. Something for you. Beck would like that.

Beside the Rehoboth Beach picture are two photos pinned next to each other. Both were snapped in Charlottesville, during the weekend I visited Beck. One was taken by Bernie, crisp and clear, its colors saturated: Beck and me in navy and red, grinning among thousands at CVU's football stadium. The Eagles went on to blow out Virginia Tech. The second was snapped early that same morning, a selfie of the two of us in Beck's dorm room, focus hazy and dreamlike. His arm is around me, and we're gazing at each other, noses practically touching.

My last weekend with him.

Our last meal, our last laugh, our last kiss.

My best weekend with him.

I will, I tell Bernie.

Early Decision

She spends the final hours of his birthday online,
researching CVU's early decision process,
jotting notes and to-dos,
  feelings and maybe-I-shouldn'ts in her journal.
The deadline is November 1st—
plenty of time to collect transcripts
    and letters of recommendation,
to contact the Office of Veteran
    Services with questions
about using the GI Bill her dad transferred to her,
to chronicle her time volunteering
    with the Key Club
and Dad's various Family Readiness Groups,
to draft a personal essay.
She's already filled out the FAFSA
    with her parents,
and there's money for the application
    fee in her checking account,
so no need to bring them into her plan just yet.

They know her interest in CVU began
    when Beck decided on the school.

Before she and he were we,

she'd planned to return to the Pacific
    Northwest for college.

She'd missed its overcast skies and the
    gunmetal-gray Puget Sound.

She was sure she wanted a semester abroad too,

a chance to explore a country
    different from her own.

But since Beck passed, she's been certain.

Four years at CVU will mend the tear in her soul.

The problem is, if her parents find out
    she's applying early decision

—if she's accepted, she's committed to enrolling—

they'll shit actual bricks.

But it'll work out.

Eventually, they'll understand.

She looks to the Magic 8 Ball that sits on her desk.

The one she and Beck used to play with,

the one they used to help with decisions
    both important and nominal.

She picks it up and whispers the
    question that's been on her mind
    since she opened her laptop.

She gives it a gentle shake, then waits
    for the bubbles to clear.

Without a doubt, the blue triangle reads.

It's settled.

She'll submit her application early decision.

She'll get word in December.

Then she'll tell her parents what she's done.

365 DAYS

Seventeen Years Old, Tennessee

On a frigid morning in November, I wake to find that a pit has opened inside me.

I endure a shower. I leave my hair down to veil my face. I dress in dark jeans and a black sweater, modern teen meets Victorian widow. And, because I'm a masochist, I open my jewelry box and take out my most treasured possession, a ring with two stones, an aquamarine and a sapphire. I stopped wearing it after Beck's wake; its pair of gems made me feel more alone than ever.

Today I need it with me.

I find Mom and Dad in the kitchen with Major, who's already inhaled breakfast and sits before his bowl, wishing for more. As I pass, he lovingly snuffles my hand. A hot cocoa sits on the counter in a to-go cup, along with a chocolate croissant peeking out of a paper bag. A special breakfast, just for me. Dad's wearing a fleece pullover and the ratty Sambas he's had since college, so he must've ventured out to pick it up. Mom leaves her chair, abandoning a mug half-filled with tea, and comes toward me. She opens her arms, zombielike, expecting a hug. I duck away. Her face crumples and I'm sorry about that, but I want to be left alone.

"I've got to get to school," I say in explanation.

She and I've barely spoken over the last couple months. I haven't said anything about texting Bernie, about *Friday Night Lights*, though I'm sure Bernie told her we're in contact. I wonder if Mom's envious or sad, and then I decide it doesn't matter—*can't* matter.

Somehow it's easier with Bernie.

Piercing me with a displeased look, Dad pulls Mom into an embrace.

She dissolves into silent tears.

Major lets out a long, low whine.

This is unbearable, I tell Beck.

I pull my backpack off its hook, take my keys from the counter, and my jacket from the closet. I put my hand on the door to the garage. I've nearly escaped when Dad says my name.

I expect him to attempt wisdom, to preach something profound. He's used to sharing words of strength and stoicism. Instead, gravely, he says, "Don't forget your breakfast."

I pick up the cocoa and croissant, then leave.

Outside it's dark and very cold. The most stubborn stars dot the sky although, distantly, the promise of daybreak smolders.

61

I lean inside my car to turn over its engine, then crank the heat before walking down the driveway to dump my breakfast, untasted, in the trash bin at the curb.

There's no way I can eat—not today.

Stalwart and effervescent, Beckett Byrne vibrated with life.

One year ago, he died alone, seized by a heart attack.

James, his roommate, found him.

God, poor James.

Bursting into their room, he was ready to drag Beck out for a night of boozing before they headed to their respective homes for Thanksgiving. He came in shouting, banging desks and bookshelves, carrying on like a fool.

Most of the time, Beck cracked up at James's antics.

On November 22nd, he didn't move.

James described that afternoon to me months later because I reached out to him, begging for details, sure they'd be cathartic. It was the unknowing that tormented me—at least, that's what I thought. In fact, it was the loss, the utter senselessness of a boy snuffed out so early in his existence.

That, and the missing.

James indulged me, recounting a scene that features prominently in my nightmares still.

Beck was on his bed.

His eyes were closed.

He had one arm at his side, one crooked behind his head.

His desk looked as if he had every intention of waking up and carrying on. His textbooks were neatly stacked, bearing a rainbow of Post-it flags. His wallet rested next to his key ring. His phone was connected to its charger. I learned later that his laptop had been open to his email; he'd recently received a delivery notification for artisan ice cream he'd had shipped to Rosebell.

"I thought he was sleeping," James told me, choking on tears. He bumped Beck's shoulder. Shook him hard. Went into the hallway and screamed for the RA. Called 911 as the RA performed CPR. Threw up in a wastebasket as seconds became minutes, as minutes became an eternity, as panic erupted, volcano-like, in his chest.

In Beck's chest, all was still.

TRANSFIXED

Seventeen Years Old, Tennessee

All day at school, I exist in a fog. I watch the floor as I navigate corridors and skip Advisory in the library to sit in my car. Since it's the Wednesday before Thanksgiving break, we're watching movies in most of my classes. Nobody seems to care that I'm zoned out.

Paloma texts: I'm here if you want to talk. Or, I'm just here.

Sophia texts: We love you.

Meagan texts: It won't always be this hard.

All the way from Colorado, Andi and Anika post heart emojis in our shared thread.

Even Macy reaches out: Thinking of you, babe.

After school, I hide in the bathroom to avoid the mass exodus. Leaning against the closed door of the stall farthest from the entrance, I draw a breath and text Bernie: Lots of love to you, Connor, and the twins. Then I tuck my phone away, waiting out the shouts and whoops that filter in from the hallway.

When it's finally quiet, I step into the corridor, which is startlingly postapocalyptic. Discarded papers are strewn across the floor. Someone dropped a full soda and left it, the upturned can floating in a pool of cola. A game-day rally pom dangles from the drop ceiling.

I feel terrible for the custodians who'll be stuck cleaning up the debauchery.

Behind me, a low voice speaks a different version of that same thought: "Gotta feel for the janitors who have to deal with this shit."

I whirl around to find a boy standing a few feet away.

The boy.

"Sorry," he says, stepping forward. "Didn't mean to scare you."

He and I've walked the same hallways for months and passed on the quad dozens of times, but I've done my best to banish him from my head. Still, every time I see him, I remember how I felt when our eyes caught that first day in the library. Like maybe there's more in store for me than sorrow. Like maybe, in some distant future, my soul might really find a second match. Now, standing in closer proximity to him than I ever have before, I allow myself a moment to take him in: his jeans, his charcoal sweatshirt, the backpack chucked over his shoulder. His skin is olive and clear, his eyes bright with concern. It's the shape of his nose, though, broken a time or two probably, that captivates me.

The hairs on the back of my neck prickle as I stare up at

65

him, breathing shallowly, lost in a memory from months ago, a wintery afternoon in Virginia. I catalog his dark hair, his height, and that crooked nose, combining his features like numbers in an addition problem.

Their sum total is like being shaken out of a deep sleep.

He moves closer, brows knitting together. "You okay?"

My bag falls to the floor. I swallow around the lump that's bloomed in my throat.

"Shit," he says with alarm, "you're not okay."

I haven't been okay all day and this—*this* is enough to eviscerate the facade I've been hiding behind.

Now, I'm exposed.

Now, I'm crying.

It's been twelve months. Three hundred sixty-five days, and I'm a fucking mess.

A weaker human would turn and run, forget the melodramatic sad-sack-weirdo making puddles at his feet.

This human, though… This human drops his bag and pulls the weirdo into a hug.

Sobs shake my frame, sparking spasms in the muscles of my neck. For a series of terrifying seconds, I can't catch my breath. In a stranger's embrace, I gasp and cry and sputter, and I'm *mortified*, but I haven't lost it like this in a long time, and now that I've given over to emotion, I'm done for.

Finally, *finally*, I get control.

Backing up, I weigh my options: explain or run.

I'm inclined to the latter when I find the courage to look up at

66

him. Anguish is chiseled into his expression, and my tears have left dark splotches on his sweatshirt. He hasn't picked up his backpack, probably because he thinks I'm going to fall apart all over again.

"Better?" he asks quietly.

We're standing so close, I can smell his wintergreen gum.

"I don't know. Maybe. I mean…" I heave the world's deepest sigh. "…no. Not even a little bit."

His mouth lifts in a hopeful smile, like, *Maybe she's not totally unhinged?* "I've seen you around," he says, gaze steady on my face. "You're new this year, right?"

I run my fingers under my eyes, trying to erase evidence of my meltdown—like he'll forget so long as I'm not rocking streaked mascara. "I enrolled in August. I'm a senior."

"Same," he says. "On your way home?"

Home. Mom and Dad. The rest of this day and its bleak, bleak night.

Begrudgingly, I nod.

He picks up his backpack and extends an arm, like he wants us to walk together.

Shit—he does.

"I'm Isaiah," he tells me as we navigate the messy hall.

"Lia," I say casually, as if I didn't just weep in his arms.

He matches me step for step until, without warning, he stops. I do too, like I'm tethered to him. Bending, he gathers a pile of papers and dumps them into a nearby recycle bin. Again, he stoops and scoops, dumping refuse along the way.

I follow his lead, collecting litter, leaping up to grab that lone pom because it's helpful. A good deed to counter the darkness of today.

At the end of the corridor, we look back the way we came. Now the hallway looks like a strong wind blew through, rather than a cyclone. Isaiah holds out his fist, and I give it a light bump, like the last ten minutes haven't upended my world.

Outside, he crosses his arms against the cold. "Need a ride?"

"No, I'm good."

He looks over at me and says, seriously, "Are you?"

"I've got a car," I say, knowing full well he's no longer asking about transportation.

When he stops at the curb, he rakes a hand through his hair, revealing a scar on his forehead, pale and V-shaped, befitting yet arresting.

...scarred on the surface and deep within...

My stomach bottoms out.

He says, "Well, Lia, it's been real."

I might as well be free-falling. Passing my keys from one hand to the other, trying hard to pull it together, I stutter out a string of words that I hope come across as authentic gratitude. "Thanks for that...in the hallway. For being decent. I know it was awkward, the way I acted."

Light finds his eyes. "I have no idea what you're talking about."

"You could've made it even more awkward," I say, calling up a smile. "I appreciate that you didn't."

His face breaks into a grin, and the neurons in my body jolt

68

awake. I see with true clarity the boy standing in front of me: the soulful depth of his eyes, the enviable height of his cheekbones, the fullness of his mouth. I feel his presence, campfire warmth on a chilly night. I bask in his kindness, in the lingering comfort of his hug. My stomach flutters and my fingertips tingle and my cheeks go hot. God, maybe I'm getting sick. But then, as my heart jackhammers, I recognize what this is.

Two magnets—north pole and south pole—drawn to one another.

He's tempered his grin, leaving his expression cloaked in mystery. His gaze sweeps my face. His tongue wets his lower lip, tasting the energy between us, and the restraint that's kept me tottering on this side of rational goes to pieces.

Woozy and overheated, I step into his space. He smells like winter: smoke and juniper and cool mint. I lift onto my toes, pressing my mouth to his. If he's surprised, he's also willing. He tilts his head, coaxing the kiss open, sighing into it. Closing my eyes, I offer and accept, lost in sensation.

When his fingertips find my face, though, I remember who I am and what I've been through. More so, I remember the significance of this day and jerk away, staggering back.

"I'm so sorry," I tell him.

I'm so sorry, I tell Beck.

Isaiah nods, touching his mouth, his expression both dumbfounded and desirous.

The sound of an approaching engine distracts us from the fuckery of the last thirty seconds—thank God. A silver Suburban veers into the lot, driven by a middle-aged Black woman in a burgundy sweater. She stops in front of us, Beyoncé's "Crazy in Love" audible even though the SUV's windows are up. She waves, grinning at Isaiah.

He waves back, then turns to me. "My ride."

"Beyoncé's the best," I say, the inanest possible observation, but our interaction is becoming more uncomfortable by the second, and commenting randomly on a pop artist seems less incendiary than acknowledging the tremendously inappropriate kiss I just initiated.

He smiles, dubious. "You sure you're good?"

Clipped, I say, "Yeah. Definitely."

He nods, unconvinced, possibly offended. "Have a good break, then."

"Okay," I say, watching him open the Suburban's door. "Happy Thanksgiving."

I drive home sobbing, salty tears mingling with traces of wintergreen left on my lips.

GLITCH

Twelve Years Old, Colorado

The baby we lost had been a boy.

My mom had gone for genetic testing shortly before the pregnancy ended.

I still can't imagine—a little brother.

That winter, we left JBLM. I was bummed. Aside from the miscarriage, I'd loved our time in the Pacific Northwest. I'd thrived in school and delighted in being down the street from Beck. All that made the move bearable was knowing that the Byrnes would have to PCS that same month. Dad had orders to Fort Carson, Colorado, and Connor had been assigned to Fort Jackson, South Carolina. Mom and Bernie hugged on the sidewalk between our houses. Beck and I didn't hug—too weird—but driving away from him felt wrong, like I'd become a puzzle with a missing piece.

My first few months in Colorado sucked. Beck and I texted a

lot and sometimes FaceTimed, but I missed our movie nights. I missed swimming at Long Lake Park. I missed the way he'd gloat when he beat me at pickleball, and sulk when I beat him down ski runs. For three years, he'd been my world.

As time went on, Colorado Springs shaped a different version of me. I made new friends. Andi, a pianist with an infectious laugh. Anika, who longed to become a screenwriter and was always happy to watch shows and movies with me. There was even a boy, Hayden, a soccer hotshot who tutored me through dividing fractions—my first real crush.

In seventh grade, I landed in Ms. Bonny's Earth Science class. She was born and raised in Australia and had the most enchanting Aussie accent. She decorated her lab with posters of koalas perched in eucalyptus trees, the teal-blue waters surrounding the Great Barrier Reef, and the rusty red rocks of Kings Canyon, and she brought Tim Tams for the class to sample. I became enamored with her and obsessed with the idea of visiting Australia. I daydreamed about being in college and spending a semester abroad in Melbourne or Sydney. Though it was years off, I pitched the idea to my parents, who thought it was fantastic—so long as I promised they could come for a long visit. With the enthusiastic approval of Andi, Anika, and Hayden, I vowed to one day make Australia a reality.

We saw the Byrnes a couple of times during those Colorado Springs years—spring break in Hawaii, a vacation during which I turned eleven, and a winter ski weekend in Park City. Mom and Bernie went to Cabo San Lucas, a getaway orchestrated by Dad and

Connor intended to pull Mom from her lingering melancholy, and to celebrate the recent news that Bernie and Connor were expecting twins. The spring of my twelfth birthday, Dad deployed to Afghanistan and, right after eighth grade started, Mom let me play hooky so she and I could fly to South Carolina to help the Byrnes with their baby girls, who were born at the tail end of August.

On the flight, I voiced the question that had nagged me since Bernie called to share that she was pregnant. "Does it make you sad knowing that Bernie has two healthy babies after what happened with our baby?"

"Sometimes," Mom said. "But my sadness never overshadows how happy I am for Bernie, Connor, and Beck. I'm so thankful their outcome was different. Does it make you sad?"

I swirled my Ginger Ale in its plastic cup. Tiny bubbles floated to the surface. "More like jealous. Two baby sisters? Beck is *so* lucky."

Mom laughed. "He might not feel that way when Bernie asks him to do diaper duty."

"Gross," I said, wrinkling my nose. "But he'll help. He's good that way."

She tucked a lock of hair behind my ear. "You're excited to see him, aren't you?"

I nodded. "And a little nervous. What if things aren't the same?"

"They might not be, lovey. But Beck is Beck and you're you, and what's between you is special. It always will be."

I swallowed another sip of Ginger Ale, hoping it would ease my apprehension.

The thing was, I'd always believed in the prediction of Mom's youth; I'd never had reason to doubt. But lately I'd found myself *really* wishing for the part about Beck and me to come true. I was smitten with Hayden—he was cute and clever and fun—but forever with a Colorado Springs soccer boy wasn't in the cards. The last couple of years spent mostly apart had cemented what I'd always known: Beck was my future. The idea of him with someone else—even hypothetically—twisted my stomach into knots. What if he'd snagged himself a South Carolina girlfriend? What if, in a decade, Bernie called to share that he was engaged? What if, one day, I had to sit through a wedding and watch Beck, wearing a suit and a rapturous grin, promise evermore to a girl who wasn't me?

After we landed, Mom rented a sedan and we made the drive to Fort Jackson, where the Byrnes had quarters. We lived on-post at Fort Carson, and seeing the neatly maintained residences with billowing American flags and baskets of geraniums, I felt at home. Connor greeted us at the door, cradling a tiny newborn. He gave me a one-armed hug, then kissed Mom's cheek as she fawned over the baby. "Mae," her daddy told us proudly.

Bernie came down the stairs, holding Mae's sister, Norah. The baby was asleep, but Bernie was crying before her feet hit the landing, then apologizing for crying because, "Ugh, my hormones are so out of whack!"

We gathered in the living room so Connor and Bernie could present Mom and me each with a bundled baby. I held Norah, who was warm and smelled of lilacs. Her features were miniature and perfect. Just a few weeks old, and she already resembled her big brother.

Her big brother, who was MIA.

"Where's Beck?" Mom asked.

Connor and Bernie traded an uncomfortable glance.

"He went out with some friends," Connor said.

"He'll be home soon," Bernie added. "We told him no later than five."

I looked at the clock that hung over the fireplace mantel.

It was five thirty.

———

Beck came home at ten after six, obnoxiously blasé. Connor and Bernie were pissed, all gritted teeth and white knuckles, but they didn't yell—I think to spare me the embarrassment. Late that night, though, I went into the kitchen for a glass of water and, on my way back to the guest room, overheard Connor getting after his eldest.

"Lia was disappointed. You should've been here."

How humiliating. Was it *so* obvious that I'd expected a warmer reception? I pressed my back to the wall, unable to step away.

"She didn't care," Beck said. "She didn't say a word to me during dinner."

"Probably because she thinks you're a chump. Look, I know it's been a rough few weeks. You're frustrated with me and that's fine, but don't take it out on Lia. Tomorrow you ought to invite her out with your friends."

"Jeez, Dad. I'm not gonna do that. She's *twelve*—a kid."

My face burned with indignation; I was twelve-*and-a-half*. Eighteen measly months separated Beck and me. Two grades. He hadn't given a rip about our age difference in the three years we spent in Washington, or when we snorkeled in Hawaii, or when I kicked his butt down the mountain, run after run, in Utah.

"Lia is family," Connor said in the no-nonsense voice he uses judiciously. "Your mother and I expect you to treat her as such. Got it?"

Beck grumbled an assent. I hightailed it down the hall before he could catch me eavesdropping, and ducked into the guest room where Mom was already racked out on her half of the bed.

I lay awake most of the night. A few times, I heard the twins fussing. Twice, I heard Connor pacing, quietly shushing one of the babies. Once, I heard Bernie singing "Beautiful Dreamer," the lullaby she used to sing to Beck and me when we were little and I'd spend the night on his bedroom floor, tucked into a unicorn sleeping bag.

Back then, things were easy.

I tossed and turned, examining the bones of my oldest friendship. Was it possible Beck had only treated me well because that's what his mom and dad expected? Had he been indulging me, a pseudo little sister who was really just a pain in the neck?

Maybe he *had* found a girlfriend.

The next morning at breakfast, he had the nerve to mumble, "Hey, Lia, you want to play Ultimate Frisbee with me and my friends later?"

"No," I said with zero inflection.

Connor raised his eyebrows. Bernie lowered her coffee mug, pursing her lips. In their nearby bassinet, the twins whimpered a duet.

"Lia," Mom said in her don't-embarrass-me tone. "Ultimate Frisbee sounds fun."

"I think it sounds boring."

Connor gave Beck a very obvious, very pointed look.

Beck sighed, rolling his eyes. "We could really use another player."

I spent a long moment staring him down. His gaze had once been warm, his invitations irresistible, but that morning he was as emotionless as I'd ever seen. And so, it was without guilt that I launched into a blistering shutdown. "Beckett, I can't think of anything I want to do less than play Ultimate Frisbee with you and your friends. Besides, I'd probably mess the game up, since I'm just *a kid*."

Connor dropped his forehead into his palm.

Bernie winced.

Mom gaped.

I flashed Beck a caustic smile before getting up and walking out of the kitchen, leaving my Cinnamon Toast Crunch to go soggy.

The day before Mom and I were due to leave South Carolina, Connor insisted on taking Beck and me to the Riverbanks Zoo

77

and Garden. "The babies will sleep most of the day. Let's give Bernie and Hannah some time together."

Time together? They'd had plenty. The zoo outing was meant to force Beck and me into interacting. We hadn't spoken in more than twenty-four hours—since I left the breakfast table in a huff—and I'd spent most of that time texting Andi and Anika diatribes about what a jerk my supposed best friend had turned out to be.

At the zoo's entrance, Connor paid our admission, then staked out a bench. Pulling his laptop from the backpack he'd brought along, he said, "I've got some work to catch up on. You two go explore. I'll meet you here for lunch."

I grimaced. The last thing I wanted to do was cruise the zoo with Beck. But Connor had hitched an ankle onto his knee and was tapping away on his keyboard, too busy, apparently, to deal with his son and me for another second.

"Let's go," Beck muttered, ambling off toward the grizzly bears.

We followed the property's perimeter, checking out the gorillas and the Galapagos tortoises, and then the African animals: elephants, giraffes, ostriches, and zebras. We saw my favorites, wallabies and koalas, before gazing in on lions, tigers, and baboons.

"Birds or reptiles?" Beck asked, consulting the map he'd picked up when we'd set off.

"Reptiles, I guess."

"I thought you'd choose birds."

"Do *you* want to see the birds?"

"No," he said. "But I don't want to see reptiles, either."

"Then don't," I snapped.

I left him standing on the path with his mouth hanging open and made my way to the Aquarium and Reptile Complex alone.

By the time he tracked me down, I'd seen more snakes, lizards, and turtles than I'd ever cared to. I was in front of the fifty-five-thousand-gallon tank, watching eels, sharks, and a rainbow of fish swim in circles when he sidled up next to me and said, quietly, "I'm sorry, Lia."

"Don't be. I don't care about the reptiles either."

"No, I'm sorry about the other day—about not being at the house when you got there. I'm sorry I didn't come after you when you bailed on breakfast."

I didn't take my eyes off the blue-and-yellow fish I'd been tracking. "Well, I'm sorry you've had to put up with me. I wish I wouldn't have come."

"I'm glad you did."

"Please. You've treated me like a pest."

"You're not a pest."

"I know I'm not!"

Everyone in earshot turned to look.

Beck led me to a nearby bench. After we sat down, he said, "I really am sorry."

"Fine. Forgiven."

He gave a humorless laugh, shaking his head. "If you only knew…"

And with that enigmatic half sentence, I got to thinking. *It's been a rough few weeks,* Connor had said to him the other night. *You're frustrated with me...*

"Beck, I *don't* know. You won't talk to me—you've barely even looked at me."

With a deep sigh, he dragged a hand over his face. "I was pissed—I *am* pissed. At my dad, though. Not you."

"But why?"

"Because he's deploying in a couple weeks."

My heart dropped; it was the worst possible news. "Where?"

"Afghanistan. Only six months, but still."

Military kids are the rare breed who'd qualify a six-month parental absence with the word *only.* Six months is better than nine months is better than twelve months—we know this firsthand.

"Why didn't you tell me?"

He shrugged in this defeated way that made the space behind my ribs feel hollow. "Your dad's there now. I didn't feel good about complaining. But my parents have these babies who've turned our house upside down, and he's just gonna peace out and leave Mom and me to deal."

It wasn't like that—Connor, I'm certain, was distraught about leaving his family. But I didn't contradict Beck because I'd had similar, irrationally unfair thoughts surrounding my dad's deployments: How dare he go adventuring on the other side of the world, abandoning Mom and me, expecting us to fend for ourselves?

80

"Is your mom upset?"

"Yeah, but she pretends everything's fine. It's gonna be hard on her though, you know? Two babies? Keeping the house together? Worrying about Dad? It's all on her."

"And you. You'll be there for her."

"It won't be the same."

That word—*deploying*—had blown my anger to bits. Beck had been distant. Beck had been irritable. Now that I knew why, all I wanted was to be there for him, the way he'd been there for me through my dad's deployments, my first days of school, my mom's lost pregnancy, and a million other instances that barely mattered until I added them all up.

I sent a prayer to the heavens: *Please, keep Connor safe.*

And then I slid closer to Beck, until my arm aligned with his. Letting my head rest against his shoulder, I said the only words that made sense. "I'm so sorry this is happening."

He moved like he might take my hand, and my pulse stumbled. Hayden and I had held hands a few times while walking home from school, and he'd kissed my cheek before I left for South Carolina. But the prospect of physical contact with Beck scrambled my brain in a way that made the fish in the giant tank seem to glitch.

He changed courses, slipping his fingers around my forearm, giving a tender squeeze before pulling away. Quietly, we sat together, watching schools of fish glide in graceful, synchronized circles through the tank's clear water.

They, too, had spent their lives swimming together.

A PATH, A PLAN

Seventeen Years Old, Tennessee

A few days after the second-worst Thanksgiving of my life, my parents take me out for lunch and what I suspect will be a conversation about The Future.

I'm still reeling from what happened at school on Wednesday: the crying, the hugging, the kissing, the crying.

Who have I become?

A drifter. A sham. A calamity.

I knew Beck more than fifteen years before I worked up the courage to kiss him.

I kissed Isaiah after fifteen minutes.

Mom, Dad, and I go to The Shaggy Dog at my suggestion, because the bread pudding really is amazing. After we're seated, I take a sourdough roll from the basket on the table and butter it. My parents do too, smiling as they wield their dull knives.

"So," Dad says, once we've ordered drinks. "Given any more thought to what happens after graduation?"

I shrug. Thought isn't required. I know what'll happen after graduation.

"Here's what I'm thinking," he says, as if I asked. "GMU and William and Mary, should you decide you want to go back to Virginia. Ole Miss, obviously. Austin Peay and UT, in case you decide you want to stay in Tennessee."

"What about CVU?"

His smile falters. "Millie, really?"

"Yes, really."

Flummoxed, he looks to Mom.

"Lovey," she says before hesitating, her gaze shifting back to Dad's, then skittering about the restaurant. We're so conversationally out of practice, she and I, that talking with her is like navigating an ice-slicked sidewalk in platform heels. Finally, with gentleness, she says, "You can go to school anywhere. Virginia, Mississippi, Tennessee. Back to Washington, like you used to talk about. Remember when you were so passionate about Australia? I'd love to see you consider a semester abroad, the way you once did. But all Daddy and I really want is for you to find happiness. You don't have to go to CVU for that."

Last year, before, when I'd bring up Commonwealth of Virginia University, my parents would give me tongue-in-cheek shit. "You've got Rebel blood," Dad used to say, and Mom would follow with, "Our years at Ole Miss were some of the best of our lives." Then they'd burst into a rousing

83

rendition of "Forward Rebels," complete with mimed cymbal strikes.

Since Beck passed, their attitudes about CVU has been less tongue-in-cheek, and more knife-hand.

Doesn't matter, though. I know where I belong. Since I kissed Isaiah—God, my chest seizes every time I think about the way I imposed myself on him—I've doubled down on the life Beck and I dreamed up. I'll throw my whole heart into honoring our plan, no matter outside opinions and unwelcome judgments.

"I already applied," I tell my parents. Judging by their reactions—the vein in Dad's temple pulsing and Mom's jaw grazing the table—they'll lose their minds if I mention it was an early decision application. "Early action," I lie, pushing my shoulders back, projecting poise I don't feel. "I took care of the fee and got in touch with the Office of Veteran Services and everything. I thought you'd be proud."

"If that were true," Dad says, "you would've told us when you did it." Brows knitted, he lets out a gusty breath. "Okay. So you applied. Early action is nonbinding. An application doesn't mean you're committed."

Versus early decision, which *is* binding.

"But I *am* committed," I tell him.

He smiles with condescension. "You'll apply elsewhere though. You'll want options."

"You've got time," Mom says. "And now that you've submitted one application, getting a few more out should be relatively easy."

"But I don't need time, or more applications, or other options."

My parents look at one another before turning their piteous gazes onto me.

Why do they always presume to know what's best?

"I'm going to CVU," I say, "or I'm not going to college."

That's when our waitress returns and, God, I'm grateful for the interruption. Dad, strained, asks for a cheeseburger. Mom, a BLT. I go for soup and a salad.

"It's foolish," Dad says once the waitress has stepped away, "to discount other schools. You'd thrive at William and Mary. And you know how we feel about Ole Miss."

Mom nods. "Of course, we'd be thrilled if you stayed in Tennessee. Austin Peay has a very good teaching program." She touches my hand. "Is that what you still want? To teach?"

"Obviously," I say, and then I recite the clairvoyant's long-ago prediction. *"She will walk a path similar to the one you blaze."*

Mom's face falls. "Oh, Lia. I hope you'll walk a path *you* choose. You can do anything. Be anything."

I shake my head. "Teaching is the plan. CVU is the plan."

My dad's posture stiffens as he shifts into his wartime persona. Gruffly he says, "Plans change."

"God, Dad, you don't think I know that?" It feels like my ribs are closing in, constricting my lungs, compressing my heart. I look at my lap, twisting my napkin in my hands, wondering how to make him—*them*—understand that to abandon my destiny is to betray Beck. "Life is random and cruel and completely

85

unfair," I say, "and last year, the most important part of my plan was stolen. Is it so wrong to cling to what I have left?"

"No," Dad says. "But be sensible. There's nothing for you at CVU. Nothing but misery and misguided obligation."

Mom squeezes my hand. "We know you miss Beck. We know you're sad. But going to CVU isn't going to bring him back."

I am so fucking frustrated with their refusal to hear me.

"Feel your feelings," Dad says. "But to march toward a dead end rather than change course... I'd hate to see it."

I've got nothing—nothing but a strong urge to scream until my throat bleeds.

The waitress arrives with lunch. We're quiet as she sets our dishes before us. We're quiet as she walks away. We're quiet as we take our first tastes of the food.

My soup is difficult to swallow.

The greens of my salad taste bitter.

I set down my fork.

"I've done my best to survive this last year," I remind my parents. "I've gotten good grades, moved to a new town, made friends. I'm getting by. But you have no idea—" My voice breaks. I exhale a tremulous breath, gripping tight to what's left of my composure. "You have *no idea* how hard it was to lose Beck. I just—I need you to trust me."

"How about this?" Mom says, eyes brimming with sympathy. "If you submit applications to at least two more schools *and* keep an open mind during the next few months, Daddy and I will stand behind your final college decision."

He nods. "See where you get accepted. We'll visit campuses—CVU included. If Charlottesville is where you want to be when the dust settles, we'll support you."

I nod, muzzled by my earlier deceit. If CVU accepts me early decision, it won't matter how many other schools I apply to. But I'm willing to concede in the name of getting my parents off my back.

Dad rests his hand on my shoulder. He sounds like he might cry when he says, "We want what's best for you, Millie. That's all we've ever wanted."

PERFECTLY NORMAL

Seventeen Years Old, Tennessee

Last Christmas, my parents were cognizant enough to tuck gifts under the tree, a few for each other, plenty for me. I didn't get them anything. My mind was too soupy for online shopping and, while Macy offered to come with me, I couldn't muster energy enough to endure a trip to the mall. Sitting in the living room Christmas morning, pulling paper from presents, molding my face into a weak approximation of appreciation, was like trying to breathe underwater.

This year, I want to do better.

The Friday school lets out for winter break, Paloma and I go to the Mall at Green Hills. It's packed, but we link arms and wade into the crowd, on the hunt for gifts.

She picks out a bathrobe for her mom, and I get mine perfume that smells of jasmine. Our dads are more challenging. After an hour of searching, we settle on wallets from Dillard's.

Then, ravenous, we pick up lemonades and soft pretzels at Auntie Annie's. We're people watching and stuffing our faces when Paloma's name rings out. A couple of boys make their way toward us, sidestepping frenzied shoppers. One, who I've seen bullshitting with friends at school, has rich brown skin and hair buzzed short.

The other is Isaiah.

"Hey, Trev," Paloma says, popping up to hug the taller of the two tall boys. She bumps fists with Isaiah, then turns to introduce me. "Lia, this is Trevor. He's one of the first people I met when I moved to River Hollow last year. And this is Isaiah."

Trevor grins. "Good to meet you, Lia."

"Yeah, same."

He knocks his shoulder against Isaiah's, an obvious prompt.

Isaiah lifts his eyes to mine and, smoothly, says, "Hey."

"Hi," I return, as if I've never before set eyes on him.

How disingenuous, considering I had my tongue in his mouth a few weeks ago.

Paloma and Trevor spend a couple minutes catching up. Apparently he's on the basketball team, which has been playing preseason games for the last couple of weeks. He's just started going out with a junior named Molly, and he's hoping like hell she likes the bracelet he just picked out for her. I gather all this with my eyes glued to the floor, thinking about how Isaiah and Trevor make an odd pair. Trevor seems gregarious, a sharer and an easy laugher. Isaiah, conversely, is kind of emo. He strikes me as a creative type. Since we met, I've wondered about him as a photographer, or a musician, or a painter—I've wondered about him a lot, truthfully—and that makes me curious about his connection with basketballer Trevor.

"Who are you shopping for, Isaiah?" Paloma asks.

He clears his throat. "Uh, Naya."

My head snaps up, my gaze colliding with his.

Who the hell is Naya?

His girlfriend, probably.

Shit. He has a girlfriend.

He has a girlfriend, and I kissed him.

He looks away.

Heat ravages my neck, my face.

"That's sweet," Paloma tells him, and then she shines a smile on me. "Should we get back to it? I've still got to find something for Liam."

I nod. My voice has fled.

"Have a good break," Paloma tells the guys.

"Merry Christmas, P," Trevor says. "Nice meeting you, Lia."

I wave slackly as they disappear into the crowd.

Paloma drops down on our bench, breaking off a length of pretzel to point accusingly in my direction. "Girl. What the hell?"

I gulp my lemonade in an effort to cool off.

She persists. "You gonna tell me what that was about?"

I balance my drink between us. "You mean…?"

She laughs. "I mean the weirdness between you and Isaiah. Do you know him?"

I sigh. "We've met."

90

"And…what? You didn't vibe?"

"Oh, we vibed."

She gives me a cat-with-a-mouthful-of-canary grin. "Tell me everything."

I do.

She reacts accordingly: sympathy as I recount how I gave in to grief, pride as I describe the way Isaiah and I tidied the hallway, hopefulness as I tell her about those few moments when I conversed like an emotionally healthy person.

"Then I kissed him," I tell her, and she nearly falls to the floor.

"Did he kiss you back?"

"He did."

"And…?"

I close my eyes. "It was good."

I feel conflicted, *awful*, admitting this truth.

Paloma squeals. "So where's the problem?"

"Problems," I clarify. "First, I spent my whole life believing I was never meant to kiss anyone but Beck."

"Lia, it was an impulsive moment during a really hard day. And look, I don't know if saying so is going to make you feel better or worse, but it's not as if you cheated. Please don't beat yourself up."

I scoff. "Too late. Besides, what about Naya?"

She arcs an eyebrow. "Naya?"

"The girl he's shopping for?"

"Yeah. His sister."

"I…oh."

91

"Did you think—?"

"I don't know what I thought."

She smiles, though her expression is veiled in concern. "I don't know him well, but he seems like a nice guy."

"Yeah," I say, remembering the way he hugged me without hesitation. The way he cleaned up after our classmates. The way he played off my meltdown like it's perfectly normal for a girl to lose her shit during a seemingly average afternoon.

Paloma's eyes spark with mirth. "A nice guy, *and* a good kisser."

"Okay," I say, pulling her off the bench. "I thought you needed a present for Liam?"

"Yeah," she says, letting me pull her into the sea of shoppers. "I guess I do."

I owe her one for letting it go.

SOMEDAY

Fourteen Years Old, Virginia

When I was fourteen, we moved once again.

I was sad about leaving Colorado Springs, but I wasn't unhappy to be heading to Northern Virginia. My final sleepover with Andi and Anika felt like reading the last chapter of a favorite book. The next day, Hayden and I hugged goodbye in the empty living room of our just-packed rental. My dad was fresh off an Afghanistan deployment, and an Army Staff job at the Pentagon wouldn't require TDYs longer than a few weeks. Bummed as I was about leaving my friends and my favorite teacher, Ms. Bonny, the thought of having Dad home consistently for the next three years was a worthy trade.

Plus, Beck was in Virginia.

The Byrnes had arrived six months before we did. Connor was working for INSCOM at Fort Belvoir, and he and his family had settled in Rosebell, so we did too. It was an easy commute for Dad with teaching opportunities for Mom and a good high school for me. I was thrilled to be back in the same town as the Byrnes.

They came over the day our household goods were delivered, toting a foil-wrapped casserole, a bottle of booze, and a spray of cut flowers. Mom and Bernie sat on a blanket in the front yard, checking box numbers off an inventory list as the movers unloaded the sardine-packed truck. Norah and Mae played with a collection of Little People in the grass. Dad and Connor were in the house, sipping whiskey out of paper cups, directing traffic as box after box was hauled inside.

After the mess that was our South Carolina visit, I'd been worried about how Virginia would treat Beck and me. We weren't kids anymore, and he'd had a head start establishing a life in Rosebell. Maybe, in his eyes, I'd be a chore.

But no way. He'd been front and center on the porch when his family arrived at our new-to-us house. His grin was incandescent. His hug was instantaneous and made me feel like I was being folded into the embrace of a grizzly bear. Since I'd last seen him, he'd shot up in height and filled out in frame. He was Herculean, suddenly, and I was a sprite in his arms.

Just like that, my time with Hayden became a dress rehearsal.

Beck and I hung out in the backyard, where a tire swing was suspended from a massive red maple, left behind by the house's previous tenants. Three years earlier, we would've squished on together, but I was halfway to fifteen and he'd just turned sixteen, so it seemed strange to jump into the physical closeness we'd shared when we were little. Instead he pushed me on the swing as we fell back into the friendship we'd known our whole lives.

He shared what he'd picked up about our new school, Rosebell High, where he'd been enrolled for the final months of his sophomore year, and the first few weeks of his junior year. I told him about the road trip I'd survived: Colorado Springs, Colorado, to Rosebell, Virginia, with my parents, newly reunited after too many months apart.

"They couldn't keep their hands off each other," I said, shuddering.

He laughed. "Six months is an epic dry spell. Who can blame them?"

"I can," I said, stretching my legs as the swing glided over the yard. "They're gross."

"They're in love," he said, catching the swing. Holding it in place, he turned it so we were face-to-face. Sometime during the last few years, his voice had become a deep baritone that reverberated through my bones. His eyes held fast to mine. "Someday you'll get it. *We'll* get it."

Maybe I already did.

Our three-year separation had made me long for Beck— his humor, our meandering conversations, the comfort of his presence. Being with him again made it easy to understand, suddenly, why Mom and Dad couldn't quit chattering, why they were always holding hands or resting a palm on the other's leg, why I'd catch them locked in a stare, like there wasn't anyone in the world but the two of them.

95

I wanted the same—all of it.

I wanted it with Beck.

They're in love, he said.

Was it love, that current of electricity raising goose bumps on my skin?

Did he feel it too?

"You're gonna like RHS," he said, turning the swing back around and sending me into the air again. "It's a good school—cool people. I'll introduce you around next week."

I wasn't sure if he was oblivious to the brain-melting realization I was coming up against, or if he was having one of his own, and deflecting.

I leaned back, letting my hair fly out behind me, shaking that idea free.

Beck wasn't in love with me. He was silly and fun. He was my favorite friend. Someday, hopefully, our fate would find us, but for now he was chosen family, same as he'd always been.

He spun the swing and flashed me a grin, and I was overcome with fondness.

We were together again, exactly as I'd wanted. I wasn't about to complicate things by giving in to my crush. For the time being, friendship would have to be enough.

My first morning at Rosebell High, Beck caught up with me and, true to his word, introduced me to his circle of friends.

Raj, a member of the Academic Decathlon Team, and hurdler. Stephen, a man-bun-sporting swimmer. And Wyatt, a third-generation Rosebell High legacy who stands five feet, four inches and makes up for what he lacks in height with humor. Wyatt's girlfriend was part of the group too. Macy favors thick-framed glasses and bell bottom jeans, and she has the cutest gap-toothed grin. She seemed accustomed to and unamused by the boys' roughhousing.

I liked her on the spot.

When the bell rang, the guys sent me off with salutes, Macy flashed an ironic peace sign, and Beck pointed me in the direction of my first class.

The day went smoothly, until lunch. Macy had invited me to sit with the group, which was so nice, seeing as I was a freshman, she was a sophomore, and the boys were all juniors. I'd made it to the sandwich line without tripping or dropping my bag or bumping into anyone, but Octobers in Virginia are warmer than Octobers in Colorado, and the cafeteria was like a sauna. I shed my sweater, draping it over an arm as I waited to collect a sandwich.

I'd dressed in a white tank that morning and the shadow of my bra, plum colored, lacier than any other underthing I owned (Mom only bought it after I'd pleaded) was visible.

But *barely.*

A couple of guys stood in the line next to mine, waiting for the hot lunch of fries and corn dogs, and they weren't discreet about noticing what I had on under my tank. I crossed my arms

97

and met eyes with the taller of the two. He had expanders in his earlobes and his hair was uneven, like he'd taken shears to it himself. His buddy wore a ratty Washington Nationals hat. I flashed my most disgusted look, hoping they didn't register the flush consuming my face.

Beck and his friends were in a far corner of the cafeteria. He caught my eye and grinned, and I felt better, knowing I wasn't on my own.

I felt better—until the oglers jumped lines and invaded my personal space.

The one with the shaggy hair bumped my bag, then said, blockishly, "Oops."

They laughed. And then they closed in, bringing their musky scents into my bubble. I heard the word *ass* and then *tits*, and I wanted to sink through the floor. Instead I hunched my shoulders, tucking in my chin, making myself as small as possible.

There were two people between me and the front of the line.

I had too much pride to let a pair of assholes chase me away from lunch.

They were right behind me, carrying on about the fit of my jeans, the scent of my shampoo, and the unfortunately sheer quality of my top. And then the taller boy brushed up against me and pressed his palm to the small of my back—actually *touched* me. I was too shocked to move. His hand slithered lower, to my butt, and the boy in the baseball hat snickered, either at my distress, or his friend's audacity.

My fear became fury.

98

I jerked away. "Don't *touch* me."

He lifted his hands in feigned innocence, his buddy looking on with a smirk. But before I could scream my wrath, Beck was there.

He grabbed the taller boy's arm and whipped him around. "What's your problem?"

"There's no problem," the boy said, wrenching free of Beck's grasp.

"I think there is."

"Hey, it's done," I said, taking Beck's hand. "Let's go."

He shook me off and leaned menacingly toward the guy. "You just felt up a girl who clearly wanted you to back off."

Worried a teacher would catch Beck yelling and assume him responsible for the commotion, I scanned the cafeteria. Aside from a couple of busy cashiers and a distracted custodian emptying a trash bin on the far side of the room, I didn't see any adults monitoring the crowded space.

The boy, who didn't look so imposing with Beck stacked against him, said, "Naw, dude. She was into it."

Beck swiveled to face me, then asked sardonically, "Lia? Were you into having your ass grabbed by a stranger?"

"No," I said with renewed confidence. "I told him to leave me alone."

"Bullshit," the groper muttered.

Beck got in his face. "Stay away from her."

"What do you care?" the boy challenged.

Beck shoved him backward, and I thought of King Kong

swatting terrified New Yorkers aside as he stormed toward the Empire State Building. The boy staggered, knocking into his buddy, who caught him, barely keeping the both of them upright.

"I care because she's my best friend," Beck said. "And if you touch her again, I'll fucking end you."

His complexion was ruddy, and there was murder in his eyes, but when I crossed into his line of vision, his expression cleared. He slung an arm over my shoulders and guided me away.

"You okay?" he asked as we made our way to the table where his friends waited.

"Totally," I said, disregarding my thudding heart and clammy palms. "Just hungry."

He smiled. "You can share my lunch."

Once we reached the table, Macy went all mama bear, checking to be sure I was okay, asking if I wanted her to walk me to the bathroom so I could collect myself.

"I'm fine," I told her, and I meant it.

At Beck's side, I was untouchable.

"Those guys are dicks," Macy told me after Beck passed over one of the two turkey and cheese sandwiches Bernie had packed for him. "Last year they harassed a girl in my English class until her parents complained to the administration. They were suspended for three days." She rolled her eyes. "Give me a break, right? They're predators. They went right back to the same shit."

"Probably not anymore, though," Wyatt said.

Raj thudded Beck on the back. "Our boy got through to them."

Beck shrugged. "My dad would've had my ass if I'd let them do Lia wrong."

I deflated. That's what motivated his chivalry? Fear of Connor coming down on him?

He bumped my shoulder, then leaned in to whisper, "Sure you're good?"

His low voice in my ear, his bulky arm against mine, the way he checked in, privately—a shiver built. I tamped it down.

I nodded. Yep, good. Totally and completely *good*.

Later that afternoon, he texted: Let me take you home?

Of course.

<hr>

The rest of the week was a lot of the same, minus the uninvited fondling. I met people in my classes, and I joined a few clubs—Key Club, French Club, and a creative writing club facilitated by my Lit teacher—but I mostly hung out with Beck and his friends. Occasionally, seedlings of doubt poked through the soil of my contentment: Did they really want an underclassman hanging around? But when I'd test them by showing up late for lunch or bowing out of our morning catch-ups, someone, usually Beck or Macy, rose questions.

I glowed.

A couple weeks after the lunchtime debacle, walking to fifth period with Macy and Wyatt, we cruised by a pretty girl with sleek brown hair. She was wearing a Rosebell Track and Field sweatshirt and a scowl, which deepened as she and I made fleeting eye contact.

"That's Taryn," Wyatt said as we rounded the corner. "She and Beck had a thing."

I'd assumed Beck had dated, though he and I never spoke of it. I wasn't so besotted I'd turned delusional. Of course he'd been interested in girls. But seeing one of those girls in the flesh clogged my windpipe for a few scary seconds.

"It's done," Macy assured me—maybe because I'd started to turn blue. "It has been since before you came to Rosebell. And it only lasted a second."

"No big thing," Wyatt confirmed.

So Beck had been drawn to a tall brunette, an athlete with an intimidating stare. A girl who was very different from me: a petite blond who will always choose community service over sweaty sports. I didn't care about Taryn—I didn't *want* to care—but I must've looked properly disturbed for Macy and Wyatt to go on about what a meaningless romance hers and Beck's had been.

Macy looped her arm through mine. "It was nothing like what he has with you."

"What he has with me?"

"You know, the way he acts when he's with you."

I lifted a brow. "How's that?"

She and Wyatt traded glances, then looked at me like a pair of deer caught in the high beams of a semitruck.

"You guys. How does he act when he's with me?"

102

Wyatt shook his head. "Beck would throttle me for disloyalty, and I'd deserve it." He kissed Macy's cheek and zipped off down the hall.

She tugged me aside, out of the current of traffic. Nudging her glasses up her nose, she said, "Boys can be too obtuse for their own good. I'll tell you what I've observed, okay? But I don't want you to freak out."

I was already freaking out.

Beck and I had been spending a lot of time together. The weekend before, we'd holed up in his room with popcorn and Red Vines to marathon *The Lord of the Rings* trilogy, then spent ages debating which were superior: the films or the novels. He favored the movies, and I liked the books. We were stuck at a stalemate when he flopped me back on the bed and tickled me until I was gasping with laughter, shrieking, "Okay—you win! The movies are better!"

He'd smiled then, hovering over me, triumphant. He brushed a lock of hair from my face and said, "Let's never fight again."

I lay awake for hours that night, analyzing his comments and scrutinizing his gestures, examining the gentle way he'd touched my hair from every possible angle.

Because...what if?

No—we were lifelong friends, and I was probably projecting. Still, my thoughts wouldn't quiet, and my stomach wouldn't settle; my deepening feelings for Beck scared me.

What if he never fell for me the way I was falling for him?

Exhausted, I fell asleep without resolution.

103

In the bustling hallway, Macy continued. "He's very…checked in with you."

"What does that mean?"

"You know…he pays attention. He gets you."

"Because we've known each other forever. Literally. Forever."

"Sure," she said, humoring me. "But he's always smiling when you come around, and he practically implodes when he thinks someone's done you wrong. I think he liked Taryn fine, but he didn't search for her when she wasn't in our circle. He didn't make grand declarations about how she was his best friend. She seemed like…a placeholder."

"Well, no wonder she shot eyeball lasers at me—she probably thinks I'm trying to steal her boyfriend."

"He's not her boyfriend," Macy pointed out.

"He's not mine, either."

She linked her arm through mine, and we started walking again. "Seriously, babe," she said, steering us around a slower-moving group. "Even before you started at RHS, I knew all about you. Beck talked about you constantly."

I bit back the smile threatening to split my face. "That must've been annoying."

"It wasn't. He liked you, so we liked you. And now we really like you, because you're just as cool as he was always going on about."

December 22

Dear Ms. Graham,

I am delighted to inform you that the Commonwealth of Virginia University's Admissions Committee has admitted you under the Early Decision Program. Allow me to be the first to commend you on your outstanding achievements. Your academic record, your volunteer work, your essay, the endorsements of people who know you, and your personal qualities stood out among a record number of Early Decision applicants. We are confident you will flourish in CVU's diverse and demanding learning environment.

The attached CVU brochure will provide you with information regarding your commitment deposit, financial aid, housing, and various other aspects of campus life. In the weeks ahead, I encourage you to learn all you can about the opportunities afforded to undergraduates at CVU. Our faculty and students are eager to share the Eagle Spirit with you!

A heartfelt congratulations, and best wishes to you and your family for a joyous holiday season. Please reach out to the Undergraduate Admissions Office with questions. We look forward to having you on campus for the upcoming Fall Semester.

Sincerely,

Laura L. Ovidio

Laura L. Ovidio
Dean of Undergraduate Admissions

A THREAD

LIA: I got into CVU.

SOPHIA: OMG!

MEAGAN: Congrats!

PALOMA: Lia! So proud of you!

MEAGAN: Can't believe you already found out.

LIA: Perk of applying early decision.

PALOMA: How excited are you?

LIA: I'm freaking out. Seems very real now.

PALOMA: I bet!

SOPHIA: You deserve it.

MEAGAN: CVU's lucky to have you.

LIA: Yeah… I guess.

MEAGAN: Are your parents psyched?

LIA: Haven't told them yet.

PALOMA: Seriously? How are you keeping it in?

LIA: I guess I'm still trying to process it myself.

SOPHIA: Tell them tonight. Then tell us how it goes.

LIA: No way. I'm going to wait until after Christmas.

MEAGAN: What? Why?

LIA: I'm not sure "psyched" is how they'll feel.

PALOMA: But it's a huge accomplishment. CVU's super competitive.

LIA: They'll be proud. Probably. It's the early decision thing.

PALOMA: They want you to have options.

MEAGAN: I get that.

SOPHIA: But if CVU is what you really want…

LIA: It is. But it's complicated.

PALOMA: You know WE'RE psyched, right?

MEAGAN: Our future Eagle. *cawCAW*

LIA: LOL. You guys are the literal best.

NO PRESSURE

Seventeen Years Old, Tennessee

After a few days spent attempting to process the CVU acceptance letter that's landed in my inbox, I come downstairs on Christmas Eve to find my parents working on our latest puzzle, an idyllic winter scene, as they FaceTime with Bernie, Connor, and the twins. I hang back, listening as Norah and Mae chatter about the holiday program their class put on; their parents confirm its adorableness.

"Your mama sent pictures," Mom tells the twins. "Will you sing us one of the songs you learned?"

Mae breaks into a lisped version of "Silent Night" while Norah tucks herself under Bernie's arm, content to let her sister take the spotlight. They look so much like their brother. It must be torture, sometimes, for Connor and Bernie to see Beck in the girls' tawny freckles, in their dimpled grins, in Mae's exuberance, in Norah's starry-eyed scheming.

I miss them almost as much as I miss him.

I shift, and the floor creaks under my feet.

My parents turn. Mom waves me over, gesturing to the iPad and then the puzzle. Dad gives me an encouraging smile.

Though Bernie and I are now halfway through the first season of *Gossip Girl* and text about it regularly, we haven't communicated about anything significant, and we haven't yet spoken on the phone. That feels like opening a box that can't be resealed.

I shake my head, then turn and trot up the stairs.

In my room, I shoulder a moment of regret, having shunned the Byrnes once again.

Later, the clatter of measuring cups and the whir of Mom's stand mixer filter upstairs. Every year, she preps homemade cinnamon rolls that spend all night in the fridge, then rise in the warm oven as we open gifts, filling the house with their yeasty scent. Traditionally we've eaten them, gooey and sweet, as midday brunch, after presents and showers, before naps and Merry Christmas phone calls to Grandma and the Byrnes.

Last year there were no cinnamon rolls.

I'm on my feet, ready to brandish a rolling pin, when my phone begins to ring. I pull it from its charger, expecting Paloma, though she texted this morning to tell me she was on her way to her tío and tía's house to help make tamales.

It's Bernie.

I answer. I don't know why, but I do.

"Girlie, hi," she says, breathless. "I wasn't sure you'd pick up."

Beck would be crushed by the way I've cold-shouldered his

family. If our fates had been reversed, if I'd left him behind, he would've put his needs aside. He would've stepped up for my parents. He was generous. Selfless. Extraordinarily kind.

I squeeze my eyes closed, barricading a rush of humiliated tears.

"Lia," Bernie says, fracturing what's become an uncomfortable silence. "I've got news. Big news that I wanted you to hear from me... Connor's decided to retire."

I'm stunned. Connor and my dad have both served more than twenty years. While Dad's talked occasionally about off-ramping, Connor used to joke that Uncle Sam would have to pry his dog tags from his cold, dead fingers.

"I can't believe it," I tell Bernie.

"Sometimes I can't either. But he's ready. He gave up a lot of time with Beck. He wants it to be different with Norah and Mae. He's going to teach high school history." I hear a smile in her voice when she adds, "Believe it or not, he's excited about getting back into the classroom."

"Wow," I say, sitting on my bed, curling my legs beneath me. "He'll be an amazing teacher. Where will you live?"

"We'll stay in Virginia." Her voice goes wistfully soft as she says, "Beck's here."

Of course. He'll spend eternity at a small cemetery in Alexandria.

"I have an invitation I hope you'll consider," Bernie says. "No pressure, though."

"Okay," I say, though I'm already on edge. People only say *no pressure* to help themselves feel better about making a pressure-backed request.

"Your mama and daddy are planning to visit for a few days in March, for Connor's retirement ceremony. It'll be during your spring break. We'd be thrilled if you'd come too."

Okay, *no*.

I'd like to support Connor and, more and more, I think I could handle seeing him, Norah, Mae, and Bernie. But I can't go back to Rosebell. Beck's spirit lingers on its streets. In Arlington's restaurants. At the Tidal Basin. Within the walls of the Byrnes' house.

Maybe memories of my time in Virginia with Beck should comfort me.

They shred me.

"Please think about it," Bernie says, putting chinks of indecision in my armor. "There's a place for you at the ceremony, and a place for you in our lives. Always."

A NEW LEAF

Seventeen Years Old, Tennessee

On New Year's Day, I jot resolutions into my journal.

I will cherish my friends.
I will try something new.
I will treat Mom and Dad better.
I will honor Beck.

Then I invite Paloma, Meagan, and Sophia over. My parents (and Major) are elated when the doorbell rings. I give them all a look—*chill*—before answering, then making introductions while my dog turns giddy circles in the foyer.

"I'll bake cookies!" Mom says as I lead the girls to the stairwell.

Up in my room, Meagan says, "Your parents are super nice."

"I guess." I lower my voice. "I still haven't told them about CVU."

Soph's eyes widen. "When will you?"

"In February. When Early Action acceptances are sent

out. I'll let them go on believing that's how I applied. What I haven't figured out is how to convince them that CVU is the school for me. They're stuck on this idea that I'm only interested because that's where Beck went."

Meagan asks, "Where'd you want to go before he landed in Charlottesville?"

I tell my friends about the Pacific Northwest, and my daydreams of a semester in Melbourne or Sydney. "But I was a kid back then. I had no idea what to look for in a college, or what I'd actually want to do after high school. CVU is a *great* school," I tack on, though I sound like I'm trying to convince myself as much as I am them.

"It really is," Paloma agrees. "But Australia! That would be so cool. You could spend a semester there through CVU, right?"

"Probably," I say, though I'm not even sure if CVU has a study abroad program. When Beck and I got together, five months spent living in a different hemisphere became entirely unappealing, and I started to think of Australia as a pipe dream.

Paloma's taken a seat on my bed with Soph, while Meagan's perched on my desk chair. I sink down to the floor with Major, who's settled now that he's had a chance to give my friends snuffles. I try to relocate my center, my good mood, but doubt's waging a storm in my head as I recall the posters I used to admire in Ms. Bonny's classroom: Kings Canyon and the Great Barrier Reef and cuddly koalas.

God—Australia is a world away from Charlottesville.

I ask Beck, *Am I doing the right thing?*

Oblivious to the uncertainty she's introduced, Megs scans the many photos tacked to the bulletin board over my desk. Disneyland, Park City, Rehoboth Beach. Major, being his lovable puppy self. A couple of me and Macy, who I haven't heard from since November, when I left her text unanswered, but who I know, thanks to social media, is enrolled at GMU and living her best life in an apartment with Wyatt. And Beck... Pictures of the two of us at The Mall, cherry trees blooming pink in the background. At Busch Gardens, hair tousled, fresh off a roller coaster. Sharing the tire swing that hung in my family's Rosebell backyard.

"This is him?" Meagan asks, pointing at a close-up taken just after Beck signed his CVU letter of intent. He's grinning, easy and disarming.

I nod.

"Okay," she says with an impish smile. "Now I get why you wanted to follow him to college."

I laugh and stick out my tongue at her.

"Hang on," Sophia says, getting up for a closer look. She puts her finger on the corner of one of my favorites. Beck, a toddler, hair carrot-orange, struggling to hold a swaddled baby who's been perched precariously in his lap. "Is this him, too?"

"Yep. And me."

Meagan's eyes get big. "When you said you'd known him all your life, you actually meant *all* your life."

Paloma catches my attention and arches an eyebrow, silently asking: *Want me to shut this down?*

114

I do—I really do.

But then, I think of my fourth New Year's resolution, lettered in purple gel pen.

My history is tied up in Beck, segmented like a series of books. Growing up, I was *Lia, Fated for Beck*. I reveled in becoming *Lia, Love of Beck's Life*. For too long, I've been *Lia, Grieving Girl*. Now it's time to morph into another version of myself, the protagonist of an unwritten story. One without a title—or plot, yet—but a story with a message: Lia, who remembers. Lia, who shares the good.

"Our parents have been friends since college," I say, because I'm not sure where else to start. "He and I met the day I was born. He was a part of all my firsts. All my best days. He was my whole world."

Paloma must realize I'm about to give in to tears, because she joins me on the floor, folding my hand into hers. Gravely she says, "He was really hot."

The humor hits its mark. Laughter fizzes in my chest, and I set it free, knowing Beck, too, would find Paloma's ill-timed observation riotously funny.

"He was," I say through a rush of giggles.

"You should talk about him more," Meagan says.

"I know. It's…it's still hard."

She tucks a lock of freshly pinkened hair behind her ear. "It was hard for me after my mom died, for a really long time. But now, talking about her feels like carrying a torch. Like keeping her spirit alive."

"She said the same thing to me last spring," Paloma says. "After my abuelo died. She got me talking. That's when I started to heal."

Meagan smiles and blows her a kiss. "Queen of Mourning, over here."

We spend a while covering less depressing topics. The holidays. Our schedules for the upcoming semester. Sophia goes on about her club volleyball team. Paloma shows us the Tiffany & Co. bracelet Liam sent for Christmas and tells us that he's got plans to visit River Hollow during spring break. Megs tells us about how her dad attempted to fry this year's Christmas turkey—with her gran's blessing—which resulted in a bird-sized hunk of char and a trip to the local pho restaurant.

We're cracking up when there's a knock on my door. Mom comes in with a platter of chocolate chip cookies. She sets it on my desk, and my friends descend. She doesn't stick around and I appreciate that, but before she ducks out of the room, she gives me a grin like I haven't seen in ages. Her eyes twinkle and her smile lines crinkle—which she hates—and I know her heart is happy, seeing me with friends after such solitude.

"Thanks, Mom," I say.

Then I shoo her out the door.

FORMAL

Fifteen Years Old, Virginia

Raiden Tanaka approached me in the courtyard while I was making my way to first period. Macy was walking beside me and, as he stepped into our path, arms laden with pink roses, we both stopped short.

"Hey, Lia," he said, lifting a hand to wipe his brow. It was February, the dead of winter, but he was glistening.

Raiden sat beside me in math class. We were in tenth-grade math, though I was a freshman and he was a junior. He'd explained early in the year that he had dyscalculia, which made him confuse numbers the way someone with dyslexia confuses letters.

"Math trips me up," he'd said, rubbing his reddening neck. "But I'm not stupid."

"Obviously not," I'd said, endeared by his openness.

We'd been math buddies since.

Raiden is a virtuoso on the cello, and cute. His parents immigrated to the US from Japan, and he has shiny black hair and intensely brown eyes. Also, he has the longest lashes of any person I've ever seen in real life.

He passed me the roses and said, "I was wondering if you'd come to formal with me?"

I was so surprised it took an elbow from Macy to prompt my response.

"Oh, wow, Raiden."

"Wow, as in *yes*?" he said, eyes lit with hope.

"Yes, of course," I said, finding my footing after the surprise of his invitation. "Thank you for asking me."

He grinned. "Can't think of anyone I'd rather go with. We'll hammer out the details in class later, cool?"

"Yeah. And thank you for the flowers."

He stepped forward and wrapped an arm around me, a hug that was as awkward as it was sweet. And then he was off, with a spring in his step.

Macy pivoted to face me. There was a waggish gleam in her eye. "Raiden Tanaka," she said, equal parts amused and delighted. She knew him from orchestra; she'd been playing the violin since fourth grade. "I had no idea."

"Don't be weird. He and I are friends."

Even in the cold, I could feel myself blushing. Raiden's invitation had been unexpected, but not unwelcome. He was very cute and very nice, and I was sure we'd have fun together.

"Still. Formal. As a freshman."

"Right?" I said, imagining myself in chiffon, curls falling around my shoulders, a fragrant corsage on my wrist. Raiden, sporting a suit, twirling me on the dance floor. "Who would've thought?"

At Rosebell High, freshman and sophomores are only allowed to go to formal if they've been invited by a junior or senior. I'd had no illusions about attending. With the exception of the casual friends I'd made in my classes, I hung out with Beck's social circle. There was no way Raj or Stephen would invite me to a dance. I'm pretty sure they thought of me as a kid-sister. Wyatt was with Macy. And Beck hated school dances, and dancing in general.

"Too cheesy," he used to say. "Too cliché."

"I wonder what Beck will think," Macy said, giving voice to the thought that'd just rooted in my head.

I shrugged. "He won't go to formal. That doesn't mean I shouldn't."

"Totally. I just wonder if he might be bummed."

"I doubt it."

She gave me a look that communicated her uncertainty, but she didn't dampen my excitement. She hooked her arm through mine, careful not to smoosh the flowers I'd be carrying around for the rest of the day, and asked, "Want to go dress shopping this weekend?"

⸻

Macy's musings on whether Beck might be upset about me and Raiden going to formal bothered me enough that I'd spent the

119

morning considering whether to swing by my locker to stash the roses before lunch.

But…why?

I'd been harboring a crush on Beck for months, and he'd given me no indication that his feelings had escalated the way mine had. I would've happily jumped into an ocean of *more*, but I was okay with the status quo. He obviously was too.

I took the roses to lunch.

When I sat down, placing the bouquet at the end of the table where it would be out of the way, Beck looked at it. Then he looked at me.

"Someone gave you flowers?"

"Yes," I said, pulling my lunch from my bag. I didn't like the way his mouth had dipped in disapproval, but I kept my expression neutral.

Side-eying the roses, he asked, "Why?"

"Why not?"

"That's not an answer."

Even though his sense of entitlement to the goings-on of my life was irritating, I used a sunny tone because I didn't feel like arguing. "I'm not sure that question warrants an answer."

"Who gave them to you?"

An uncomfortable tension had descended on our table. Raj, Stephen, Wyatt, and Macy had paused in their eating to observe Beck and me.

"Why do you care?" I said.

"I don't. I'm…curious."

Folding my hands on the tabletop, I met his gaze. "Raiden Tanaka gave them to me when he asked me to formal."

In my periphery, I caught Raj grimace, while Stephen let out a low "Oof."

"Formal?" Beck parroted, like the tradition was alien.

"Yes. It's a school-sponsored social event. Everyone dresses up and spends the evening dancing and posing for photos and having a fabulous time. I was invited. Does that satisfy your curiosity?"

"No. Who the fuck is Raiden Tanaka?"

I sighed. "He's in my math class."

Macy reached across Wyatt to pat Beck's arm. "He's a good guy."

"Sure he is," Beck said scornfully. And then, to me: "You told him you'd go?"

"Yeah. I think it'll be fun."

He balked. "You're gonna spend your birthday at formal with Raiden Tanaka?"

The dance was scheduled for the third Saturday in March. I knew this. But I hadn't realized that the third Saturday in March was the day I'd turn fifteen. Distress quickened my pulse as understanding took hold: I'd committed to celebrating my birthday at a dance with a relatively unknown boy, instead of with my parents and the Byrnes, like I had years past.

Misgiving must've been written across my face because, smugly, Beck said, "It'll be a *fantastic* birthday."

He didn't speak to me for the rest of lunch.

I didn't look at him.

I took the bus home, roses and all, because screw Beck for stealing my joy. He texted once—You coming?—and I ignored him because I was feeling petty and vengeful. I hoped he was standing in the parking lot. Waiting for me. Worrying about me.

When my mom got home from work, I showed her my flowers and told her about Raiden and formal. She was delighted and started tossing out ideas for dresses and hairstyles.

"You don't care that I won't be home for my birthday?"

"Of course I care. But formal is exciting. We'll spend the day celebrating while we get you ready. And we'll have the Byrnes over Friday night, or Sunday afternoon. It'll work out."

I was so overwhelmed by clashing emotions, my eyes welled with tears. "Beck's mad."

Mom zipped it about the dance. She gave me a hug and listened as I recounted the lunchtime squabble in a voice full of despair.

"Oh, Lia," she said once I'd finished. "I'm sorry that happened. Sounds like Beck is—"

She pressed her lips together, like she was having second thoughts about voicing whatever theory was spinning through her head.

"Sounds like Beck is what?"

"Jealous, maybe?" She said it quietly, as if betraying a confidence, which made me wonder how often she and Bernie discussed Beck and me.

I harrumphed. "Or maybe he's a jerk. He's not even planning to go to formal!"

"Regardless, he shouldn't have given you a hard time. But more often than not, there's a reason people behave the way they do."

"And you think Beck is jealous. Of what?"

"I'm not going to speak for him, lovey. But he's usually very good to you. He gets news that you're going to spend time with another boy, and suddenly he's, as you put it, acting like a jerk? Maybe he regrets not asking you to formal himself. Maybe he's disappointed that he won't get to spend your birthday with you. Maybe he's starting to realize something about himself. About *you*. Whatever the case, I'm sure the two of you will sort it out."

Her phone chimed in its familiar way: a text from Bernie.

I knew without having to look that its subject was formal.

I spent my fifteenth birthday getting all sorts of spoiled. My parents took me to brunch, where Dad promised he'd start teaching me to drive as soon as I was ready. Then Mom and I went for manicures and pedicures. Afterward we visited a fancy salon in DC where my hair was braided into a romantic updo. Bernie came over to help with my makeup and, bless her, didn't mention her son even once.

Over the last couple weeks, things had been weird between Beck and me. We were back to speaking, but stiffly. Formal and my birthday never came up. His grizzly bear hugs were no more. He'd quit poking my ribs and ruffling my hair and grabbing my hand in moments of amusement. I'd started riding the bus pretty regularly, because sitting beside him in the 4Runner his parents bought him—used and abused—for his sixteenth was too much.

When Raiden picked me up Saturday night, my parents escorted him inside for pictures. His suit complemented the ivory gown I'd picked out during my shopping trip with Macy. He brought a corsage, as I'd hoped. The white roses, stephanotis, and delicate baby's breath were perfect, and his hands shook a little as he slid it onto my wrist. He brought my mom peonies, her favorite flower, and a box of beautifully frosted cupcakes.

"Happy birthday," he said, presenting them to me.

I was surprised. I hadn't told him about my birthday.

We ate the cupcakes with my parents. He held his own with my dad, answering questions about current events as if he'd been previously briefed, and he was super polite to my mom. She flashed me more than one approving smile.

The dance was held at the Washington Hilton near Dupont Circle. The ballroom was gorgeous, and Raiden could not have been nicer. We spent several songs on the dance floor with his circle of friends, mostly from the orchestra, laughing and matching each other ridiculous move for ridiculous move. I saw Wyatt and Macy, who was wearing an elegant floral gown, and Raj and his date, Aimee, who went to Mount Vernon High School and was his on-again, off-again. I saw Stephen, who'd come stag and was clearly glad about it. I soaked up tons of birthday wishes from my friends and Raiden's.

I tried not to think about the birthdays I'd celebrated before, with the Byrnes. I tried not to think about the sense of missing I couldn't seem to shake. I tried not to think about the tension that had wedged itself between me and Beck.

And then I *saw* Beck, standing near the dance floor.

He was wearing a suit—a nice one. I'd never seen him in anything dressier than a blazer, and those rarities occurred because Bernie is good at threats. His tie was loosened, the top buttons of his shirt undone. His hair was in its usual charming disarray. He had one hand in a pocket, and the other was holding a cup of punch. I wondered if it'd been spiked, because how else could he tolerate something as *cheesy* and *cliché* as a high school dance if not with a steady drip of booze?

He was talking to Taryn, the girl he'd dated before I moved to Rosebell. The placeholder, Macy had called her. She looked stunning in a floor-length black dress, her hair pinned with a pearl barrette. It was easy to see why Beck had been drawn to her: she was beautiful, poised, and confident. I couldn't help but steal glances at them as Usher's "Yeah!" faded out.

I was imploding, heat and energy and *envy* razing me from the inside out.

As the music transitioned to a slow and sentimental Tim McGraw song, Beck looked away from Taryn to capture my gaze.

He was a struck match, blazing.

Raiden stepped into my line of vision. He smiled, circling his arms around my waist, positioning his hands politely. It was probably unintentional, the way he turned us so Beck was to my back, but it was certainly for the best. I brought my palms

125

to rest on Raiden's shoulders and tried to reclaim the happiness I'd found before Beck showed up. Raiden had given me a nice evening, after all, and that's what you're supposed to do at formal: dance with your date.

As soon as I'd found a rhythm with him, though, I felt a tap at my elbow.

I turned to find Beck.

"Is it cool if I steal a dance with Lia?" he asked Raiden.

Raiden's mouth bobbed open, then closed again. I had a feeling he wanted to suggest that Beck pound sand, but he seemed to lack the courage to tell off a guy who outweighed him by a solid fifty pounds.

When he'd been silent too long, Beck's gaze fell to me. "Lia?"

I nodded before Raiden could work out a response. Hoping my expression didn't appear too eager, I watched him shuffle off the dance floor to join a few of his friends near the refreshment table. Then I turned to face Beck.

I'd expected him to say something, whether it be an explanation as to why he'd come or an apology for the way he'd acted after finding out that Raiden and I were coming to formal together. He didn't speak, though. He strode forward and drew me against him. There was nothing hesitant about the way he initiated the dance—it was the opposite of how Raiden had timidly placed his hands along my spine. Beck and I had hugged a thousand times, but that night, he held me like the contact between his body and mine was life giving.

Maybe my mom had been right: maybe he *had* been jealous.

Or maybe he'd had an epiphany about himself, or me, or the possibility of us—the same as I'd experienced over the last several months. Whatever the case, that night he made it clear that he cared enough to dress up, come to a school dance, and move about the floor with his arms around me.

I closed my eyes, pressing my cheek to his chest, wholly at peace in his embrace.

During the song's final melodies, he dropped his chin, touching his cheek to mine. He smelled so good, like himself, but with an added note of cologne. His hands skimmed up, up, up, until they rested warmly against my neck.

He murmured, "Happy birthday, Lia," and, as the song ended, he let me go.

After the dance, Raiden drove me home. We skipped the various after-parties because I had a curfew, which I was secretly glad for. He'd spent the evening treating me like a princess, even after I was finished dancing with Beck. Still, I was ready to be alone with my journal and the newest layer of understanding I had regarding my feelings for Beck.

"That was fun," Raiden said as he walked me to the door.

"I thought so too. Thank you for the cupcakes."

He shrugged. "You should thank your friend for clueing me in about your birthday."

I smiled, making a leap. "Macy's considerate that way."

"No, not Macy. Your other friend, the dude who cut in on our dance."

It took me a second, though there'd only been one person

to interrupt Raiden and me on the dance floor. I spluttered, "Beck?!"

"Yeah, he pulled me aside last week and told me about your birthday. He also told me your mom likes peonies and that I should educate myself about what's going on in the world, unless I wanted to make an ass of myself in front of your dad."

I blinked, dumbstruck.

Beck had coached Raiden?

After the drama he'd stirred up a couple weeks before?

"It was cool of him to fill me in," Raiden admitted, taking hold of my hand.

"Yeah," I said, struggling to reclaim speech. "It was."

He ducked forward, pecking my cheek, and then he was off.

I floated into the house and up to my room, romanced not by Raiden, my date, but by Beck, who'd swallowed his pride to ensure that my night was special.

Sitting on my bed, I pulled out my phone and sent him a text.

Thank you. <3

UNABASHED

Seventeen Years Old, Tennessee

Second semester, senior year.

I'm taking Ceramics.

Second semester, junior year, my very darkest months, Mom and Dad stood by, eyebrows doubtfully lifted as I shuffled my schedule, transferring into the most challenging classes Rosebell High had to offer. They failed to hide their incredulity when I aced every single one, though I'm not sure why they were so surprised. After Beck passed, I gave up friends and clubs. I took a break from volunteering, and I quit on the Byrnes. I sank everything I had into school; it only made sense that I'd excel.

Last month, when Paloma suggested we sign up for Ceramics together, I vacillated. How would CVU perceive such a slack course? I went for it, though, partly so my parents will start to think of me as healed—whatever that means—and partly so I can hang out with Paloma last period of the day.

I beat her to the classroom, an outbuilding behind the library. She coasts in three seconds before the bell. Ponytail swinging, she hurries to the table I've claimed. It has stools for four, but none of the underclassmen have opted to join us, which is just as well.

"This is gonna be *excellent*," she says, settling onto a seat. She's still waiting to hear from USC, though I'll be shocked if she doesn't get in. Her GPA's even better than mine. She pulls her bag onto the table, unearths a tube of lipstick, and uses the reflective screen of her phone to paint her mouth a glossy pink. When she's satisfied, she turns her voluminously mascaraed gaze on me. "So? How was the first day of your last semester?"

"Better than expected. Yours?"

She grins. "The beginning of the end. Want to celebrate with bread pudding later?"

I nod, flashing her a smile as the bell rings.

Our teacher, Ms. Robbins, sports goldenrod nail polish and wears her sandy curls in a nest atop her head, reminding me of Ms. Frizzle from *The Magic School Bus* books. I listen as she talks about her grading policy, which is an A for effort, basically, and scope out the classroom. Cluttered shelves skirt the perimeter, a gallery of completed projects donated by students from semesters past. To the left there's a closet storing jars of glaze. To the right sit a half-dozen pottery wheels, dusty with dried clay. Behind Paloma are bricks of fresh clay, ripe with potential, and tins that hold potter's needles, sponges, and modeling tools. The air smells earthy and lush.

Ms. Robbins's space is the antithesis of *classroom*, and I kind of love it.

She's passing out the course syllabus when the door bangs open. Isaiah—

who I kissed

—blows in with nonchalant confidence.

Paloma catches my eye and smirks.

"Sorry I'm late," he tells Ms. Robbins.

She smiles shrewdly, making me suspect that she's had him in class before. "Don't let it happen again, Mr. Santoro." Scanning the room for seating options, her gaze lands on the table Paloma and I share because—*shit*—we've got empty stools. "There's a spot there, back by the clay."

Isaiah's attention lands squarely on me.

He smiles the most unabashed grin I've ever witnessed.

Fire consumes my face.

He makes his way over, looking comfortable and cool in jeans, a Memphis Grizzlies sweatshirt, and beat-up black Chucks. On one white rubber toe, someone's drawn a smattering of pink stars.

Ms. Robbins tells us to take a few minutes to read over the syllabus as Isaiah drops his backpack on the floor and pulls out the stool nearest mine. With a last-period-of-the-day sigh, he sits. "What's up, Paloma?" he says, tipping his chin in her direction.

"Nada. Excited to get my hands on some clay."

He turns his smile on me, milder now, more inquiry than salutation. I give a slight nod—*let's play it cool*—before looking

131

down at my syllabus, pretending to focus on its bullet points while I get lost reliving the warm want of our November kiss.

It's confusing and embarrassing and really freaking distressing to admit that I've thought about Isaiah Santoro a hell of a lot since that day.

"Lia," he says. "You ready to get your clay on?"

I let my eyes rise to his. "Sure. Ms. Robbins seems cool."

He gives me a quick once-over: my ponytail, my fleece, the aquamarine-and-sapphire ring I resumed wearing the day he and I met. He says, "She's the best. She advises Art Club."

"You're in Art Club?" Paloma asks.

"Yeah. I talked Trev into joining this year too."

"Like you guys don't have enough going on with basketball."

I furrow my brow and say to Isaiah, "You play basketball?"

As if I should be keeping tabs on his extracurriculars.

"He's captain of the team," Paloma tells me. "He's been varsity since he was a freshman, which is very unusual."

"That's me: very unusual," he says, charmingly self-deprecating. "League games start next week. Hope to see you both in the stands."

"Obviously," Paloma says.

Isaiah looks to me.

"Oh. I don't really know basketball," I say, leaving out the part about how my deceased boyfriend was a football fan. "But I guess I could come watch."

"You don't *watch*," Paloma says. "You scream your face off."

"You don't have to scream your face off," Isaiah tells me, his

132

voice quiet and focused, as if we're a lone pair on this vast, vast planet. I'm trying to figure out what to make of that when he adds, "Showing up's enough."

VOLLEYING

Seventeen Years Old, Tennessee

A couple days later, my good sense is nowhere to be found. I stay after Ceramics to talk to Ms. Robbins about Art Club.

"I like your class," I tell her. "If you've got room in the club, I'd love to be a part of it."

She smiles, eyeing me over her glasses. "We've got plenty of room. If you're carrying at least a C average and can join us during Advisory on Thursdays, you're in."

"I am, and I can."

"Then we'll see you tomorrow. Happy to have you, Lia."

Before I leave campus, I swing by the library to check out a few books for the research paper that was handed out in my Contemporary Lit class. We've got to include at least two physical books in our citations, even though the Internet is *right there*. It takes me forever to find sources, and by the time I'm on my way to the parking lot, basketball practice has wrapped for the day.

I spot Isaiah waiting on the sidewalk near the pickup loop in gym shorts, a Nike hoodie, and black-and-white Jordans. He's got his phone pressed to his ear.

Even from afar, I can tell he's unhappy.

I have to walk right by him to get to my car. He ends his call as I pass.

"All good?" I ask.

He pushes his phone into his pocket. "My ride fell through. Car battery's dead, and she's waiting on a jump. Otherwise yeah. All good."

Before my brain has a chance to catch up to my mouth, I say, "I can drive you."

"That's okay. I'll walk."

"Where do you live?"

"West side of town, near the post office."

"That's, like, five miles from here. Come on—my car's over there."

In the Jetta, he gives me his address and I punch it into the GPS before pulling out of the lot. His house is zoned for Rudolph High. I know because I joined my parents on house hunting trips when we arrived in River Hollow, and they asked the realtor about a million school-centric questions.

I ask Isaiah, "How come you go to East River if you live on the west side of town?"

"Open enrollment, freshman year. East River's a better school

135

than Rudolph, and since I can throw a ball through a hoop with a decent rate of accuracy, they were happy to have me."

"A decent rate of accuracy? I thought you were some kind of prodigy."

He flashes a grin. "Your word, not mine. You like East River?"

I shrug, flipping the Jetta's blinker. "It's different from my last school. A lot smaller. But I adore Paloma. I'm not sure what I'd do without her, Meagan, and Sophia."

I don't feel much like talking about myself, so I set loose a question I've harbored since November. "That woman who picked you up before Thanksgiving... Is she your mom?"

"No. I live with her, though."

"Oh. Why don't you live with your actual mom?" And then my manners resurface, having taken a hiatus equal to the length of this conversation. "I'm not trying to be nosy. I'm just..."

I'm interested.

"You're not being nosy," he says. "We're volleying—it's cool. The woman I live with, Marjorie, is my foster mom."

I'm surprised, and I don't think I'm going a very good job of hiding it.

The light flashes green, and I give the Jetta some gas. "She looked nice, that day in the parking lot."

"She's an angel," Isaiah says, his voice steeped in fondness. He laughs wryly. "You know, except for the dead car battery thing."

It's sweet how he talks about his foster mom. Endearing. I keep thinking about how I'm not sure I'm ready to open my heart up again, about how I should maintain emotional distance, yet I'm disarmed. "How long have you lived with her?" I ask.

"Almost six years."

"Is she married? Like, is there a foster dad in the picture?"

"No, but there's a foster sister. Naya. She's nine. She's lived with us nearly a year."

We're getting close to his house, and my head has become crowded with queries—so many, I'm not sure which to launch next. He must think my curiosity's satiated, though, because he says, "My turn?"

I glance at him. "To...?"

"Ask about you. 'Cause that's how conversations work."

The events of our first interaction, I'm sure, left him with a slew of questions. Only perilous inquiries can follow melting down and making out. But it'd be super weird to decline.

"Yeah," I say. "Okay."

"The day we met," he begins, and I brace myself, tightening my grip on the wheel as my pulse picks up its pace. "Had something specific happened, or were you generally sad?"

Turning onto his street, I say, "I was generally sad. Last year kicked my ass. But that day was also significant. It was the first anniversary of why last year kicked my ass."

I slow the Jetta as the GPS announces our arrival and shift into park. The house is a ranch-style with a brick facade. A café table and a pair of chairs sit on the front porch. The concrete walk is covered in softly illuminated chalk: rainbows and fire-breathing

137

dragons and a castle with a moat. I wait for Isaiah to toss another question my way.

His gaze is like a sunbeam. I feel it on my cheek...my hair.

He says, "I'm sorry you've had a shitty year."

I look at him, taken aback. "You don't want to know more?"

"Oh, I do." He drags a hand through his hair, allowing me another glimpse of the scar on his forehead, and a recollection jars me: *long limbs and ebony hair.* "The thing is," he says as I try to get a grip on my composure, "I know what it's like to be sad. I've had my ass kicked more times than I can count. Tell me more when you feel like it."

He climbs out of the car, stretching his arms over his head a second, showing off a sliver of skin below the hem of his hoodie. I look away because I'm feeling it again—that stirring of attraction that scares the hell out of me.

He dazzles me with a grin. "Thanks for the ride, Lia."

ENDEARMENT

Fifteen Years Old, Virginia

Beckett Byrne was, as far as I was concerned, a god among teenage boys: capable and strong; smart and outgoing; kind and funny. He earned varsity letters and had college track and field scouts vying for him. His smile was knee buckling. His loyalty was unwavering. He was cocksure on his mildest days, but he possessed an indefinable charisma that made people—made *me*—revere him.

By the midpoint of my sophomore year, the crush I'd harbored had morphed into full-blown infatuation.

When Beck would come over with his family, he was adorable with his sisters, sweet to his mom and dad, and respectfully chummy with my parents. Together, we baked cookies for the twins, burned through movies, and metro-ed into DC to take superlong walks. We had a route from the Capitol Building to the Washington Monument to the Lincoln Memorial to the Martin

Luther King, Jr. Memorial to the Jefferson Memorial, where we'd land on a bench and talk, looking out over the Tidal Basin.

After formal, my birthday, and our dance, I'd catch myself staring at him, daydreaming, pining. But I held back from acting on my feelings, too afraid of rocking our rickety boat. Sometimes, though, I'd catch him looking at me. He'd grin and give my ponytail a tug, or stick out his tongue, or wink, and I'd inwardly swoon. He'd resumed his grizzly bear hugs. He drove me to and from school. He showed no interest in other girls. But, despite our foretold destiny, we were still just friends.

I was frustrated. I wanted to set up house on his planet, not orbit it.

The first day of winter break, he was scheduled to have his wisdom teeth removed. He was pissed at Bernie for making the appointment at the beginning of what was meant to be a vacation, but Bernie didn't want her eldest to miss class. That morning, on their way to the oral surgeon's office, Beck texted me from his mom's Subaru.

I'm bored. And then: If I die today, go into my closet and find my nudie magazines. Box on the top shelf, under GI Joes. Trash them before my mom sees them.

I shuddered. Boys could be so gross.

You disgust me, I replied.

He returned: You delight me.

I smiled and asked: Why do you have nudie magazines during this, the Age of the Internet?

An ellipsis appeared as he worked on an answer. Same reason

you like books more than movie adaptations. Our imaginations are superior.

I snorted out a laugh.

If I survive, he texted, let's never speak of my nudie magazines again.

I typed: You'll survive, and I'll tease you about them forever.

The conversation went quiet. I resumed *The Vampire Diaries*, the show Bernie and I had recently started watching, assuming she and Beck had reached their destination. I didn't envy him. The thought of having teeth with massive roots pried out of my head made my stomach roil.

My phone vibrated. Come over later? Promise I won't bleed on you.

My heart, the silly thing, gave a flutter of excitement.

I typed back: Can't wait to see your chipmunk cheeks.

Late that afternoon, Mom drove me to the Byrnes.' Bernie ushered me inside. Norah and Mac were camped out on the couch, engrossed in *Encanto* and a shared bowl of Cheez-Its. I kissed their rose-gold curls before turning back to their mom.

"He's in his room," she told me, rolling her eyes. "He's a wimp, Lia. A big ol' wimp. Here—take these down, would you?"

She handed me a pair of gel ice packs, then waved me off.

I skipped downstairs to the basement, where Beck's bedroom was, along with a family room that served as the twins' play space. I knocked on the door, wary after that morning's talk of nudie magazines. Voice gruff, he called for me to come in.

The shades were drawn and the lights were off, save the small nightstand lamp. Beck reclined on his bed in sweats and an RHS T-shirt. He looked up from his laptop, positioned on a stack of pillows next to him. His expression was so pitiful, I couldn't help but laugh.

He wasn't noticeably swollen yet, but he looked feeble and pale, more exhausted than after a morning at the gym. Swatting indiscriminately at his computer's keyboard, he paused the movie, *Elf*, a mutual Christmastime favorite, then patted the spot beside him. I sat, biting my lip to keep my amusement from further announcing itself.

"You survived," I teased.

His answer was a mumbled, "Barely. They tortured me."

"You had a dental procedure, you baby. How are you feeling?"

"Terrible. Fucking *terrible*."

"Baby," I said again. This time, though, my voice lacked bite. My face warmed as I rewound and replayed those two syllables: *baby*. The word sounded tender, like an endearment. Hoping he was too hopped up on painkillers to evaluate my tone, my blush, or their combined implications, I offered him the gel packs.

He folded his arms over the barrel of his chest and tipped his head back. "Will you?"

I sighed like I was put out but really, I was glad to scoot closer. He smelled of the same deodorant he'd used since he was ten, the Dove shampoo he'd been lathering all his life, and the Tide detergent Bernie favored. I placed the gel packs against his freckled cheeks, careful about how much pressure I applied.

He sighed.

He closed his eyes.

He brought his hands up to cover mine.

That was new.

"Amelia," he whispered.

My given name—also new.

"Better?" I asked.

"So much better." He turned his head, opening his eyes to look at me, trapping one of the gel packs between his cheek and the pillow beneath. I slipped my hand free, but he caught it.

"Lay with me?"

My head was spinning like a top. Beck trusted me to see him through his recovery, to dote on him, and to comfort him. But there was more to it: a mutual sense of awareness, a feeling of shared acceptance. We were stepping toward something new.

It felt *right*.

I curled up beside him.

Because everything that'd happened since I sat down on his bed was undeniably surreal, I asked, "How high are you?"

He laughed, warm and sleepy sounding. "I've taken eight hundred milligrams of Ibuprofen."

The Army's cure for whatever ailed—like a Band-Aid to a bullet hole.

"No wonder you're hurting. They didn't give you anything stronger?"

"They did, but I wanted to be awake while you're here."

He circled his arm around me. With one hand, I held a gel pack in place. With the other, I reached up to massage his calloused palm, the pads of his fingers, the velvety skin of his wrist.

He exhaled. "That feels so good. I'd kiss you if my face didn't hurt so bad."

My breath caught.

He noticed.

He gave my fingers a gentle squeeze. "Soon?"

"Yeah," I whispered. "Soon." I paused, smiling into his chest. "And when you're ready for solid foods, I'll make you pancakes with Nutella."

Slurred but sure, he said, "You really do delight me, Amelia Graham."

He fell asleep a few minutes later.

I stayed by his side, finishing the movie he'd started, settling into my new reality.

In the space of an afternoon, I'd become the girl Beck wanted, the girl Beck needed, the girl I was always meant to be.

I Miss...

1. absolute trust
2. the combined scent of Degree, Dove, and Tide
3. grizzly bear hugs
4. the deepest, most self-assured laugh
5. The Mall
6. big hands, calloused and gentle
7. trust in the future
8. army-green eyes
9. quick wit
10. his shamelessness
11. his reflexive blush
12. his freckles
13. pancakes with Nutella
14. being part of a whole

DENYING THE MOON

Seventeen Years Old, Tennessee

I don't tell Paloma, Meagan, and Sophia about Art Club. They'll wonder when I don't show up in the library, but I'm not ready to tackle questions about why I've randomly decided to join a club more than halfway through senior year.

I send a quick Can't do the library! text to them, then head toward the outskirts of campus. By the time I'm slipping through the door of Ms. Robbins's garage, the bell trills. A couple dozen heads swivel to see who's arrived, a sea of unfamiliar faces—with the exception of Isaiah Santoro's. He's at his usual spot, alongside Trevor.

"Welcome, Lia," Ms. Robbins says from up front. "Pick a seat, and we'll get started."

There's an empty place at Isaiah's table. He notices as I do and flags me down, sliding the stool out with his foot.

"I hear you gave my boy a ride home the other day," Trevor says as I get settled.

"I did," I say, trying to decide whether it matters that Isaiah told his buddy about the ten minutes we spent in my car.

Isaiah sends a grin my way. "Saved my ass."

My cheeks flush warm.

Ms. Robbins explains the day's activity: blind line drawings. "You'll draw while focusing on your subject. Don't look at your paper until you're finished." She holds up examples: landscapes and fruit bowls that look like they were drawn by first graders. "It's a great exercise to help you learn to draw what you see, rather than what you think you see. We'll start with portraits and continue at our next meeting, so no need to rush. I'll hand out materials while you sort yourself into pairs."

Before I can panic about who I'll work with, Isaiah drags his stool closer to mine.

"Really, dude?" Trevor says. "You're gonna do me dirty?"

"Make a new friend," Isaiah tells him. "Like I have."

Trevor looks between us, then affably rolls his eyes and saunters toward a table of three by the glaze closet. Isaiah and I sit in unwieldy silence until Ms. Robbins stops by with newsprint and pencils.

"No peeking," she reminds us.

He pushes a sheet of paper toward me. "You want to draw first?"

"Promise not to be offended if I make you look like an ogre?"

He smiles. "Promise."

I square the paper and choose a pencil, centering its point near the top of the page, where the crown of a drawn head should be. Then I look up, appraising Isaiah's features; it's not the worst thing, being instructed to study his face for as long as it takes to sketch his dark hair and strong jaw and imperfect nose. He's looking back at me, statue-still, eyes extraordinarily bright.

He asks, "Aren't you supposed to be drawing?"

The room is noisy, full of activity, but his question arrives as though it traveled a direct line to my ear, two cans linked by a length of string.

"I—yes. Yes, I am." Flustered I glance down at the blank paper, my hand poised, white-knuckling the pencil.

"Hey, now," Isaiah mock-scolds. "No peeking." With two pointed fingers, he directs my attention back to his eyes. "Look here."

I huff out a laugh, as if this is the silliest of exercises, as if I'm not deeply uncomfortable connecting with him this way. But as the moment lengthens, I settle into his gaze and begin to draw. I don't have to look at the paper to know that my attempt is nightmarish. But I press on, sketching wavy hair, a square chin, and prominent brows. I try to capture his eyes: round and slightly upturned, fringed by dark, thick lashes. Purple smudges live beneath, the telltale sign of a bad sleeper. Lightly, I shade them in. Wondering what keeps him up at night, I move to pencil in his asymmetrical nose.

He breaks eye contact long enough to assess my work-in-progress. When his gaze returns to mine, his mouth is lifted in a smirk, so I draw it, full lips, curved mischievously.

I think I might be finished, but I scrutinize his face for another

148

moment to be sure. That's when I remember his scar. Today it's hidden beneath his hair, but leaving it off feels wrong, like denying the moon because the sun is shining. With the lightest touch, I add it to my portrait.

"There," I say, putting down the pencil.

I slide my work toward him, afraid to look.

He lifts the paper to give my effort careful perusal. I expect him to guffaw because the examples Ms. Robbins shared were bad and my finished product must be too, but he says, "This is good. I mean, it's absolute shit, but you added details that make it obvious it's me."

He places the drawing between us and, yeah, it's dreadful, but also, I understand what he means. He points to the shadows beneath his eyes. "You made me look tired. And my nose. You fucked it up in the most accurate way."

I smile. "Has it been broken?"

"Repeatedly, yeah."

I point to the graphite scar on my sketch. "What happened here?"

He pushes a hand through his hair, uncovering the real thing. "Smacked my head into the corner of a coffee table."

I gesture to the outer corner of my left eye, where there's a scar the size of a lemon seed. "When I was four, I was jumping on my parents' bed and my foot caught on a pillow. I hit my face on the headboard. Had a shiner for a week."

"It's a bad-ass scar, but let's give you a cooler story. How about...you were in a bar fight on your way to preschool."

I laugh, relaxing into our banter. "That *is* better."

149

Isaiah grins. "I'll remember to add your scar when I do your portrait."

"You're planning to make me look like a goblin, aren't you?"

His smile sweetens, honey in hot tea. "Even if I wanted to, that'd be impossible."

JUST A BOY

Seventeen Years Old, Tennessee

I'm the last one to make it to lunch at our picnic table outside. It's sunny but crisply cold, and I zip my jacket to my chin before I take the spot beside Paloma.

"Where were you during Advisory?" she asks as I pull my lunch from my bag.

"I went to Ms. Robbins's room for Art Club."

"Oh," she says. And then: "Why?"

"I don't know... It sounded fun."

Her expression says *Spare me the bullshit.* "Isaiah's in Art Club."

"Isaiah Santoro?" Sophia asks.

Paloma smiles. "The one and only."

Meagan arcs an eyebrow. "Are you guys—?"

"No!" I yelp. Then, more calmly, "We're nothing."

"They're friendly," Paloma amends.

Meagan and Soph swap a skeptical glance.

"Seriously," I say. "He's just a boy."

"And a clubmate," Paloma says.

"And a basketballer," Soph says.

"And a *hottie*," Meagan adds, waggling her eyebrows. Sophia acts aghast, and Megs laughs. "What? I'm a lesbian. I'm not blind."

"You guys are the worst," I tell them, but what I mean is that they're the outright best. They're making me laugh even though I want to crawl under the table and spiral. It's all wrong, the way my heart stands at attention when Isaiah's around. My cheeks shouldn't bloom pink when our eyes meet. Those butterflies that flitted around in my stomach earlier? I thought they were dead and buried—they're *supposed to be* dead and buried.

And yet...

My expression must scream of internal conflict because Paloma circles an arm around me. "It's okay if, one day, he becomes more than just a boy."

Soph nods. "I once read that falling for a new person after the death of someone you love means the first relationship was truly special. Otherwise, why would your heart risk trying again?"

"Maybe," I say. "But this...it just seems too soon."

Is it? I ask Beck.

He doesn't respond.

"Lia," Meagan says. "No one expects you to grieve forever."

That might be true, but Beck and I were so interwoven, it often feels like he's still living and breathing—like he's at CVU, or like a PCS forced him and his family to a state far from mine. When

152

the sadness is so intense it threatens to bore a hole through my chest, I let myself imagine we'll be reunited during spring break, or when summer comes. Sometimes I pretend he's a phone call away. Sometimes my heart talks to him.

Is that grieving?

Meagan tosses a blueberry. It pings my shoulder. "What's going on in your head?"

I sigh. "I just—I wish there were rules about this stuff. Hard rules. Universally accepted rules. Like, let's say I *do* want Isaiah to be more than just a boy. How am I supposed to tell him about Beck? How am I supposed to introduce him to my parents? How could I possibly tell Beck's mom and dad that I've moved on?"

"Tackle that as it comes," Paloma says.

Soph nods. "First decide if you're ready."

"And then," Meagan says, "decide if Isaiah's the one."

Paloma grins. "I think he is. You two have been making all the heart eyes at each other during Ceramics."

"Hey—I make heart eyes at no one."

"All I'm saying," she goes on, "is that there are plenty of people who'd be all over that boy if he so much as glanced their way. Except I've never seen him show anyone anything more than polite regard. Until you came along."

"He shows me polite regard," I argue weakly.

"No," Paloma says, smirking. "He looks at you the way a starving man looks at a double bacon burger with cheese."

Meagan, Sophia, and I dissolve into giggles.

153

A Diversion

One dreary Thursday, in Art Club, a
   boy draws a picture of a girl.
The girl is a knot of anxiety.
The intimacy of his focus, of his attention…
HOLY SHIT.
She needs a distraction, somewhere to
   funnel her nervous energy.
She takes her journal from her bag,
props it on her knees
—so he can't see what she's writing—
and pretends to be Very Busy.
He draws, humming a melancholy refrain.
He's in-tune, and she's unsurprised.
Her fingers tremor,
her script like chicken scratch compared
   with its usually neat flourish.
He draws, his gaze a flame's caress on her
   forehead, her cheek, her throat.
When will he finish?

The problem isn't that she's miserable—
    it's that she's NOT.
The melody of his tune quickens.
Has he found happiness in sketching her face?
His gaze snags hers. He smiles.
Her heart pirouettes.
She's confused. She's flustered. She's afraid.
Not of him—of her feelings.
Contradictory but fierce, new but undeniable.
He draws and she writes and he hums
    and she goes to pieces.
Their teacher cruises the room, offering
    compliments and critique.
She pauses to watch him work.
The girl stops writing to study the
    teacher as she studies the boy.
There's a dazzle in her artist's eye.
"You're lucky," she tells the girl,
which is wild because the girl hasn't
    felt lucky in a long time.
The teacher moves on.
The boy holds out his drawing.
"It's yours," he tells her, then points.
    "I remembered your scar."

He watches her, hopeful.

She takes the portrait.

The overall effect is abstract, yet his
    choices seem intentional.

Her resolve, once infinite, is beginning to deplete.

Is this right?

Is this okay?

Is THIS her fate?

She wishes she could be sure.

Gazing at his drawing, at her face,
    she says, "It's beautiful."

SUNRISE

Fifteen Years Old, Virginia

Beck bounced back from his wisdom teeth removal quickly, motivated by a desire to enjoy the holidays, his need to lift five times a week, and the promise of hanging out with me.

Our families celebrated Christmas Eve together anytime we were living in the same zip code. That year, we met up at the Byrnes' house. By nine o'clock, we'd eaten homemade pizzas and dozens of cookies and played a few rounds of Pictionary. While Bernie and Connor tucked the twins into bed, my parents selected Settlers of Catan from the Byrnes' game collection and arranged the board on the dining room table. By the time Connor and Bernie came back downstairs, they were giggling. Bernie whispered something that made my parents laugh too. On holidays, Dad and Connor like to pretend they're reliving their fraternity days, but with microbrews instead of Natty

Lights. Mom and Bernie let the wine flow. And so, it was easy for Beck and me to sneak downstairs to his room.

"I have something for you," he said, closing the door.

"I have something for you too."

We sat facing each other on the bed. I handed him a rectangular box wrapped in silver paper. I'd gotten him a pair of noise-canceling earbuds, using a chunk of the money I'd earned babysitting his sisters over the last couple years. He drew a pleased breath when he opened them, and I was relieved. He and I had given each other silly gifts over the years, as well as gifts picked out and purchased by our mothers, but it was a first to formally exchange presents the way we did that Christmas.

He passed me a small package wrapped sloppily in red and green. Knowing that he'd sat down with paper and tape rather than asking Bernie to help raised a lump in my throat. He watched, drumming his fingers on his knees as I unfolded the paper. Inside, tucked into a layer of tissue, was a ring: white gold, set with two stones, each a shade of blue.

"Our birthstones," he told me.

I touched the aquamarine, then the sapphire, and breathed, "Wow."

"Right? There's this jeweler in Georgetown who makes custom stuff, special order. I found him online last year."

I lifted my eyes to his. "Last year?"

His cheeks flooded red. He was an easy blusher, a deep blusher, and I'd always loved the way this strong, confident boy wore embarrassment plainly on his face. He cleared his throat.

"Yeah. That's when I bought it. I was gonna give it to you for your birthday, but—I don't know. Formal. Raiden. The timing felt off. So I held on to it."

"And now?"

He shrugged, eyes alight. I thought he might lean in to kiss me—our first kiss; I'd been beside myself, imagining it—but instead, he said, "Now the timing's right. Don't you think?"

"Yeah. I do."

He fit the ring onto the third finger of my right hand.

I was sure that someday he'd slide a ring onto the third finger of my left hand.

The next morning, Christmas, my alarm blared early. I rolled out of bed and into Uggs, plus the downiest jacket I owned. Tiptoeing past Mom and Dad's dark room, I lit the tree that stood in the living room's bay window, moved the cinnamon rolls from the fridge into the oven, where they could rise, then filled two travel mugs with hot cocoa—the good kind. Beck pulled up in the 4Runner, and I slipped out the door to meet him.

The drive into DC was quick, and parking near The Mall was, for once, a breeze. Beck took a blanket from the backseat, then we walked to the Lincoln Memorial. We climbed all the way to the top of the empty steps, paid our respects to President Lincoln, then sat facing the Reflecting Pool, bundled into the blanket. In the distance, the Washington Monument stood proudly, casting its illuminated image into the inky water.

The sky was just starting to lighten.

We sipped cocoa and talked in hushed tones about the coming year, the last half of my sophomore, the last half of his senior. He'd applied to several schools on the East Coast, but he had his sights on Commonwealth of Virginia University. It was competitive, academically, but their track and field team was in desperate need of a good thrower.

Beck was an excellent thrower.

"You'll get in," I said as the heavens faded from purple to pink. I wanted him to; CVU was close compared with the other schools he'd applied to.

"I hope so." He took my hands in his, rubbing warmth into them. "You'll visit, right?"

"Beck, obviously."

"And you'll apply too?"

Back then, I was only starting to consider colleges, but I liked the idea of a small school in Seattle or Tacoma, close to where we'd once lived. I pictured myself on a campus like Seattle Pacific's, or University of Puget Sound's, someplace intimate and picturesque. CVU is city-huge, with a pulsating Greek row and a football stadium capacity of more than seventy thousand, which is the very opposite of the collegiate experience I was after.

I told Beck, "Of course I'll apply."

Because I'm in love you, I could have said. *I've loved you as long as I've known you.*

160

His face shone golden in the day's first light. And then he said his version of what I'd been thinking, softly, without modesty. "I fucking adore you, Lia. I have—well, forever, I think. But lately...I just really want us to be together."

Words I'd waited all my life to hear.

Words that steeled my resolve.

I didn't need to go to school on the West Coast. I didn't need rocky beaches or rainy skies or a small campus. I didn't even need a semester in Australia. I had a lifetime to see the world. I could go to CVU and be happy. I would be, because I'd be with Beck.

As the sun crested the horizon, bathing the city in amber light, I kissed him.

He was, at first, surprised, but it took only a second for him to react as I'd hoped. He released my hands and found my face, kissing me back, then kissing me anew. I burrowed into him, asking for more with an insistent palm on the back of his neck. He gave me more. He gave me everything I wanted that Christmas: devotion, warmth, and laughter. A windfall of *good* washed over me, over us, like the morning sun's radiant glow.

We were inseparable during the week that followed. We went on long drives, ate our combined weight in burritos at District Taco, and holed up in Beck's room to watch our best-loved holiday movies—anything to keep us away from of his mom and dad, and mine.

161

We weren't discreet because we were worried our parents would disapprove. Mom and Dad loved Beck. They always had. And Bernie and Connor loved me. I had no doubt they'd all be thrilled at the news that Beck and I were together. The response to *us* would be elation. And that was just it: I was in the midst of my own elation. I wanted to share the newness and excitement with Beck—only Beck.

I found out later that our parents had suspected. Bernie guessed something was up the day Beck had his wisdom teeth removed. Connor caught on when his son passed up a Shenandoah hike to help me with my family's puzzle-in-progress: the elves' North Pole workshop. During Christmas dinner, as my parents and I dunked soft bread and fresh veggies into a steaming pot of fondue, Mom asked about my ring. When I told her Beck had given it to me, she gave Dad a smug smile. But, to their credit, no one said anything.

On New Year's Eve, Connor, Bernie, and Beck came to our house, leaving the twins with their second-favorite babysitter, a sweet, grandmotherly neighbor. Dad grilled Prime Rib, Mom boiled lobsters, and Bernie brought her peanut butter sheet cake. We stuffed ourselves full, and then the board games came out. Dad insisted we play Pandemic, which he and Connor love, and Beck hated for all its complicated rules. Scattergories was more fun, and for the first time ever, I managed to beat everyone at Ticket to Ride.

When the games were done, when midnight was nearing, I went to the kitchen to fill a pair of flutes with sparkling wine. My dad had

162

picked up a bottle of cider for Beck and me, but ringing in the New Year with juice seemed too childish for the person I was becoming.

Beck followed, leaving our parents to clean up the games and fill their flutes in the living room. As soon as the door to the kitchen swung shut, he swept my hair off my neck and nuzzled his nose beneath my ear.

"This blows," he murmured, the tickle of his breath making me shiver.

"Right? I had no idea it'd be so hard to keep my hands to myself."

He grinned, hooking his fingers in the waistband of my jeans to tow me closer. "Let's tell them. They'll be happy—at least, my parents will be."

I looped my arms around his neck. He was shelter and safety and happiness. He always had been. "Mine will be too."

He arched a brow. "Your dad?"

"Beck, of course. He loves you."

"Yeah, 'til he finds out that now I think about his daughter instead of flipping through my nudie magazines."

I laughed and swatted him. "Doesn't it feel dramatic, making a New Year's Eve announcement? That's what people do when they're engaged. Or pregnant."

I expected him to recoil at both scenarios. I wouldn't have blamed him.

He didn't even blink. He opened his mouth, expression thoughtful, eyes full of longing, but before he got a chance to speak, my mom called, "Countdown's about to start!"

We took our drinks to the living room and stood with our parents, watching masses of people in New York City cheer the upcoming Times Square Ball drop on TV. When the clock read ten seconds till midnight, we counted down together, as we'd done in years past. The nostalgia of it, combined with the euphoria I'd experienced since Beck and I'd gotten together, had me blinking back a rush of joyful tears.

He set our flutes on the coffee table, then took my hand. I laced my fingers through his, lost in the moment, and, in unison, we called out, "Three, two, one—"

He dipped me back and gave me my first kiss of the New Year. There was heat behind it—there was always heat behind Beck's kisses—and when we drew apart, four pairs of eyes gaped at us. Our parents spent a moment in slack-jawed silence. Then Connor whooped. My mom cried, and Bernie did too. My dad looked like he was caught somewhere between genuinely pleased and deeply confounded until Connor clapped Beck on the shoulder and said, "Treat her right, buddy, or Cam will bury you."

Dad laughed.

Connor laughed.

Even Beck laughed, after nodding solemnly.

He dipped close to whisper, "See? Told you."

I let the coming year unfold in my imagination: Beck and I dressed up at prom, spring break at the beach, his graduation in June. And then summer. Months of sunshine and freedom. He'd go to college after that, but we'd make it.

We were Beckett and Amelia.

We were meant to be.

OLIVE BRANCH

Seventeen Years Old, Tennessee

The portrait Isaiah drew during Art Club finds its way onto my bulletin board. It's weird to see it adjacent to photographs of Beck, but I like the way Isaiah sees me: a girl with a sparkle in her eye, a girl with a tiny scar and a bounty of secrets.

The portrait lives in my room for a few days before Mom comes in to leave a pile of folded laundry on my desk. She bends to peer at it. "Did you make this?"

I'm sitting on my bed, slogging through Physics homework. "No. It's from Art Club."

"You're in an art club?"

"Yes. At school. During Advisory, every Thursday."

There. All the information. Hopefully she'll move along.

She sits on my bed, jostling Major, who's snoozing. "You didn't need parental permission?"

"To draw and paint on school grounds, during school hours? No."

She points at the portrait. "Who's the artist?"

"Another club member."

"A friend of yours?"

"God, Mom. What's with the interrogation?"

She flinches. My sharp pitch might as well have been a raised hand. After blinking hurt from her eyes, she says, "Reminds me of Picasso. She did a good job."

"He," I correct without thinking.

Her breath catches, that male pronoun like a thunderclap on a clear afternoon.

"His name is Isaiah," I say in explanation, my tone gentler now. "We're in Ceramics together. When he mentioned Art Club, I thought it sounded like fun. So I joined."

"Oh… Well, that sounds like a productive way to spend Advisory."

She's taking care with the olive branch I've offered. It's weird, interacting with her, all caution and courtesy, after so long spent keeping her at a distance.

I shrug. "More productive than hanging out with my friends in the library."

Now she smiles. "Don't discount the value of your friendships. Bernie and I'd be a mess without each other. Speaking of, she told me she mentioned spring break to you. Connor's retirement. Daddy and I hope you'll come. We're going to stay with the Byrnes. They'd love to have you too."

166

I'm hung up on *stay with the Byrnes.*

I haven't been to Connor and Bernie's since the week after Beck's wake, when I woke up in the middle of the night, covered in a sheen of cold sweat. It was hours before daylight, but I was too wired to do anything but get out of bed. I tugged on a fleece and pulled wool socks over my leggings, then slipped my feet into Birkenstocks. Tiptoeing into the kitchen, I filched my dad's keys, then escaped through the front door.

There were patches of black ice on the ground. My parents would've gargled paint thinner before letting me drive slippery streets while exhausted and mourning, but I was on a mission. I'd startled out of sleep remembering a text from Beck, deep in the thread he and I'd once shared: If I die today, go into my closet and find my nudie magazines... Trash them before my mom sees them.

I texted Bernie to tell her I was on my way.

I drove hunched over the wheel of the Explorer, testing the brakes every ten feet, worried the SUV would go skidding across a patch of ice, leaving me in a ditch with my face buried in an airbag. More than once I thought about turning back, but I swear to God, it was as if Beck's magazines were summoning me from across town.

Bernie was waiting on the front porch in a flannel robe, the oversized sweatshirt she had on underneath peeking out: *Rosebell High School Track & Field.*

It'd been Beck's.

After I'd navigated the slick porch steps, she gave me a long hug, then led me into the house and to the living room, where she'd made a nest for herself on the couch. On the coffee table sat a half-empty mug with a tea bag's string trailing over its rim. "I can make you some," she said when she noticed me looking.

"That's okay."

"Hot cocoa?"

"No thanks."

"You want me to put on the TV?"

"Actually, I was hoping I could go down to Beck's room. I won't mess anything up," I added.

In the nearly two weeks since her son's passing, I'd seen Bernie shatter once: the day before the funeral, when she'd caught the twins under their big brother's bed, using flashlights to look for him. Her hands went to her hair, her face went crimson, and her eyes filled with rage. *Stay out of Beck's room!* she'd screamed with such savagery, Norah and Mae burst into tears. I'd looked on from the top of the stairs, stunned, while Connor comforted the twins and my mom led Bernie, sobbing, to her bedroom.

"I just…" I said, shaking off the memory. "I want to feel close to him."

"Lia," she said. "Of course. Go on down."

I hadn't been in Beck's room since the morning after he passed, and it must have been a full minute before I found the courage to push open the door. It felt as if he'd come barreling in any second, kicking off his shoes, flopping onto the bed, pulling me down with him.

I wanted that more than I wanted my next breath.

I crossed the room and, kneeling on the rug, pressed my forehead to his comforter.

It smelled of him, clean and familiar.

My chest constricted with the realization that it wouldn't always.

I rose and flipped on the desk lamp, then shuffled to the closet and slid open the door. As I took in the clothes, the sports equipment, the many pairs of sneakers, all so quintessentially Beck, the air fled my lungs.

It was the beginning of a panic attack, I think, my body at last surrendering to the assault of grief.

I could not make myself inhale.

My pulse raced and my head spun. My vision swam—

—and then a faraway echo: *Amelia, breathe!*

I sucked in a shuddering gasp that wasn't enough but was also, somehow, too much.

Lightheaded, I waited for my heart to slow, for my breathing to even out, before peering up at the top shelf. There was a box labeled *GI Joes*. Taking it down, I set it on the floor. Hands trembling, I pulled back the flaps to find Beck's GI Joes. It was an impressive collection. I'd spent hours playing with them alongside him, acting out romances between soldiers and Barbies while he set up battle scenes, blowing apart bunkers fashioned out of Bernie's *Real Simple* magazines.

One by one, I took the action figures—Beck would never call them dolls—from the box, piling them on the carpet until I unearthed three *Playboys* and a *Hustler*, showcasing women who were very beautiful, very augmented, and very naked. All four magazines had publication dates older than me, and their once-glossy covers were rife with tears and creases. They looked well loved, which was so gross but, even in my emotionally battered state, kind of funny too.

Where'd Beck get them?

I'll never know.

"Lia?" Bernie called.

I jumped, slapping a hand over my heart. God—if she caught me in her dead son's room looking at porn, she'd never speak to me again.

I whisper-shouted, "Be up in a sec!"

I stacked the magazines, folded them once, then slid them into the waistband of my leggings. Pulling my fleece over the top, I gave my reflection a check in the mirror that hung on the back of the door. My face was wraithlike, but the magazines were undetectable. Bernie would be none the wiser. Then I set the GI Joes in their box, heaved it back onto its shelf, and swung the door open.

Bernie stood at the top of the steps, looking down at me. "You okay?"

I nodded, linking my hands, further shielding the magazines I intended to smuggle through the front door. "I'm going to head out."

"Oh—okay. Come visit again soon. Norah and Mae will be sad they missed you."

I nodded. "Of course."

On my way home, I stopped by a gas station and dumped the magazines into a rank dumpster, weeping as if I was disposing of something really and truly precious.

I haven't braved the Byrnes' house since.

"I'm not ready to go back to Rosebell," I tell my mom. "I'm not sure I'll ever be ready."

"Think about it," she says, patting my arm. "It might be cathartic."

Or it might be traumatizing.

Our eyes meet. Optimism shines in hers. She thinks she's getting through to me, except now I'm questioning her motives.

Did she come in just to work me over about visiting the Byrnes?

"I don't want to go to Rosebell," I say. "Not ever."

JUST LIA

Seventeen Years Old, Tennessee

On a breezy Wednesday in late January, Paloma, Isaiah, and I arrive in Ceramics to find a substitute teacher at Ms. Robbins's desk. He takes attendance with the roster she left, cruising through the first third of the alphabet before calling, "Amelia Graham?"

My breath catches.

Paloma glances at me, her gaze inquisitive.

The substitute lifts his chin to scan the room.

On the first day of school, I'd prepared myself to be called Amelia as each of my teachers took attendance for the first time. I'd braced for the squall of sorrow, and the necessary correction.

Today, *Amelia* is a blow to the back of the head, painful and disorienting.

"Lia, please," I manage, though the words do their best to stick in my throat.

The sub nods, then moves on while I hear my name over and over, in Beck's baritone.

My phone buzzes. I slip it discreetly out of my pocket and give it a glance.

A text from Paloma: You okay over there?

Yep, I reply, working to adjust my expression from grief stricken to indifferent.

You look like you're gonna be sick.

I'm fine, I text back, then pocket my phone.

The sub finishes attendance and sets the class loose on our works-in-progress. I shoot out of my seat, nearly knocking down a pair of sophomores on my way to the shelves where prefired projects are kept. My lopsided coil pot sits on a board beneath protective plastic. I pick it up and head for my workspace, knowing full well that I'm acting weirder than usual and hoping my tablemates won't mention it.

Paloma and Isaiah lackadaisically chat about last night's basketball game, a win, as they head to the shelves to collect their projects. They give me matching looks of bewilderment as I hurry past.

I love you, Amelia Graham.

Oh, Beck.

I'm perilously close to crying when laughter bursts from the table behind me. My classmates, having a fantastic time on the sub's watch.

I should be doing the same.

I straighten my spine and draw a fortifying breath. I'm getting better at sliding from brink-of-tears to an approximation of composure, I realize as I roll a new coil from a lump of clay. What a travesty, that this is a skill I've had to hone.

I enjoy sixty seconds of restorative quiet before Paloma and Isaiah return with their coil pots. I watch from the corner of my eye as he pulls the plastic from his project. It looks so much better than mine, like actual art.

He assesses my pile of coils and says, "Looking good, Amelia."

It's the most benign comment, but it unravels all the mending I managed in the last couple minutes. Fire awakens in my chest, burns up my neck, and singes my face as I meet Isaiah's cheerful gaze.

He sobers immediately.

I leave my stool—just get up and walk away, without a word to him or Paloma, whose mouth has opened in disbelief.

Weaving through tables and stools and people carrying their fragile projects, I end up in the space's only private place: the glaze closet. It's cool, lit by a single bulb. Standing with my back to the entrance, I pretend to consider shades, though my pot isn't ready for its bisque firing, let alone a coat of color.

My devastation is embarrassing.

My embarrassment is devastating.

There's a shuffling sound behind me.

I expect Paloma, but—no.

My heart beats differently in Isaiah's company.

I hate it. I *hate* the way he makes me feel.

I turn as he steps into the closet, bumping the door just closed enough.

174

"I'm sorry," he says. "Whatever I did... Whatever I said."

I sigh. "You didn't do anything."

"I must've, because you're acting—"

He cuts himself off, which stokes my frustration.

"I'm acting how? Immature? Bitchy?"

Both, for sure.

His eyes go big. "No—shit. I'd never call you either of those things. Jesus, Lia. I was going to say that you're acting like I fucked up. I'm trying to fix it."

"Why? Why do you even care?"

He shakes his head, letting his gaze fall to his Converse, and I think, *Fine. Point out the way* I'm *acting and don't take accountability for the way* you're *acting.* But I'm wrong because he *is* trying to take accountability, and I'm so freaking messy and self-involved, I can't accept an apology like a normal human being.

I step toward the door. The closet is so small I have to brush by Isaiah to get to the exit and, when I do, he catches my hand. I freeze, breathing hard for no good reason.

His fingers curl loosely around mine.

"I don't like how this feels," he says quietly. "You, pissed at me."

"I'm not pissed at you. I'm just...pissed."

"Why?"

I'm not sure how to articulate an answer, but I try. "Because life sucks."

He laughs, dry as dust. "Yeah, I get it. Life's fucked me over a thousand times."

175

I know so little about him. I like to think that's because I'm chill, a cool girl, the opposite of intrusive. But truthfully, learning about him, learning to like him, makes me profoundly uncomfortable.

"You never seem angry," I say.

"I've figured out how to deal. Most of the time."

He presses his palm to mine.

My heart is beating *so* fast.

Isaiah is taller, leaner than Beck.

His skin is olive, freckle-free.

He smells like wintergreen gum and juniper.

His hand fits differently around mine.

Beck would hate me for this—hate me for wanting this.

After everything I promised you, I tell him.

"I don't like to be called Amelia," I say to Isaiah.

I feel stupid, voicing it, but he doesn't leave me time to wallow.

"Then I'll call you Lia."

"Just Lia?"

"Just Lia," he repeats, his voice filling the closet with reassurance. "And listen—you're obviously going through some shit, but you should know...I look forward to this class 'cause I get to spend it with you. If it were up to me, I'd see you outside Ceramics."

I have no idea how to respond; the truth is shameful.

I decide, haltingly, on "Thank you."

He smiles. "Will you let me know if you ever want that too?"

I shift, letting my arm graze his. "I promise I will."

Reasons to Avoid Isaiah Santoro

1. I'm not ready.
2. I'm not ready.
3. I'm not ready.

FOREVER

Fifteen Years Old, Washington DC

When school resumed after the New Year, Beck started bringing me to parties, where he'd stick by my side, making sure I never missed curfew. Holding hands, we watched Raj kick ass at Academic Decathlon tournaments and Stephen set district-wide records in the pool. We went to Macy's orchestra concerts with Wyatt and to late-night diners with the two of them, sharing stacks of pancakes while cracking each other up with good-natured bickering. We joined Beck's family for hikes at Great Falls Park and Sugarloaf Mountain, as well as my parents for day trips to Richmond, where we visited the Capitol Building and walked through Hollywood Cemetery.

My favorite times, though, were when I got Beck to myself. More often than not, we found ourselves at The Mall, snacking on whatever was up for grabs at the food trucks parked near the Washington Monument.

"Do you think we should see other stuff?" he asked one Saturday afternoon in early March, just before my sixteenth birthday. We sat on a bench alongside the Tidal Basin. It was cold and windy, and the cherry trees hadn't yet blossomed. Aside from a few die-hard tourists, we were on our own.

"Like what?"

"I don't know…around the city. We always hang out here."

"I like it here," I said, smiling up at him. "It's our spot."

He pulled off the knit beanie he'd been wearing and tugged it onto my head, covering my ears with an attentiveness that made my heart swell. "I thought our spot was the Lincoln Memorial. Where we kissed the first time."

"That can be our spot too."

He laughed. "Let's claim the whole Mall."

"Done. But if you want to see other places, we should."

"I just think we should take advantage of what's around. We won't always live here."

He'd been accepted to CVU. He was going to throw for them. He'd leave for Charlottesville in August. I was thrilled for him, but I'd grown used to having him down the road. His hugs had become sustenance, his kisses oxygen. I didn't like to think about him three hours away. I didn't like to think about how much I'd miss him.

"We could go to the National Zoo," I said to spare myself premature sadness.

He nodded. "And maybe Ford's Theatre."

"That'd be cool. We should get ice cream at Pop's Old

179

Fashioned. My dad says people at the Pentagon call it a DC institution."

Beck grinned at the suggestion of ice cream. "Let's do that one soon."

I pulled my phone from my jacket pocket and opened my Notes app, since I didn't have my journal handy. "I'll start a list."

"Of course you will," he teased.

It was an easy list to make; our area was full of interesting history, quirky landmarks, and good food. I had plenty of ideas, and Beck tossed out suggestions as fast as I could type.

1. Ford's Theatre
2. Ice Cream at Pop's Old Fashioned
3. Smithsonian National Zoological Park
4. Ted's Tarts at Ted's Bulletin
5. The Kennedy Center
6. Smithsonian National Museum of Natural History
7. Embassy Row
8. Theodore Roosevelt Island
9. The Exorcist Stairs
10. Frederick Douglass's House
11. Library of Congress
12. The National Cathedral
13. Lincoln's Cottage
14. Half Smokes at Ben's Chili Bowl

"There," I said, titling the list, Things to Do in DC.

"Things to Do in DC—Before Beck Leaves for CVU," he

corrected, peering over my shoulder as I revised the name with a despairing sigh.

Laying a hand on my cheek, he turned my face up to his. "You're not already sad about me ditching Rosebell, are you?"

"*No*," I said with overblown emphasis.

"Aww," he said, his tone playful. "You're gonna miss me."

I shook my head. "Nope. Not even a little."

Serious now, he leaned in and whispered, "Lia, tell me how much you'll miss me."

It was silly to pretend I'd be anything but inconsolable while he was at CVU. "I always miss you when you're away—you know I do."

He pulled back, wearing a smile. "Yeah, but it's nice to hear."

"I wish I could go with you," I said, feeling pouty, preemptively abandoned.

"You will. In a couple years."

"Do you really want that? Me at CVU?"

"Hell yeah. Are you still planning to apply?"

"I am…it's just…what if I crowd you? What if you get sick of me? What if it's not everything we expect?"

He was looking at me like I'd sprouted a second nose. "It will be. You're my favorite person on the planet. Graduate high school. Then come to CVU."

Small schools on the West Coast hardly tempted me anymore. The once-bright light that was a semester abroad had dimmed almost completely. I was growing up and realizing how fanciful they were, my childhood aspirations.

At least, that's what I tried to convince myself that day at the Tidal Basin.

Beck regarded me pensively, sensing, maybe, that I was on shaky ground. Sensing, maybe, that I was working to merge the girl I once was with the girl I'd become since he and I got together. The way his eyes swam with solicitousness made me wonder if he understood that I felt a little empty, a little sad, when I thought about what I'd have to sacrifice to attend CVU with him.

He feathered his lips along the shell of my ear as he whispered, "Be with me, Lia. Be with me forever."

That's what I wanted: Forever with Beckett Byrne.

We met in a kiss, a promise, and even though my heart hurt when I thought about him moving away, I was comforted by my certainty that Beck and I would always find our way back to each other.

STAY

Seventeen Years Old, Tennessee

A week after Isaiah and I have our heart-to-heart in the glaze closet, I'm out on a Friday afternoon, walking Major through the neighborhood. I hear a basketball bouncing on the pavement even before I round the corner leading to the recreation area.

Trevor, who I've gotten to know during Art Club, is on the court with Isaiah. There's a girl, too, sitting on a nearby bench. She has brown hair twisted into a bun, and she's wearing a puffer jacket. I've seen her at school, though we don't have classes together.

I've no choice but to walk past the trio, and I'm torn about whether I want them to notice me or not. Being around Isaiah kicks my nerves into high gear. I find myself thinking about him at the oddest times: halfway through a journal entry, pen poised above the page; or in the middle of a show, while the keystone characters are making up or making out; or in the dark of night, before I slip into sleep.

I don't dwell on what my preoccupation suggests.

As I stroll by, the boys grapple over the ball, laughing and shoving. Isaiah comes out victorious, then takes off toward the basket, leaving Trevor to stand at half-court. Shielding his eyes from the low winter sun, he spots me and shouts, "Lia!"

Isaiah's mid-shot. By the time the ball sinks through the net, he's looking my way.

"What're you doing?" he calls, his voice pitched with surprise.

I hold up Major's leash and shrug.

"Come hang out," Trevor says, waving an arm.

My dog's already tugging toward the court, intrigued by potential new friends. I let him lead me to Isaiah. "I meant, what are you doing *here*," he clarifies, bending to greet Major.

"I live here." I point toward the far side of the pond. "That way."

"No shit?" Trevor says, trotting over with the basketball under his arm. "Same. I mean, out by the clubhouse. But hey—we're practically neighbors."

By now, the brunette has left the bench to join us. Trevor hooks an arm around her shoulders. "This is Molly," he tells me. "Molly, Lia. She joined Art Club this semester."

"Nice," she says, flashing a smile. A silver charm bracelet peeks out of her jacket's cuff. I bet it's the one Trevor picked out at the mall before Christmas. "Are you an actual artist," she asks me, "or are you in it for the résumé building, like Trev?"

"Neither," I say. "It just sounded like fun."

Isaiah gives Major a final pat before straightening. "It is fun."

"Nothing like playing hoops though," Trevor says, underhanding the basketball to Isaiah, who catches it smoothly.

Their team won again last night, an upset against the top-ranked school in the district. I've started paying attention now. And yeah, according to ERHS's morning announcements, the basketball team's social media accounts, and the local news, Isaiah is a phenom. He and Trevor are cocaptains and apparently an indomitable duo on the court.

"You guys are kicking ass this season," Molly says, looking at Trev, smitten.

"Yeah, we are," he hollers, thumping Isaiah's shoulder, "thanks to my boy."

Isaiah whacks him back. "Okay, high scorer."

"Don't let him fool you with his meek bullshit," Trevor tells me. "He's a straight *baller*."

Molly rolls her eyes, laughing. "If you guys are done with the ego stroking, Trev and I've gotta go." She gives me a scheming look. "We're going out to dinner with my parents soon. He's *so* excited."

Trevor groans, but drolly. "Can't. Fucking. Wait."

She takes his hand and leads him off the court. "Nice meeting you, Lia!"

"See you around," Trevor calls as they take off down the block.

Isaiah watches them a second, then spins the ball on his

forefinger like it's easy as winking. He ought to be watching its balance, but his eyes are on me. "Want to shoot around?"

"Oh—but my dog."

He looks down at Major, who's curled up at my feet.

"He seems okay to chill." His eyes meet mine. "Stay."

FAIR GAME

Seventeen Years Old, Tennessee

I loop Major's leash around a nearby bench, then tighten the laces of my Nikes and step onto the court with the captain of the basketball team, the humblest hotshot I've ever encountered.

"Wanna play a game?" he asks.

"Basketball's not really my sport."

"Yeah, you said. Ceramics. First day. And I didn't mean an actual game of basketball. Do you know Horse?"

Beck and I used to play when we lived in Washington. Connor put up a hoop in the Byrnes' driveway because Beck was the tallest kid in his class, and his dad was sure he was going to be NBA material. But when it came to athletics, Beck was more brawn and determination than speed and finesse. We had fun with the hoop, but he never played basketball beyond PE.

"I know it," I tell Isaiah.

"Cool. Instead of earning letters, we'll earn questions."

I lift an eyebrow. "You'll crush me."

His smile becomes mischievous. "And I'll learn a lot. Where's the problem?"

He tosses me the ball.

I catch it—barely.

He nods approvingly. "There. You're warmed up. You game?"

I send the ball back and slip the elastic from my wrist. Tying my hair up, I say, "I'm game."

He turns and, from where we're standing—like a million miles from the basket—launches the ball. It hits the square on the backboard before banking into the hoop.

Okay. I'm done for.

He rebounds, then passes me the ball. Shaking my head, I take aim, then hurl it into the air. It drops like a stone, landing with a bounce well before the basket.

Isaiah camouflages laughter with a cough. "We'll work on it," he tells me, rebounding. "First, though, I've scored a question."

He pauses, scrutinizing my face before asking, "What do you think of the coil pot I'm working on in Ceramics?"

I smile. A blander question than I'd expected. "It's very good. You could sell it."

He accepts my compliment in his unassuming way, then moves toward a line painted on the court, in front of the basket. I watch how he lifts the ball, right hand beneath, left acting as support. With a flick of his wrist, he sends it toward the hoop, tracking it as it swishes through the net.

I set up while he rebounds. After he passes me the ball, I try to mimic his stance.

"Bend your knees," he says. "You're a spring. Shoot with your body, not your hands."

I do as he says, giving my knees an experimental bounce.

"That's better. Don't look at the ball though. Look where you want it to go. That square on the backboard? That's your target."

I focus on the square. I keep my knees bent. I shoot with my body, not my hands.

Not a basket, but the ball hits the rim, ricocheting back.

"Better," Isaiah says. "You'll sink one in no time. How's senior year treating you?"

I scrunch my nose at his second earned question. "Okay, I guess."

"Really? Because sometimes you look miserable."

"Sometimes I feel miserable."

"But not because of school?"

"No. I like school. I like my friends. I like my classes, mostly."

"Ceramics?"

I love Ceramics. I love Ms. Robbins and her cluttered garage. I love that the only expectations are creativity and effort. I love the cool, damp clay, and all its possibilities. I love capping my day with an hour spent under Paloma's warmth. And I love that Isaiah sits by my side, rolling coils, smoothing nicks and bumps with damp sponges, peering over at me every so often, all dancing eyes and inquisitive smiles.

"Ceramics is cool," I say.

189

He sets up another shot, which he makes and I go on to miss. The game continues.

"Favorite junk food?"

"Fritos. Or brownies."

"Least favorite book?"

"*The Catcher and the Rye.* Holden Caulfield is insufferable."

"Best animal?"

"Foxes. Because they're cute and smart."

"Favorite season?"

"Summer. Obviously."

He grins. "Me too."

He sinks another basket. I swear, he hasn't choked once. On my turn, I miss—but barely. "So close," he says. And then: "What are you gonna do after high school?"

Another easy question. "Commonwealth of Virginia University."

At this, he tucks the basketball beneath his arm. "Not a Tennessee school?"

"I've lived here less than a year. I have no allegiance to the Volunteer State."

"But you've got allegiance to Virginia?"

"Yes." I sound uncertain, even to myself.

"Your parents aren't on your ass, trying to get you to stay close?"

"Oh, they're on my ass, but not about staying close. Just... the future in general." I smooth a hand over my hair, flustered by the turn this afternoon has taken. I never would have guessed, leashing Major up for his walk earlier, that I'd end up getting deep with Isaiah on the neighborhood basketball court. What's strange about opening up to this boy, though, is that it doesn't actually feel strange. I'd happily shoot hoops with him until the sun sets. I ask, "Does Marjorie get after you about college?"

"Nah. She doesn't care what I do after high school, so long as I have a plan and graduate with intelligence, independence, and generosity of spirit—those three things specifically. Since the day I moved into her house, a punk-ass kid who snickered at her attempts at discipline, she's preached about how I'm gonna grow up to be the sort of human who makes a difference. At some point, I started to believe her."

"She sounds incredible."

His eyes go soft. "She is," he says before firing another shot at the hoop. He showboats a little this time, posing with his hands in the air, making a zealous *aaaaah* sound, an arena full of fans screaming for him.

I rebound, boot him out of the way, and copy his shot.

The ball swishes through the net.

I'm so surprised, I stand motionless, staring at where it bounces under the basket as Isaiah hollers an elated, "Holy shit!"

I turn a grin on him. "I did it."

"'Course you did," he says, offering me his fist.

I give it a bump, considering my first question. I could ask about school, or basketball, or his life with Marjorie and Naya, but first things first: "Did you know I live in this neighborhood?"

His expression becomes quizzical. "How would I?"

"I don't know. You mentioned that you wanted to see me outside Ms. Robbins's garage and then you turn up around the block from my house. Seems coincidental."

He lifts a brow. "Some might say coincidental. Some might say fated."

That word, *fated*…it leaves goose bumps in its wake.

He notices the way I shiver, the way I chafe warmth back into my arms, the way my mouth lifts in the tiniest smile. He's good at listening, at watching, at picking up cues. Holding my gaze, he says, "I had no idea you live in this neighborhood, but I've gotta say, I'm not bummed to have found out." Then he shoots the ball, his eyes locked on mine and, as it has every other time, it drops through the net.

I throw up my hands. "For fuck's sake!"

He laughs, going after the rebound, then returns to me, handing over the ball, his mouth turned up in a challenge. "Your turn."

"Do I get to look at my target?"

"Did I?"

Frowning, I lift the ball, then hurl it sightlessly at the hoop.

It smacks the backboard, but misses the rim.

"Not bad," he says. "Before long, we'll be a fair match."

I smile. "Liar. Question…?"

"Yeah. You ready to tell me about how last year kicked your ass?"

WHAT-IFS

Seventeen Years Old, Tennessee

I walk away, caught off guard, and sit on the bench near where Major's snoozing.

Pressure builds behind my ribs, where my heart used to beat steady and true.

Isaiah follows. He sits beside me, setting the basketball in the grass, propping his sneaker on it. There're those pink stars, a miniature galaxy twinkling on a scuffed toe. "I'm curious," he says. "I'm trying to understand."

"I know. It's just...not easy to talk about."

"I get that. I shouldn't've—"

I hold up a hand, cutting him off. Drawing a breath, I come right out and say it: "Last year, on the twenty-second of November, my boyfriend died."

The light behind Isaiah's eyes blinks out, and I worry that I've stolen something—his spark, his spirit.

"Jesus, Lia. I'm sorry. I had no idea. You're—you're so steady."

"No. I'm miserable, like you said."

"You knew him in Virginia?"

I nod. "And Washington and North Carolina. His dad's in the Army, like mine. Our parents have been friends since before either of us was born."

I have no idea why I'm offering unsolicited details. That day in the hallway, a rash kiss, a few weeks of Ceramics, and a few Art Club meetings...my time with Isaiah is a collection of moments. We have a connection—I can admit that now. But it's nothing like the years of shared experiences, the tome of inside jokes, and the lifetime-spanning history Beck and I had.

Still. I trust Isaiah.

More than that, I don't hate the butterflies-in-my-stomach feelings of *excitement* and *tenderness* and *hope* I experience when I'm with him.

My heart aches as I think about how Beck would feel if he knew that I've been experiencing prickles of attraction for another boy.

Once, when we lived in Colorado, when my dad was getting ready to leave for Afghanistan, I heard him and Mom talking behind their closed bedroom door. Mom was crying. The sound of her sorrow stopped me in my tracks.

"What if you don't come home?" she asked, voice trembling.

Dad's tone was gentle, but his response was firm. "Then you'll find someone else."

"I could never."

194

A moment of heartbreaking quiet passed before he said, "Hannah, I'd want you to."

I went to my room and cried myself. I pitied my parents; how excruciating to be forced into such a conversation. Beck and I never spoke of what-ifs—we were young, spontaneous, invincible. Yet time and again, I torture myself with this incomprehensible question: If it had been me who died, would I expect him to suffer forever?

Or would I want him to rediscover love?

"What happened to him?" Isaiah asks.

"He had a heart attack," I say in a small voice. "A sudden, massive heart attack."

"God. How old was he?"

"Eighteen."

"Had he been sick?"

"Not at all."

He draws a heavy breath. "Shit, Lia. I'm so sorry."

The wind ruffles my ponytail. Major sighs and curls into himself. I look at Isaiah, who's gazing out over the court. His profile is angular. Broad forehead. Thick brows. Sharp cheekbones. His nose has a bump on its bridge that might bother a vainer person. His mouth is downturned, making his expression weary.

He's like Beck in this way. His features make his emotions public.

"Are you okay?" I ask.

He meets my gaze. "Not really. You?"

195

"I haven't been okay in a long time."

He swivels, drawing his knee up, turning to face me. "I feel like an asshole. Knowing now what you're going through... I should've given you space."

"You have."

"Bullshit. I hugged you before I knew your name. I followed you into a closet. And here I am in your fucking neighborhood. You must think I'm out of my mind."

"Isaiah, if I didn't want your attention or your friendship or your company in art supply closets, I'd tell you. I swear I would."

He bends to smooth his hand over my dog's head. "What's his name?"

"Major."

"He's a good boy."

"Isn't he? My dad brought him home last year, hoping he'd make things better."

"Has he?"

I consider. "More survivable, maybe. I can't check out, even on the really bad days, because I have a dog who'll eat my shoes if I forget to walk him. For a long time, I needed that sort of incentive."

Isaiah says, "The bad days can really stack up."

I want to ask how he navigates his bad days. I want to know how he came to live with Marjorie. I want to know his favorite junk food and his least favorite book and his post-high-school plans. But the sun is beginning to drop, and my parents are probably expecting me. Still there's something I can't leave unsaid.

Looking at the stars on his shoe, I confess, "I want to see you outside Ceramics too. I'm just—I'm still figuring stuff out. I don't know what right looks like yet, but I'm trying to get there."

"You're telling me to be patient," he says.

"I'm asking you to be patient. I'm telling you I like you."

He smiles. "Then you set the speed. I'll hang beside you."

INEVITABLE

Sixteen Years Old, Virginia

We didn't waste time tackling our Things to Do in DC—Before Beck Leaves for CVU list.

The restaurants were easy. Beck had an enormous appetite, and I made a game of keeping up with his ridiculous caloric intake. Given that Connor and my dad were both history nerds, we took them with us to Lincoln's Cottage and Frederick Douglass's House. As spring marched on, we found the Darth Vader grotesque and the Space Window—with a tiny, embedded moonstone—at the National Cathedral. At the Library of Congress, we saw the Gutenberg Bible. We found the Exorcist Steps, a narrow set of stairs adjacent to an Exxon station in Georgetown, where the climactic scene from *The Exorcist* was filmed—poor Father Karras. We went to the Kennedy Center, where we had tickets to see *The Sleeping Beauty* ballet. I loved it; Beck fell asleep.

In May, we took Norah and Mae to the Smithsonian National Museum of Natural History. They were thrilled to be out with their big brother and their favorite babysitter, while Connor and Bernie were glad for a kid-free afternoon.

We rode the Metro into the city, then walked the girls to the museum, where we *ooh*ed and *aah*ed at the elephant statue in the rotunda before venturing into the mammal exhibit, with its thousands of preserved specimens collected by Theodore Roosevelt in the early 1900s. Upstairs, we saw mummies, and then walked through the Butterfly Pavilion. We explored the geology and gems section next.

I was showing Norah the Hope Diamond—"I want one!" she exclaimed, eyes glittering—when Beck grabbed my shoulder and whirled me around.

"Do you have Mae?" he asked, breathless.

"I—no. Just Norah."

"God*damn* it." He raked his hands through his hair, scanning the dark hall. "I turned around for a *second*."

"She's here," I told him, but my gaze was sweeping the exhibit too, and I didn't see her. "She couldn't have gotten far."

He was already on the move, calling, "Mae? Mae!" as he looked behind each display, around every corner. I searched where he didn't, pulse surging as I dodged museumgoers, tugging Norah along behind me.

After a frantic but futile search, Beck and I met at the entrance to the Hall of Geology, Gems, and Minerals. He was wrecked, sweating and scarlet-faced. I was terrified. Only a few minutes had passed, but those minutes might as well have been centuries.

"Beck," Norah said, looking fearfully up at him. "We have to find Mae!"

He nodded, scooping her up. "We will. Don't worry, okay?" To me, he said, "I'm gonna search the rest of this floor. Will you find security and let them know we've got a missing kid?"

I nodded. "Call me when you find her?"

When—not if.

"I will." Then he was off, shouting for one sister while carrying the other.

I ran for the information kiosk I'd seen in the rotunda. There, in a harried rush, I gave a fractured account of what had happened to the silver-haired woman working the desk. She contacted security and, holding the phone to her ear, asked for a description of Mae.

"She's four," I said. "Strawberry-blond hair. She's wearing black leggings and a purple T-shirt. Wait, no! A pink shirt! Her sister is in purple."

"Pink shirt," the woman repeated into the phone. She finished with security, then hung up, and reached across the counter to pat my hand. "It'll be okay," she told me. "Kids slip away all the time."

"But she's so little."

"They always are. The good thing about that is when they realize they've been separated from their grown-ups, they cry. Red flag. We've never *not* found a kiddo."

I nodded, feeling infinitesimally more hopeful, then gave her my phone number, which she wrote beside Mae's description. "Her brother is looking upstairs. I'm going to search this floor. Will you please call if—"

My phone, clutched in my hand, began to ring.

Beck.

I scrambled to answer. "Tell me you found her," I said in greeting.

"I did," he said with a disbelieving chuckle. "With the mummies. She said she likes the way they're all bundled up."

I laughed, a surplus of adrenaline combined with joyful relief. "She's okay?"

"She's perfect."

My information desk ally whispered, "Shall I call off the hounds?"

I nodded, mouthing *thank you*.

"Lia," Beck said. "Look up."

I did. He and the twins were looking out over the rotunda from the second-floor balcony. Norah waved. Mae shouted, "Lia! Beck found me!" He shrugged sheepishly while looking phenomenally proud.

So clearly, I remember thinking, *How lucky I am to call him mine.*

"My mom's gonna go apeshit," he said on our way back to his house. He'd driven Bernie's Subaru to the Metro station, and as soon as the twins were buckled into their booster seats, they were asleep. "My sisters and I are her whole world. She'd never recover if something happened to one of us."

He wasn't being hyperbolic. Bernie didn't work outside the house like my mom. Every second of her every day was spent catering to Beck, Norah, and Mae, and I'd never gotten any indication that she wanted it another way.

I reached for his hand. "She'll understand. Sometimes kids wander off."

"I bet you didn't."

"Wrong. When I was seven, I got lost at Bed, Bath and Beyond. My mom was shopping for a toaster and while her back was turned, I drifted away. When she found me, I was admiring the bath towels. You know how they fold them into those cubbies on the wall, all color coordinated and aesthetically pleasing?"

He turned to give me an endeared smile. "You're adorable."

"My mom didn't think so. She was hysterical. I never walked away from her again."

"She loves you," he said. "Same as me."

When we got back to the Byrnes', he called his dad into the kitchen where his mom was watering houseplants, a dish towel thrown over her shoulder, and came clean about what happened with Mae. Connor acknowledged the incident with an easy "Kids will be kids." Bernie was, as Beck had predicted, horrified, but only briefly. After recovering, she smothered him with a hug and told him he was the best big brother, an accolade he accepted in stride.

202

"They'll always remember that you and Lia took them to the museum—it's special, the way you let them tag along."

"We like them," Beck said with a shrug.

Connor clapped his shoulder. "They idolize both of you."

"What time do you need to be home, Lia?" Bernie asked.

"Eleven." Since I'd turned sixteen, my parents had cut me some curfew slack. Generally I was expected home by ten, but so long as I was with Beck, I got a bonus hour.

"We're taking the twins to Uncle Julio's for dinner," Connor said. "Leaving in thirty. You two want to come?"

Beck looked at me, torn. He loved Uncle Julio's guacamole, made fresh at the table, but if his parents were going out with the twins, the house was ours.

"I don't know," I said, holding his gaze. "The museum kind of zapped me."

He grinned, knocking his knuckles against the countertop. "Same. Want to order food and watch a movie here?"

"Yeah," I said. "That sounds good."

Bernie frowned. "That sounds dangerous."

My face went warm.

"They'll be fine," Connor said in a *don't embarrass the teenagers* tone.

She glowered at her husband. "Define *fine*."

"You can trust us," Beck said. "Best behavior. I swear."

Bernie arched her eyebrows. "I'll call Hannah to see what she thinks."

Beck took my hand and towed me to the basement, where we

pushed a menagerie of plush Disney characters out of the way so we could get comfortable on the couch.

"Gotta love that at this very second, our moms are talking about whether you'll jump my bones if we're left unsupervised for more than five minutes," he said.

I laughed. "Do you ever wish they didn't know each other so well? Because then we could sneak around without them checking in with each other."

"That'd be cool," he said, twining a lock of my hair around his finger. "Most of the time though, I like that our families are tight. Constant intrusiveness aside."

Bernie came trotting down the stairs. "Okay, Lia. Your mom said it's fine for you to hang out here. She asked me to remind you to make good choices."

I nodded, pressing my lips together, trying not to spontaneously combust. *Make good choices* was *don't have sex* in Mother Speak. Couldn't my mom have sent me a text?

Bernie looked at Beck and said plainly, "Don't have sex."

He burst out laughing. "Jesus, Mom. A little subtly? Hannah managed it."

"Subtly has never worked with you."

"Fine. If I promise to keep my pants on, will you leave now?"

"Don't push your luck," she said, whipping the dish towel from her shoulder to throw at him.

Bernie, Connor, and the twins did leave soon after. Beck ordered Uncle Julio's for two, and while we waited for the delivery, we spent a while kissing on the couch. But my hair ended up beneath his arm and he was balancing on the edge of the cushion and we were both uncomfortable.

He pulled back with a grumble. "Want to go to my room? There's a—" He cleared his throat. "—bed."

"Is there? In your bedroom? I had no idea."

He poked my waist. "I promise to make good choices."

"Well, then. Let's go."

It was easy with Beck. It had been since Christmas, since our sunrise kiss. We were good at reading each other; we understood when to fill silences with conversation and when it was better to settle into them. He sensed when my introvert battery needed a recharge and let me be. I recognized that he was a wimp when it came to discomfort and babied him accordingly. He knew that when he ran his fingers through my hair, I'd dissolve into a full body shiver. I knew that when I kissed his neck, he'd simultaneously squirm and nestle closer.

That evening in his room, though, it was awkward.

The interruption was partly to blame, as well as the general expectation of what's supposed to happen on a bed between two people who're wild about each other. My mom obliquely discouraging sex and his mom coming right out and forbidding it was the same as stepping into a cold shower.

Beck rolled onto his side, propping his head on his hand. "You okay?"

"Yeah. Totally."

He gave me a lopsided smile. "I think you're spooked."

"I think *you're* spooked."

205

"Yeah, I am. I've been cockblocked by our mothers."

I laughed.

"I'd like to know what makes them think we *wouldn't* make good choices," he mused, cheeks reddening. He and I had talked about a lot over the years, but not about sex. I loved him so much that I was often dazzled by the intensity of my feelings. I knew he loved me—he said so all the time. But more significantly, he showed me: in lingering looks and gentle touches, in considerate gestures, and in letting me set the pace while we were walking, or teasing, or kissing.

"I don't know," I said. "I guess they figure it's inevitable."

He smiled bashfully, and I edged onto his side of the bed. He took my hand, turning the ring he'd given me in a slow circle. "Do you talk to your mom about this stuff?"

"A little. She asked me a while back if you and I were...you know," I finished, cringing. I'd set my mind to being mature. Mom and Dad raised me to believe that if you're considering sleeping with someone, you and your partner had better be able to navigate a discussion on the subject. But the idea of uttering *having sex* to Beck felt akin to stripping naked while he watched.

"She wasn't being nosy," I went on, building a blush that rivaled his. "Or maybe she was. But mostly she was asking because she wanted to be sure I know to be safe." I ran a hand across my scorched face. "God. Why am I so embarrassed right now?"

Beck laughed, pulling me to his chest and wrapping his arms around me. "I wish you weren't. I'm embarrassed enough for the both of us."

"Do you talk to your mom about this stuff?"

He snorted. "Fuck no. Can you imagine?"

I couldn't. Bernie often lacked the nuance that was inherent to my mom, who'd been pretty cool about the topic of sex. While it was clear she hoped I wouldn't sleep with Beck anytime soon—she hit beats about pregnancy and emotional complications hard—she also offered to make me a doctor appointment so I could get a prescription for birth control.

Burying my face in Beck's shirt, I told him as much, mumbling, "I'm on the pill as of last month. Just so you know."

He smoothed a hand over my hair. "Okay."

I drew back to meet his gaze, which was a mix of tenderness and amusement.

"Okay?" I echoed.

"Yeah. I'm glad you told me. Nothing has to change though."

"Do you want things to change?"

His eyes gleamed as he leaned in and kissed me, a sweet, chaste kiss that, nonetheless, made my stomach flutter. "'Course I do. But not until you're ready."

"Have you ever? Before you and me?"

"No."

"Seriously?"

"Seriously." He sat up, a little indignant. "I only ever wanted it to be with someone I love, and I've been in love with you all my life."

I smiled. "So when I ask you to drop your pants, you will?"

He laughed again, gathering me close to whisper in my ear, "Without hesitation."

FLIMSY

Seventeen Years Old, Tennessee

For the last few days, I've thought of little more than how to share my CVU acceptance with Mom and Dad. They haven't asked about notifications because, as far as they know, I shouldn't hear anything until February.

Until now.

On a foggy Saturday morning, I get up early, let Major into the backyard, and then lose myself measuring brown sugar, cinnamon, and pecans. I'm not a baker—the kitchen is Mom's domain—but I'm hoping warm coffee cake will soften the blow of what I suspect will be an unwelcome collegiate acceptance.

Not long after the pan goes into the oven, the house fills with a sweet, buttery aroma. I set a pot of coffee to brew before letting Major in and giving him breakfast. He dives face-first into his bowl. Working a few pieces into the puzzle that sits half-finished on the dining room table, I listen for signs of life up in my parents' room and, yep, there's running water and murmured voices.

The oven timer goes off. As I'm setting the pan on a cooling rack, footsteps descend the stairs. Dad's in sweats and a Star Wars T-shirt. Mom's wearing a flannel pajama set.

She smiles, though there's wariness in the lift of her eyebrows as she catches sight of the coffee cake.

"You're up early," Dad says, cautiously optimistic.

"I made breakfast."

Mom scopes out the cake's crumb topping. "Smells good. What a thoughtful surprise."

Dad retrieves mugs from the cupboard, while Mom gets out creamer. Drumming my fingertips anxiously against the countertop, I watch them prep their coffee, hoping beyond hope that this goes better than I anticipate.

We sit at the table with wedges of coffee cake.

I charge forward, before my nerve dips out: "I heard from CVU."

Mom's loaded fork pauses midway to her mouth, hovering while she regards me with blatant trepidation. Dad, who's only just taken a bite, looks like he's chewing sawdust. He swallows with effort. "And?"

"I got in."

I used to daydream about this moment, before Beck passed, before I understood how quickly plans can be upturned and expectations can be thwarted. I'd make my announcement, then pull off my sweatshirt to reveal a CVU Eagles T-shirt beneath.

My parents would gasp with joyful astonishment. They'd hug me and tell me that CVU is lucky I applied and wow, what a life I have ahead of me! Then we'd go to dinner with the Byrnes, who'd be just as pleased. I used to see it all through starry eyes: my future unfurling before me.

This, *reality*, is nothing like that.

Dad crosses his arms.

Mom folds her hands.

Major comes to the table, which he's been trained not to do, and rests his chin in my lap. I stroke his head, waiting for someone to say something.

Dad breaks the gloomy silence. "Well. I'm not surprised."

Mom nods. "You *are* the sort of student CVU is looking for."

With a lift of his shoulders, Dad adds, "You're the sort of student most universities are looking for."

Mom says, "Have you heard about any of your other applications?"

I didn't submit other applications.

"Not yet." I brush a few granules of brown sugar from the tabletop. For months, I've been eaten up by guilt at having lied to them, but now that guilt is eclipsed by hurt. My parents' complete lack of excitement, of pride, is a terrible blow. It's no simple feat, getting into college, let alone into one of the best-ranked colleges in Virginia. Yet Mom and Dad are looking at me like I asked them to bail me out of jail.

Is a *well done* too much to ask? A *congratulations*?

"CVU is a good school," I say quietly.

"Of course it is," Mom says.

"But is it the right school for you?" Dad asks rhetorically.

"You promised to keep an open mind," she says.

He nods. "You promised to consider your options."

My stomach churns.

He'd be furious if he knew I don't have options.

But...what if he's on to something?

I should've applied early action to CVU and saved myself the binding commitment of early decision. I could've sent applications to GMU and UT and Austin Peay and Ole Miss and Seattle Pacific. I would've had nothing to lose reaching out to other universities. Instead I dug in my heels and shrugged off my parents' advice—which wasn't even *bad* advice—and now I'm going to CVU, whether I want to or not.

I should tell them. Come clean right now. Stand by my decisions.

I'm obligated to CVU. I didn't send applications anywhere else. I'm nearly eighteen. It's my choice.

I'd sound like a brat. An irrational, egotistical brat.

I *do* want to go to CVU.

Pressure builds in my chest, a balloon expanding beneath my ribs. I feel trapped in this house. Trapped in my life.

"Lia, take a breath, lovey," Mom says.

The kitchen's overly warm from the oven, and the cloying air clouds my head.

"It'll work out," Dad tells me in a tone meant for a toddler who's dropped her ice cream.

I'm about to blow up at him—at them.

"I'm going upstairs," I say, shoving back my chair.

My parents look at one another, their expressions clouded with concern.

Now they're worried about my feelings?

"How about finishing your breakfast first?" Dad says.

I shake my head. "I've lost my appetite."

AFTER TWENTY-TWO YEARS OF FAITHFUL
AND HONORABLE SERVICE,

COLONEL CONNOR F. BYRNE

IS RETIRING FROM THE UNITED STATES ARMY.
PLEASE JOIN US TO CELEBRATE AND WISH
HIM WELL IN HIS FUTURE ENDEAVORS.

CEREMONY TO BE HELD ON
MONDAY, THE EIGHTEENTH OF MARCH
AT EIGHT O'CLOCK IN THE MORNING.

GEORGE WASHINGTON'S MOUNT VERNON
3200 MOUNT VERNON MEMORIAL HIGHWAY
MOUNT VERNON, VIRGINIA 22121

RECEPTION AT CAFÉ AMERICANA TO FOLLOW.

PLEASE RSVP BY THE FIRST OF MARCH.
BERNADETTE.C.BYRNE@MAIL.COM

PIECE OF CAKE

Seventeen Years Old, Tennessee

I find the invitation on the kitchen counter when I get home from school. Its envelope, already opened, is addressed to my parents and me in Bernie's loopy handwriting. A formality. Mom's been helping with ceremony planning, and Dad's been asked to speak.

A celebration for Connor. Well-earned and a long time coming. I'm as glad for him as my parents surely are. But it stings, considering the way they shit all over my CVU news.

Shouldn't that have been a celebration too?

I snag the invitation, printed on cream-colored cardstock, and take it up to my room, where I tuck it into my journal.

After dinner, I feed my parents a story about studying at Paloma's, though in truth, Isaiah's invited me to his house for dessert. It's not that Mom and Dad will tell me I can't go, but there's a murmur in the recesses of my conscience that keeps reminding me of loyalty. I'm not doing anything wrong—I *want* to go to Isaiah's—yet it unsettles me, visiting a boy who's not Beck.

It'd unsettle my parents too.

His house is lit from inside, modest, warm, and welcoming, like Isaiah. I sit in my car a minute, gathering emotional implements the way a child plucks flowers from a garden: chrysanthemum for truth, snapdragon for graciousness, geranium for friendship, and crocus for good cheer. Using the rearview mirror, I fluff my hair, which I've blown out smooth. I'm wearing more makeup than I do to school, with a second coat of mascara and tinted gloss rather than balm.

Maybe I want to feel pretty.

Maybe I want to feel confident.

Maybe I want a shield, a mask, a disguise.

All of the above.

None of the above.

Who am I, sitting outside a boy's house, preening?

I leave my car, then march up the walk, stepping over another gallery of chalk drawings: starfish, dolphins, sea turtles, sharks, and a tentacled octopus rendered in maroon. On the porch, I ring the bell. When the door swings open, I exhale.

"You look like you're about to face a firing squad," Isaiah says, waving me inside.

"I know—I'm sorry. It's…a lot."

"It's cool. Have a piece of cake. If you're hating life after, you head home."

Marjorie's kitchen looks a lot like ours, with white cabinets, stainless steel appliances, and vining plants on the windowsill over the sink. A multilayered, richly frosted chocolate cake sits on the island like a centerpiece.

Naya, who's perched on a stool at the counter, looks older than her nine years, and not particularly happy to be a part of tonight's meet and greet. Her skin is ocher and her hair is dark, secured in a long French braid. Her eyes, a sun-faded brown, study me with guarded curiosity. I remember Marjorie from that awful afternoon back in November. She's older than my mom but younger than my grandma, with hair styled in shoulder-length twists. She's traded her red sweater for a lavender cardigan, and her glasses hang on a cute pearl chain.

"Lia," she says, rounding the island to hug me. "We're so happy to have you."

She smells sweet and summery, like cotton candy, and her cardigan is cashmere soft. While maybe it should be awkward to embrace a stranger in a new-to-me home, my bones are no longer jittering and the intrusive thoughts have quieted.

Marjorie, like Isaiah said, is an angel.

Over her shoulder, his eyes find mine. "She's a fan of the premature hug."

"Well. Now I know where you get it."

Marjorie steps away, her smile like strewn glitter. "He hugged you too soon?"

"Not too soon. But within sixty seconds of meeting me."

She laughs and returns to the counter to slice the cake.

"Isaiah told us you were accepted at CVU. That's quite an achievement!"

My friends have been so nice about CVU. So supportive. The girls have been hyping me up since December, and when I told Isaiah about my official acceptance as we were walking out of Ceramics the other day, his eyes lit up like supernovas. Marjorie's the first adult to acknowledge the news with enthusiasm, though. Appreciation makes my heart swell; I could cry, thinking about how this family has been so gracious in saluting my accomplishment, while my own labeled it a mistake.

My voice is unsteady when I tell her, "Thank you."

She grins. "We thought chocolate cake was the perfect way to celebrate."

Isaiah must sense that I'm in a precarious place emotionally, because he moves to his foster sister's side, giving her braid a tug. "Naya did the baking herself."

"Did you really?" I ask, glad for the deflection. "That cake looks like it came from a fancy bakery."

"It wasn't hard," she says with a shrug.

"Maybe not for you," Marjorie says. "But baking is reading and math and science—one mismeasured ingredient, and you've got a pan of chocolate soup instead of a beautiful cake. Our Naya is a whiz in the kitchen."

I don't doubt it. The slices Marjorie's plated look delectable.

"Did you do the chalk drawings outside too?" I ask.

Naya nods. "Isaiah helped."

217

"They're so good. Did you know Isaiah and I are in Art Club together?"

"Lia draws me under the table," he says.

"Lies. The portrait I did of you looks like I drew it left-handed and under duress."

Naya brightens, turning to Isaiah. "The portrait hanging in your room?" He nods, making a goofy face that closely resembles my rendering. She giggles. "The eyes and nose and mouth are all out of place!"

He makes his wonky expression even wonkier. "She captured my likeness exactly."

Their camaraderie keeps me from dwelling on this new knowledge that Isaiah hung my drawing and doesn't appear embarrassed by the fact that I know.

"If you can draw people as well as you draw sea turtles and hammerhead sharks," I say to Naya, "I could use some tips."

She grins. "I can help you."

"Later," Marjorie says. "First we feast."

STARTING OVER

Seventeen Years Old, Tennessee

During dessert, Marjorie asks about school, about our move from Virginia, and about what my parents do. Normal questions from a normal woman in a normal home. I answer like I've done this dozens of times: meeting the family of someone who interests me. Except I never imagined myself in this starting-over place because it was never, never, never supposed to be this way.

After cake, Isaiah and Marjorie clear plates. Naya, true to her word, spends a few minutes teaching me how to draw a realistic eye, using negative space to create the illusion of reflecting light, before scampering upstairs to study spelling words. As Marjorie wipes down countertops, Isaiah gives me an inquiring look: *Want to go?*

I shake my head.

I'm…good.

He smiles, then tells Marjorie, "We're going upstairs."

"Have fun. Door open?"

Isaiah aims a smirk at me, and I drop my jaw in mock horror because what does she think we're going to get up to under her nose?

"Door open," he promises.

As I follow him upstairs, my attention catches on the wall, which is lined with framed photos. I recognize Isaiah, of course, in a series of six eight-by-tens. Naya's framed once, which makes sense, since she's been with Marjorie for less time. There are photos of a dozen others spanning childhood—chubby infants, rosy-cheeked toddlers, schoolkids with cowlicks, preteens with braces—an array of genders and races and expressions and style choices.

"Marjorie's been a foster mom for a long time," Isaiah tells me as I look. "She thinks of all of us as her kids, no matter how long we stay, or how much shit we give her."

"Where are they all now?"

"Some went back to be with their parents. Some were adopted by other families. Some are adults now, aged out of the system. Marjorie stays in touch with most of them. She has them for holidays, sends birthday gifts, helps out when they need it. You know."

No, not really.

What a privilege, to have such limited awareness of the child welfare system.

Isaiah leads me to the door at the end of the hall. "If you

have questions," he says as we step into his room, "I'll answer them."

I sit on the floor, leaning against the bed. He joins me, stretching his long legs across the rug. His space is orderly; his comforter is green plaid, and the curtains, which are pulled closed, match. On his desk sits a school-issued laptop, a mug of pens and drawing pencils, and a stack of sketchbooks. Sure enough, the picture I drew in Art Club is tacked to the wall. A nearby bookshelf is stocked with nonfiction: adventure stories by Jon Krakauer, Bryan Stevenson's *Just Mercy*, plus biographies on basketball players—Jordan, Bryant, Bird.

"Naya stole my Percy Jackson books," he says as I scan the spines.

"Smart girl." I nudge his shoe with mine, indicating the pink doodles I noticed the day we met. "Did she draw those stars?"

"Yep. That girl leaves drawings everywhere."

I lower my voice and ask, "What'll happen to her?"

His mouth dips into a frown. "The plan is for her to reunite. Marjorie thinks the judge will hand down an official decision next month."

"Reunite with her parents?"

"Her mother, Gloria, yeah." He's speaking softly. I suspect he's not supposed to be telling me this. It's none of my business, and there must be rules about confidentiality. But I'm glad he is. I've already taken a liking to his foster sister. I hope her future is sound.

"Naya came into the system because of neglect," he goes on.

"Gloria's a single mom with a hell of a past, but she was trying. Problem is, for her, trying looked like leaving Naya alone while she worked a slew of shitty jobs. I'm not saying it's cool for a little kid to spend nights by herself, but what's a mom in that position supposed to do? DCS stepped in, and Naya ended up here. But now Gloria's doing everything right. Taking advantage of services, showing up for visits, for court. She loves Naya, and Naya wants to go home. Sometimes parents backslide, though."

"If that happens, will Marjorie adopt her?"

"I doubt it. She got into foster care because she wants to preserve families, help kids short term. She's not interested in parenting indefinitely."

"But you've been here six years," I say, wondering what it's been like for him. Marjorie is awesome, but he's spent a significant chunk of his life in limbo. Even I know that foster care is meant to be temporary; kids aren't supposed to languish for years.

He shrugs. "My case was complicated. There are exceptions to every rule."

"Would Marjorie adopt you?"

"Nah. I turned eighteen in October, so it'd be pointless. She and I've worked it out though. I'm here through the summer, and back again when I want to be."

I'm grilling him—I know I am. Once upon a time, I thought it'd be best to keep him at a distance, to maintain a buffer of indifference. But now that I've stepped into his world, I can't imagine backing out.

"What happens after this summer?" I ask.

"I'm gonna travel."

"But what about college?"

"Someday, maybe. First, I want an adventure."

I sink back against the bed, feeling like the wind's been knocked out of me.

It's never occurred to me that college can wait.

"What about basketball? You must've had recruiters after you."

"Some, yeah. But basketball's a hobby. An outlet. Marjorie signed me up for a team when I was thirteen and full of rage, and I've loved it ever since. But it's not my future."

"What is?"

"No idea—it's too scary to think about. I've got a short-term plan, though," he says, his timbre sparking with excitement. "As soon as basketball season's done, I'll get a job, and save for a car. Marjorie's gotten a stipend every month for as long as I've been with her. It's meant to go toward my care, but she's put it all away for me. Done the same for every kid who's been with her, no matter how long."

"Because she's an angel," I say, nudging him with my elbow.

He smiles. "Exactly. By now, she's saved more than enough for me to live on for a year. At the end of this summer, I'm going on a road trip. I'm gonna see every state in the lower forty-eight."

"Whoa," I say, surprised by the immensity of his goal, and how wildly unconventional it is. "Where are you heading first?"

"Don't know. I'm gonna see where the highway takes me. Kind of like of *Into the Wild*."

I frown. *Into the Wild* ends in tragedy.

Isaiah goes on. "After my year on the road, I might go to art school or look for an internship. Or maybe I'll apply to universities. Whatever feels right."

Okay, but that's not really a plan. A plan involves an itinerary. Strategizing. Advanced bookings. Debating pros and cons. To-do lists scribbled into notebooks.

Isaiah's is an idea, wide open and fuzzy-edged, optimistic but amorphous.

Yet, he doesn't seem daunted.

The day we shot baskets in my neighborhood, he told me I'm steady.

He's steady. To set out on a country-crossing escapade all on his own? To see where he ends up? To possess the faith, the confidence, to do *whatever feels right*?

I'm lost for words, thinking about the way he makes decisions—with his gut, with his heart—and agonizing over my own rigid plans for the future.

Have I gotten it all wrong?

It's a question to angst over tomorrow.

Tonight, I want to try living in the moment. For once letting my instincts lead, I take Isaiah's hand, weaving my fingers through his. I've been tasked with setting our speed, and this—holding his hand in the quiet warmth of his bedroom—is the beam of light I need to ride out the storm of uncertainty that's rolled in.

He moves closer, until his arm aligns with mine. Taking a pen from his nightstand, he begins to draw on the hand he holds.

A tiny flower on my first finger. A butterfly below my pinky. A basketball on the inside of my wrist. I wonder if he picked up doodling from Naya, or if she mirrors him.

"I've never invited anyone here," he tells me, inking a lightning bolt onto my palm. "Not even Trev."

"How come?"

His voice is low as thunder. "The house I grew up in was a nightmare. My first few foster placements weren't much better. For a long time, school was my only safe place. I got used to compartmentalizing and never really stopped."

"God, Isaiah," I say, my stomach turning over. "I can't imagine."

"I wouldn't want you to. Point is, it's taken years of therapy and a hell of a lot of patience on Marjorie's part, but I finally trust that my relationships are secure. This house is safe. The life I've built is solid. I want you to be part of it."

He pauses doodling to smile sweetly at me, and I feel so welcomed, so cozy and so comfortable with him in his room and in his home, with the people who make up his family.

Would it be so bad to stray from the pothole-riddled path I've been trying to navigate?

To veer toward Isaiah instead of a future that no longer feels like *me*?

Would it be so wrong to let myself settle into his world?

Buzzer Beater

She waited for an official invitation
    to watch him play.

It came as they sat at neighboring pottery wheels.

He was throwing a gorgeous vase.

She was starting over, her previous effort
    collapsed beneath her muddy hands.

"We're playing Rudolph," he said. "Friday
    night. Huge rivalry. Will you come?"

He didn't look up from his clay,

but hope glowed phosphorescent in his voice.

"Okay," she told him, though rooting
    a second boy to victory

is another step away from her first.

Two days later, she's squished
    onto a crowded bench,

flanked by her friends.

The game is fast paced, exciting.

The players are aggressive.

She's never known this side of the boy.

She's used to his contemplative glances,
    hands covered in clay.

His even voice and his piercing gaze.

On the court, he's dynamic, a leader,
    a flare of white-bright light.

He's a step ahead of his teammates and
    miles ahead of his opponents.

Even so, the game is close.

Rubber soles squeal against polished wood.

Players whoop, spectators shout.

The lead shifts with each possession.

The girl and her friends are on their
    feet, hands in the air,

hollering like victory depends on
    the racket they make.

She shouts the boy's name because
    the ball is in his charge.

Seconds remain.

He pulls up short, just outside the three-point line.

Rudolph's defenders descend.

He shoots.

A buzzer beater, barely.

Time screeches to a halt as the ball
    arcs through the air.

She squeezes her eyes closed—it's too much.

She hears it: the whisper of leather
    through nylon netting.

The East River High crowd explodes.

The girl's feet leave the ground, the gym's
    energy propelling her skyward.

She claps, she cheers, she hugs her friends.

She's _so glad_ she came.

On the court, the team celebrates in a huddle.

The boy has transformed again,
    grinning, triumph in his eyes.

And then his eyes are on her.

He stares at her, intentionally, intently, intensely.

She stares back.

He furnishes her with confidence,
    autonomy, a desire to feel.

Her vision goes soft.

She thinks of the day they met, of kissing him.

"I'll hang beside you," he told her.

She believes he will.

CAPRICIOUS

Sixteen Years Old, Virginia

Beck graduated high school on a sun-soaked Saturday afternoon at the EagleBank Arena at George Mason University. My parents and I went to the ceremony with the Byrnes, and when Beck marched across the stage to claim his diploma, he looked so grown up, so accomplished. He beamed when he heard our cheers. I grinned and waved and cursed summer's end, when he'd leave for CVU.

Afterward, while we waited for Beck outside, Mom, Bernie, the twins, and I snapped selfies. Dad and Connor looked on, glad, probably, that we hadn't yet roped them into posing. When the graduates appeared, there were more pictures: Beck with Raj, Stephen, and Wyatt. Beck with his parents, and with his sisters, and with me. Bernie insisted on snagging a passing stranger to get one of our whole group.

I'd never been so ardently happy, and so utterly woebegone.

Love is confusing.

Hearts are capricious.

Growing up is a pain in the ass.

As we were on our way to the parking lot, headed to dinner, Beck's name rang out. There was Taryn, prancing toward us in her robe and wedge sandals.

Beck pulled me to a stop as Bernie, shepherding the twins along, called, "We'll meet you at Bellisimo!"

I would've been cool hitching a ride with my parents or the Byrnes rather than watching Beck engage with Taryn, but he squeezed my hand and murmured, "Just for a minute."

A minute was long enough for Taryn to snare Beck in a hug. Long enough for her to tell him that she'd loved being his track and field teammate, and that she was sure he'd do amazing things. Long enough for her to compliment my dress, a blue fit and flare with a halter neckline. For a whole minute, she was genial.

And then she said to Beck, "I hope we'll get to hang out this fall. CVU and the University of Richmond are only an hour apart."

I scowled. I'd had no idea that Taryn would be in Richmond. That she'd be physically closer to my boyfriend than I would be.

"It'll be nice to see a familiar face every so often," she said before she kissed his cheek, then skipped off to find her friends or her family or the hole in which she'd crawled out of.

On the way to Bellisimo, Beck asked if I was okay.

"I'm *great*," I said.

He chose to play along.

All through dinner, I faked pleasantness.

Internally, I lost my shit.

After dinner our families went home. Beck and I went to the graduation party that'd been the talk of school for the last month. It was hosted on the outskirts of Fairfax County at the home of one of Beck's classmate's uncles, who lived on acreage and had promised to confiscate keys and let graduates pitch tents in his cleared fields before tapping kegs. I'd told my parents I'd be spending the night with Macy, which was true: Macy would be at the party.

Beck and I managed to get our tent staked without saying more than ten words to each other, though all around us, vehicles rumbled and mallets struck stakes and graduates hollered and whooped. When we crawled inside to unroll our sleeping bags, he hooked an arm around my waist and pulled me close.

"You're pissed," he said.

"I'm not."

"I know you are." His lips brushed my neck, his words tickling my skin. "You're shit at hiding your feelings."

True to form, I failed to swallow an amorous sigh as he threaded his fingers into my hair, tipping my head to expose my throat. His breath was warm.

Weakly I said, "I am not."

He swirled a kiss below my ear before saying, "Are you mad because, for the next two years, you're stuck at RHS without me?"

"That'll suck," I admitted, trying not to shiver as his mouth mapped my neck. "Doesn't make me mad, though."

"Then maybe you're grouchy because you chose a shitty salad for dinner, and you wish you'd ordered a steak, like me."

I smiled despite myself. "My salad was fine."

His lips grazed my jaw. His voice was low and sure. "Okay... Then you're angry because Taryn wants to visit me next fall."

"*No.*"

He kissed my lying mouth, then pulled back to look into my eyes. "Lia, I'd be pissed if I was standing in your shoes. I'd be jealous and irritable and really fucking sad."

I softened, leaning into him.

He said, "You don't have to be any of those things, though. You know that, right?"

I nodded. Beck was loyal and Beck was honest. He loved me, not Taryn, and he'd never given me reason to think otherwise. Still, in a few minutes' time I'd turned into an insufferable drama queen. I had nothing to worry about—I knew that. So why were we holed up in a tent when we could be partying with our friends?

"Let's go have some fun," I told him.

Fun, that night, involved loud music, hundreds of people, and free-flowing booze.

"I might have sex with Beck later," I divulged to Macy, loose and languid.

She hooted, then took a swig from her cup. It was filled with

232

Boone's Farm Fuzzy Navel, one of several flavors acquired for us by Wyatt's older sister, a senior at Marymount—much better than the keg beer most were drinking. "In a tent?"

"Yeah. So romantic, right?"

"I mean, maybe if you guys were on a mountaintop or at the beach or something—*alone*." She looked around the field, which was strewn with Solo cups and lit by what I now recognize was an ominously full moon. Bass beats blared as various speakers competed. There were people everywhere. I had no idea where Beck and the boys had gotten off to, but I didn't much care. I was having fun with Macy.

"This is a *nice* setting," I insisted, my words running one into the next.

"Bullshit."

"But, Mace, it's graduation."

"Yeah, Beck's. Not yours."

I sipped my Fuzzy Navel. It tasted like nectar, sweet and syrupy; I *loved* it. "I want tonight to be special for him."

Macy arched a judgy eyebrow. "I want your first time to be special for you."

"It will be, because *Beck*."

She laughed and clanked her cup against mine. "It will be *anytime*, because Beck. You do you, but I'd save first-time sex for a bed. And really," she said, waving a hand to indicate hordes of partiers far as the eye could see, "do you want a field full of people to hear you? Or worse—interrupt?"

"Oh, we'd be quiet," I said.

She snorted. "Sure you would. Except you're literally shouting now."

Swallowing another gulp of my drink, I considered her concerns because she was Macy, and she had my best interests at heart. Then I pulled her close, so I could speak more softly—*not* that I'd been yelling. "You really think I should wait?"

"If you're asking for my opinion, if you're not one hundred percent sure, hold off. You've got all summer."

"And then forever," I said, raising my glass like *Cheers!*

We went in search of the boys and found them not far from where we'd been talking. Raj and Stephen were shotgunning beers while Wyatt, Beck, and a group of girls from their graduating class cheered them on. Taryn was there. She'd swapped her dress for shorts and a tank and was holding a Solo cup, as were her friends. Macy and I pulled to a stop at the fringes of their circle, where we could mainline our Boone's Farm without intruding on the boys' fun.

Macy then proceeded to describe, in dirty detail, the first time she and Wyatt had sex. Had I not been three-quarters of the way through a bottle of malt liquor, I would've blushed all the way to my toes. As it was, I giggled, took a few mental notes, then glanced over at Beck. He was waving off a turn to shotgun. He'd been nursing the same bottle of Bud Light since he'd wandered off with the guys. I knew because earlier, I'd watched him peel back the label. I was pretty sure he was taking it easy so he could look after me, and that made me want to blow off Macy's advice about waiting.

As he kicked empties into a pile, I took a step in his direction. But before I could break into the circle, Taryn leapt toward him and threw her arms around his neck. He staggered, surprised, a geyser of beer erupting from his bottle as he caught her. He lowered her to the ground, and when she was back on her feet, his arms fell to his sides.

Hers did not.

She hung on him like a cutoff-wearing sloth, saying something into his ear. He laughed. She did, too, tipping her chin back. She was on her toes again, the way she'd been that afternoon when she'd pressed a kiss to his cheek. She was closer than I would've stood to another girl's boyfriend, hip to hip, cheek to cheek. I was torn between wanting to retreat, or pour what was left of my drink over her impossibly shiny hair.

"Ugh," Macy said, tracking my gaze. "The placeholder."

They'd become engaged in what appeared to be an actual conversation. She was still touching him. He still wasn't moving away. In fact, he leaned in to hear what she was saying, his eyes bright with interest. He'd looked at me that way thousands of times. It never occurred to me that he might wear the same captivated expression while conversing with other girls.

I thought I might throw up.

Instead I squared my shoulders and pounded what was left of my drink. "Will you come back to the tents with me?" I asked Macy.

"You know I will," she said churlishly.

She had a zero-tolerance policy when it came to girl-on-girl shadiness.

235

I spun on my heels. Tears pooled in my eyes as my name broke the din of the party.

Beck was behind me, nudging Macy out of the way so he could grab my hand.

"Hey," he said, breathless. "Where are you going?"

"What do you care?" Embarrassingly, my voice broke. I pulled my hand from his and said, "You're having tons of fun without me."

He glanced at where Taryn was standing, watching us. When he turned back to me, his expression was one of regret. "We were just talking."

"Yeah. I saw."

"Hey," he said, "don't be like this."

I huffed. "How would you feel if you saw me hanging all over some dude?"

He looked at Macy. "How much has she had to drink?"

She shrugged. "Enough."

"I'd be pissed sober," I snapped.

Tottering a little, I fled, a malady gurgling in my stomach.

Macy followed.

Beck did not.

SOMETHING REAL

Seventeen Years Old, Tennessee

The girls and I make our way down the bleachers, savoring the last sips of victory.

My pulse races.

Isaiah found me.

Mid-celebration, he sought me out, a face among hundreds. His eyes met mine, and he grinned. In that moment, my heart did something it hasn't done in ages.

It soared.

The gym's air is humid, thick with musk and fervor. I'm so warm, my makeup is likely voyaging down my face, but I don't care. My skin tingles, my vision shimmers, and my ponytail swings; I feel *good*. Better than I have in more than a year.

We step into the gym's lobby, which is lined with trophy cases and dozens of portraits, Athletes of the Year spanning decades. There's a similar Hall of Fame at Rosebell High. Beck's senior portrait hangs there, snapped during autumn, two years ago. His auburn hair complements the trees' red and gold leaves. Cheeky grin, broad shoulders, freckled skin. It's the same photograph that hangs in his parents' home, framed in dark wood.

I falter a step, as if Beck has extended a phantom hand to hold me fast.

Paloma pauses, looking back to where I've stopped. She's been wearing a perma-grin since this afternoon, when she found out she was accepted early action to USC. Now she gives me an inquisitive look.

I shake it off—the memory, the sense of obligation, the guilt.

"Lia?" she asks. "You okay?"

I nod, but I'm not sure.

Is it okay to be okay?

Once we step outside, I feel lighter, clearer. This is what it's like for me. Highs and lows that come and go, sudden reminders of what I've lost and what I've found. The winter wind surrounds my friends and me, rekindling the excitement that sadness tried to extinguish.

Meagan and Soph lead the way, hands linked, as we cross the dark campus. We rehash the game: *did you see when...? and I can't believe...* and *holy shit—that shot!*

"Molly's party?" Paloma asks, confirming the night's plan.

"Totally," Meagan says. "Who's driving?"

She and I rode with Paloma to Rudolph. Sophia met us, thanks to a club volleyball practice that didn't end until just before the basketball game. Tonight we're all sleeping at her house because her parents don't wait up to administer breath checks.

238

"I will," she says. "We can pick up your car tomorrow, Paloma."

As we near the parking lot and its bus loop, Meagan spins a circle, arms wide. Sophia joins her in a series of twirls that leave them cracking up. Paloma laughs, then pulls me in.

"I saw that, back there in the gym," she says into the space between us. "Isaiah. After the buzzer. He looked for you."

I could pretend I don't know what she's talking about, but after half a year of friendship, she knows me well.

"Do you really think—?"

She cuts me off, grinning. "Yes. I really think."

We emerge from between buildings, Sophia and Meagan making a commotion up ahead, Paloma and I giggling because, God, there's something between me and Isaiah. Something more than ceramics and flirting. Something more than joint loss and hard times. Something fresh and promising. Something real.

My name cuts through the night.

I whirl around, dragging Paloma with me. Scanning the parking lot, I search for the source of the shout. There's an idling school bus dumping billows of exhaust into the parking lot. East River's basketball players are visible through the open windows, and they're making fantastic noise.

Isaiah isn't on the bus. He's standing a few feet from it, hands on his hips, head high, back straight, eyes locked on me. He smiles and calls, "Come here."

Butterflies awaken in my belly.

Paloma nudges me forward.

Meagan purses her lips in a kissy face.

239

Sophia smiles. "We'll wait for you by the car."

My heart spills over with love for the three of them.

I skip toward Isaiah.

CRESCENDO

Seventeen Years Old, Tennessee

He takes long strides in my direction, making quick work of the dark pavement. When a few feet separate us, he opens his arms.

Tonight, I'm a girl who's impulsive, who lives in the moment, who's falling for a boy—a different boy. I leap into his embrace, looping my arms around his neck, letting go of the bullshit baggage I've been lugging around.

He catches me, laughing, hair shower-damp and smelling of juniper and mint.

"You were amazing," I say.

He grins. "I'm glad you came."

"I told you I would."

"Yeah. Not everyone keeps promises though."

I cradle his face in my hands. Softly I say, "I do."

His gaze is steady on mine. I lean forward, close enough to see the many shades of brown in his bottomless eyes.

I want to kiss him so badly and I think…maybe…

No, he gathers me close, hugging me tight, comforting in a way I didn't know I needed.

The night's gone strangely quiet.

I pull back to find the basketball players on the bus glued to the windows. Every last one of them is gawking—Trevor wearing the most self-satisfied smirk of all.

They break into a chorus of cheers.

Isaiah turns and, with a low laugh, says, "What a bunch of assholes."

I smile. "They're rooting for you."

"They want a show," he says, rolling his eyes. He loosens his hold and, regrettably, I do too. As my feet find solid ground, he catches my hand. "Are you going to Molly's?"

"Yeah. Are you?"

"I am now."

At Molly's house, a Victorian by the river, there are bottles of booze lined up across the kitchen countertop. She's supplied canned soda, along with bags of chips and crackers. When the girls and I arrive, she's in the kitchen, passing out cups like a legit hostess. She hugs me. We're friends now, because Isaiah and Trev are, and I'm glad about that. Paloma, Megs, and I end up with root beers spiked with generous splashes of vanilla vodka. Sophia, our DD, swigs her soda straight as the four of us toast Paloma and her USC acceptance.

I'm halfway through a refill, gossiping with the girls in the living room, when there's an eruption of whooping and clapping near the front of the house.

"The team has entered the building," Meagan says in a put-on announcer's voice. She taps her cup against mine. "You ready?"

I'm a little tipsy, a little nervous, but thanks to the lingering high of the team's win and a bit of liquid valor, confidence comes easy. "Totally."

"We've got your back," Paloma says, as if I haven't been one hundred percent secure in that knowledge for the last six months.

I wrap the four of them in a vanilla-vodka-infused hug. "I'm going to find him."

Isaiah's in the kitchen with a few guys from the team, including Trev. They're passing around sodas and inhaling snacks and making a ruckus. I hang back, sipping my drink, watching as Isaiah laughs with his friends. They're all good looking, all jovial and winsome, but he's a light among them, a full moon in a star-speckled sky.

Trevor spots me. He throws his elbow into Isaiah's side.

Isaiah turns, then ditches his Coke and crosses the kitchen.

I set my cup aside and step into his arms, linking my hands at the small of his back, resting my head on his sternum. He holds me like he did the day we met, like he did earlier in the parking lot: like letting go is unthinkable.

The kitchen clears out—probably because Isaiah and I are hugging like a pair of weirdos.

He pulls back to find my gaze.

243

"I've been waiting for you," I tell him, because I can't with pretenses—not anymore.

He smiles. Picks up my cup. Peers into it. "You need a refill."

I follow him to the makeshift bar. Choosing a dry section of countertop, I hop up to sit while he sniffs the dredges of my cup. "Root beer?"

"Yep," I say, pointing to the Smirnoff Meagan used to spike my drink. "And this."

"Classy," he teases, popping open a can of soda. He finds ice in the freezer, then fixes my drink, a little less generous with the vodka than Megs was. After opening three different drawers, he finds flatware. He uses a soup spoon to stir, then passes over my cup.

I take a sip. It goes down syrupy smooth. "You're not having anything?"

He gestures at the Coke he abandoned a few minutes ago. "No boozing during the season."

"You're very responsible." We are—for once—the same height, thanks to my perch on the countertop. I like looking directly into his eyes.

He steps closer. "I've no choice but to be."

"I used to be."

"Now you're not?"

I lift my cup, shrugging. "Less so. The Lia of before wouldn't have wasted an hour of her school day taking Ceramics, that's for sure."

"I like the Lia of today," he tells me, very serious.

244

"I think I'm starting to."

His attention drops to my mouth, and he frowns. His eyes close in a series of rapid blinks, as if he's trying to clear his thoughts.

"What's happening in your head?"

He rests his hand on my knee. The warmth of his palm bleeds though the denim of my jeans. "I'm thinking about kissing you." He gives a reticent laugh. "I think about it a lot."

"What's stopping you?"

He hesitates, taking his hand back, crossing his arms over his chest. "I don't know if you're ready."

"You could ask if I am."

He shakes his head. "Not sure I need to. You miss him. You ought to. But I can't kiss you and wonder if you're remembering him. Stacking me against him. Wishing I was him."

"I would never do that."

"Did he call you Amelia?"

"Sometimes."

He studies my right hand, with its band of white gold and two sparkling stones. Gingerly, as if it might burn him, he touches my ring. "Did he give you this?"

"Yes."

"Do you ever take it off?"

"I did, after—" My words bump up against the lump in my throat. I swallow, holding tight to his gaze. It's imperative that I explain, that he understands the ring's evolving symbolism. "I didn't wear it for a long time. It was too hard to look at. A reminder of what I've lost. But I put it back on in November."

"Because you love him."

"Because I wanted to go back to believing in a future full of promise."

Voice soft, he says, "And then you met me."

He'll appear when you least expect it.

"And then," I repeat wistfully, "I met you."

I grasp the hem of his sweatshirt and tug him forward, until he's settled in the space between my knees. I could lean in, put my mouth on his, but if he wants to talk this out, if he wants to be certain, I want the same.

I whisper, "I think about kissing you too."

He blinks, canting his head the way Major does when he's puzzling out the meaning of my words. "Since when?"

"My first day of Art Club. When I drew your face." Reaching up, I let my fingertip skate the bridge of his nose. "I knew I wanted a redo. I wanted to kiss you the right way, for the right reasons. I wasn't ready, but I thought about it. A lot. And honestly, that terrified me. But...it also gave me hope." I brush his hair off his forehead, revealing his scar, a sharp contrast to the olive tone of his skin. "All those afternoons in Ceramics, that day on the basketball court, the other night at your house... Don't tell me my crush isn't obvious."

His mouth quirks into a smile. "Maybe it is."

"Maybe it is, but...?"

"But, historically, I'm not so lucky."

246

I smile. "If luck is catching the attention of a girl who sometimes feels really fucking sad even though life's starting to come through for her, then yeah. You are *blessed*."

He uncrosses his arms to hold my face in his hands. "Tell me what you want."

My response comes without contemplation. I lean forward and kiss him.

He answers back, and it's nothing like that first time back in November. Tonight we're gentle and sweet, mindful of the soap-bubble-frailty of the moment—until Isaiah's hands slip from my face to my throat, and what started out as careful slowly builds, crescendoing in flushed faces and shallow breaths.

If loving Beck was a serene snow dusting, falling for Isaiah is a blizzard: fierce, disorienting, thrilling. I shiver, burrowing into his hug, committed to riding out the storm.

Magic 8-Ball

Would Beck hate me if he knew?
REPLY HAZY, TRY AGAIN.

Will Mom and Dad go ballistic if they find out?
WITHOUT A DOUBT.

Will Bernie's heart break?
YOU MAY RELY ON IT.

Am I doing the right thing?
CANNOT PREDICT NOW.

Am I a terrible human?
MY SOURCES SAY NO.

Should I give up on fate?
BETTER NOT TELL YOU NOW.

NONSENSICAL

Sixteen Years Old, Virginia

The morning after Beck's graduation party, I woke up in a tent, in a field, sick with shame and also *sick*. My memory was hazy, my head throbbed, and my throat convulsed with the need to throw up. Crawling woozily to unzip the flap, I got my head outside before I retched rancid peach liquid into the dirt.

A hand squeezed my shoulder, then gathered my hair from where it fell around my clammy face.

Macy, bless her.

"Shit, Amelia," a groggy voice said. "Are you okay?"

Not Macy.

Beck.

"No," I said pitifully, crying over the puke. "I'm dying. Already dead, maybe."

He laughed, shifting to kneel beside me. Adoringly he said, "Baby."

"I think I need to throw up again."

He slipped the elastic from my wrist so he could secure my hair in a ponytail, then rubbed my back while I emptied the contents of my stomach like the Boone's Farm rookie I was. When it was over, he gave me tissues he found in my bag, then made me sip water until I was no longer green.

Feeling infinitesimally better, I collapsed on top of my sleeping bag, sweaty and stinky. I flung an arm over my face to block the light. Beck lay beside me, running his fingers over my palm until my breathing evened out.

"Did you sleep in here all night?" I asked, eyes closed.

"Yeah. I came in, like, fifteen minutes after you walked away."

It was hard to believe that only fifteen minutes had passed between my temper tantrum and conking out. The night before seemed a thousand lifetimes ago. "I thought you were Macy," I told him. "I assumed you wouldn't want to be near me after the way I acted."

"Lia. I'm not gonna hold a drunken outburst against you. You were...dealing."

I pried my eyes open, tilting my head so I could see his freckled face. "I know you don't like Taryn—not like that. I'm insecure. And kind of an asshole."

"You're not an asshole."

"Well, Taryn must think I'm out of my mind."

"Who cares what Taryn thinks?"

I didn't—not really. "What do *you* think?"

His fingers trailed over mine, along my palm, my wrist. "I

250

think I don't like fighting with you. I could've handled last night better. You've got no reason to feel insecure with me, though."

There was tension in his jaw and doubt in his eyes when he asked, "Lia, don't you trust me?"

"I always have."

"Do you trust us?"

I mulled over his question. If I trusted him but not *us*, where was the problem?

With me.

The problem was with me.

It took me a second to work up the nerve to voice this new realization. "I don't know who I am without you. We've been Beckett and Amelia for as long as I've been alive. We've had two years of high school together, but now you're leaving and I have to learn how to get by on my own and…I'm feeling very lost."

"You think I'm not?" he asked quietly.

"Maybe you are. But you're the one who gets to leave."

"And you're being left behind…kind of like a deployment." His expression clouded over and, with such sadness, he said, "We could take a break."

A strangled gasp escaped me. "Like, *break up*?"

"I guess, yeah. Until we figure our shit out. I don't know… maybe some space would make things easier for you."

"Is that what you want? To break up?"

"Fuck no. But if that's what you need, I'll figure it out."

His suggestion was nonsensical—absolutely bananas. The

notion of being without him physically *and* emotionally was intolerable. I would *never* choose life without him.

"I don't want to take a break," I told him. "That's the opposite of what I want."

His shoulders fell from his ears, his face relaxing into its usual good humor. "Then I'll sneak you to CVU with me. How about that?"

"I wish you could."

He leaned in, pressing a kiss to the top of my head. When he drew back, he said, "You smell like puke."

I laughed, which made the tent spin. I squeezed my eyes closed and, in the darkness, let go of another confession: "I had plans to have sex with you last night."

He barked out a laugh. "Seriously?"

"Yes, seriously. Until...you know."

"Until I fucked it up?"

"More like until I got sloshed."

He floated his fingers over my hand again. "Our first time shouldn't be in a tent."

"That's what Macy said!"

He laughed and laughed, then walked me to the 4Runner and let me sit in the passenger seat with all the air conditioner vents aimed at my face while he tore down our tent, cleaned up our mess, and packed the SUV.

Even suffering through a hangover, I felt so happy, so lucky, to exist in the world with Beck.

A THREAD

PALOMA: You guys. USC deferred Liam to regular decision. ☹

MEAGAN: Oh shit.

LIA: God, I'm sorry.

SOPHIA: But that isn't a NO.

MEAGAN: It's not a yes, either.

LIA: What's his plan B?

PALOMA: Safety schools he's still waiting to hear from.

SOPHIA: What's your plan B?

MEAGAN: She doesn't need a plan B. She got in.

SOPHIA: I mean…would you go anywhere other than USC?

PALOMA: Girl, no. I'm a Trojan through and through.

SOPHIA: I bet he gets accepted regular decision.

LIA: Me too. But wait, you'd really go to USC without Liam?

PALOMA: I mean, yeah. I'd be bummed, but I won't ditch my dreams for a boy.

LIA: Megs, would you go to Austin Peay without Soph?

SOPHIA: Yeah. Megs, would you?

MEAGAN: I plead the fifth.

SOPHIA: I'd want you to. I wouldn't hold you back.

MEAGAN: Ditto. What about you, Lia? If things had been different?

LIA: Would I have chosen a school other than Beck's?

PALOMA: Yeah. Did you ever consider it?

LIA: I did until we got together.

MEAGAN: Did he ask you to apply to CVU?

LIA: He did, and I wanted to go. I honestly didn't think I could survive being away from him. But now...

SOPHIA: Now...what?

LIA: Now I know I can.

RAMPARTS

Seventeen Years Old, Tennessee

Sunday evening, I meet Isaiah at Over Easy, a diner downtown. It's small and kitsch, with a checkered floor and album covers adorning the walls. The air smells of fry grease and grilled meat, and though I had lasagna with my parents after texting with the girls, my stomach rumbles as I slide into the booth across from him.

We order sodas and slices of blueberry and chess pie. When I tell him my Virginian friend, Macy, didn't known what chess pie was until after she met Beck and me, the offspring of two proud Mississippian women, he laughs.

"Did your mom—?" I start before cutting myself short.

Somehow I doubt his mother is an apron-in-the-kitchen type.

He finishes for me. "Did my mom bake pies?"

I fiddle with the saltshaker. "Or anything?"

"No. Does your mom?"

I shrug, not wanting to boast about homemade pastries.

"She does," Isaiah concludes. "Don't feel bad about it, Lia. Marjorie bakes all the time. So does Naya. But growing up...my childhood was different from yours."

"What do you think my childhood was like?"

He regards me as if I've asked a loaded question.

I bump his foot with mine. "I'm serious. If you had to make three assumptions about the way I grew up, what would they be?"

After a few seconds, he ticks them off on his fingers. "You've never worried about whether you'd get dinner. There've always been presents under your Christmas tree. And your parents gave—still give—you hugs."

I regret asking.

Like, deeply.

Because if our childhoods were different, as he just said, then he did worry about whether he'd get dinner and he didn't receive Christmas presents and his mom and dad didn't hug him.

"You grew up the way every kid should," he tells me after the waitress drops off our sodas. "Don't question whether you're worthy of your experiences."

I nod, though I can't help but question.

"You can talk about it," I tell him. "Your past. Your parents. Any of it. All of it."

"I do. With a mental health professional."

I smile. "I mean you can talk to *me*."

"Yeah, except I'm not about to heap my trauma onto your shoulders."

My gaze falls to the tabletop, worn smooth by decades of patrons. This conversation has gone deep quick, and I give my words careful consideration before lifting my eyes to his. "My shoulders can bear a lot."

He reaches for my hand, holding it in both of his. "I know. But there's this too: If I tell you how I grew up, why I ended up in the system, the way you see me...it'll be different."

"No, it won't."

"Lia. You'll end up feeling sorry for me."

"I already feel sorry for you." He flinches and I feel terrible, but I can't *not* finish my thought. "I don't need details to hate that your parents weren't able to give you what you needed. I already wish with my whole heart that things had been different for you. Knowing the story isn't going to change that."

He takes thoughtful audit of my expression, then says, "Why's it so easy to trust you?"

In you, he'll find a confidant. In your heart, faith will regain its footing.

Emotion swells in my chest. A wave rolling toward shore, gaining speed, height, and intensity, curling then cresting, a spray of fine, salty mist sending rainbows into the air.

"I could ask you the same thing," I say. "Instead I'll ask you this: Why were you taken from your mom and dad?"

He sighs, a sound like surrender. "There were a lot of reasons. They were addicts. Our house was a dump. Food was a pawn. Hygiene was nonexistent. My attendance at school was shit. I never had what I needed: supplies, permission slips, lunch. I

257

raised myself while my parents pumped poison into their veins."
He pauses to look at our joined hands. When his eyes find mine
again, they're empty. I worry he's taken himself back to his
parents' home, to the psyche of the boy he used to be, suffering
but surviving.

"They hated me," he says. "I was an obstacle standing between
them and their next fix. If they gave me something—breakfast,
shoes, the time of day—and I didn't show enough gratitude,
there was hell to pay."

"What does that mean?" I ask in a small voice.

He waves a hand before his face. "My nose isn't jacked because
I was a clumsy kid."

Crooked as a woodland trail.

My heart swims into my throat, beating too hard and too fast.
I ache thinking of little Isaiah, hungry for food, attention, affec-
tion. Hurt by hands meant to nurture.

"Teachers are mandated reporters," he says. "They have to
call when the abuse is as obvious as a kid coming to school
with a dislocated shoulder. But DCS didn't pull me right away.
There's a process, a push for family preservation, a bunch of
bullshit bureaucracy. A social worker checked in every few
weeks. My parents got clean and put on a convincing show.
The case was closed in six months. Not long after, they were
using again. And then when I was eight, my mom had another
baby. A girl."

Dread surges through me.

The waitress approaches with our pie. We release hands as

she places the plates in the middle of the table, along with forks and napkins.

"Enjoy," she says brightly.

My appetite has fled.

Isaiah doesn't acknowledge the pie or the waitress. There's a rigidity to his posture, and his expression is still terrifyingly dull.

This exhumation of his past has come at a cost.

"Her name was Emily," he tells me. "She was colicky. That's a word I learned later, from Marjorie. Means she cried all the time. My parents were usually too high to deal, so I tried to keep her calm—meet her needs or whatever—but she never settled. One night I slept, like, eight uninterrupted hours, which hadn't happened since she was born. I woke up panicked, sure in my gut something was wrong. I found her in her crib, so quiet. So still. She looked like a little doll."

I swallow, nauseated, my cheeks consumed by heat. "Your parents...?"

"Shook her until she quit crying. Then they got wasted and passed out. I still don't know if they didn't realize she was gone, or didn't care."

I leave my seat and slide in beside him. His hand finds my leg, and I thread my arm through his, resting my head on this shoulder as he breathes shallowly. He's impossibly strong, but behind the ramparts his childhood raised, he's all softness, a boy who wanted nothing more than to protect his baby sister.

"When's the last time you saw them?"

"When I was ten, in court. I was a witness for the prosecution.

They'll spend decades in prison. What's fucked is that for a long time, I felt guilty for turning them in."

"That's not fucked, Isaiah. It's human." I shift, so I can meet his eyes. "You were a good brother to Emily, and you're a good brother to Naya. You have to know that."

He smiles, but the sorrow in his eyes says he's unconvinced.

"I'm serious," I say vehemently. "What happened could have made you cold. Instead you're this…this *light*."

He lifts a hand to tuck a lock of hair behind my ear. "That's the nicest thing anyone's ever said to me."

Then he retrieves our forgotten desserts, and we share pie like two people who know nothing of heartache.

LABELS

Seventeen Years Old, Tennessee

He's a good kisser," Meagan says when I walk into the library Monday morning. "Isn't he?"

I claim the chair across from her with a coy lift of my shoulders.

"Come on," Soph says. "Spill."

"You guys, she doesn't have to," Paloma chides before turning a smirk on me. "Unless she *wants* to."

I grin. "He's a *very* good kisser."

Their laughter is enough to summon the librarian, who hushes us with a benevolent roll of her eyes. Softer now, Sophia says, "You seem happy."

"I feel happy."

Paloma squeezes my hand. "Have you told your parents about him?"

"Not yet." I never used to keep things from Mom and Dad,

but now I've got a growing list of secrets. Hiding Isaiah away as if he doesn't matter… I don't feel good about it. "They loved Beck, and they're super loyal to his parents. I'm not sure they'll understand."

"There's only one way to find out," Meagan says.

"I know. I'll tell them, eventually. I mean, Isaiah and I haven't even defined our relationship yet. I don't want to get my parents worked up over something that might be casual."

"You and Isaiah aren't casual," Sophia says.

"But I don't know that we're together."

"You're together," Meagan says with conviction.

I shrug. "For now, I want to keep him to myself."

"Then that's what you should do," Paloma says with a resolute nod.

Later, in Ceramics, I'm sitting on my usual stool. I'm starting a new project today, the slab house that's next on Ms. Robbins's syllabus. I've collected a hunk of clay, a rolling pin, and guides, but I haven't started working because I'm busy offering Paloma moral support as she texts Liam, who's being the world's biggest dick—her sentiment, not mine.

"He's still worked up about being waitlisted," she tells me.

"I get that."

"Me too, but he wants me to be all mopey with him. Shouldn't I be able to celebrate my acceptance?"

"You absolutely should. Is he still coming for spring break?"

"That's the plan. Everything feels so up in the air right now though, you know?"

I give her a sympathetic smile. "I really do."

Her phone buzzes with another text. She glares as she skims the message. "I swear to God," she mutters. "I'm dating a toddler." She looks at me, her exasperation palpable. "If he were sitting here—if we could have an actual conversation—this would be so much easier."

I reach over to loop her ponytail behind her shoulder. "Long distance is tough."

Her thumbs move furiously over her phone. "*Liam* is tough."

"Liam doesn't know how good he's got it," a sage voice says.

I turn to find Isaiah. The combined scents of juniper and wintergreen settle over me, and anticipation scatters like sparks on my skin.

"Hi," he says.

"Hey," I return, a greeting that lights his face.

He touches my neck with a warm hand, bending to kiss me like it's the most natural thing in the world.

Paloma clears her throat.

She drops her phone into her bag, then raises her eyebrows at me. "Casual, huh?"

As the bell trills, she leaves the table to retrieve the slab house she started last week.

Isaiah takes the stool next to mine. He pokes my shapeless clay and asks, "Casual?"

263

"The girls wanted a status update during Advisory."

His mouth lifts in an uncertain smile. "And you told them we're casual?"

"I told them we hadn't talked about it."

Gripping the base of my stool, he hauls me closer. Quietly he asks, "Is that what this is for you? Casual?"

Being with him is like holding my beating heart in my hands. He makes me happier than I've been in more than a year. He makes me wonder if I might actually be able to do it: start over again. But I'm terrified—absolutely *petrified*—of the unknowns. How will my parents react? How will Bernie and Connor respond? How will he and I survive beyond our time at ERHS?

Is admitting the seriousness of my feelings for Isaiah a final goodbye to Beck?

"I'm not really into casual," I tell him.

"Me neither," he says, his shoulders relaxing. "Do you think we need, like…a label?"

I'm trekking through uncharted territory. Beck and I never required a conversation like this. We were assumed. We were requited. With Isaiah, question marks abound. I like that he's asking, though. I appreciate that he gives as much as he takes.

"I don't hate the idea of a label."

He pulls a pen from his backpack. He extends his open palm, his eyes meeting mine. I slip my hand into his, and he begins to draw. "So, I'm into you and…you like me okay."

"I like you more than okay."

Focused on the winged insect he's inking onto my wrist, he smiles. "What if I call you my girlfriend?"

"Then I'll call you my boyfriend."

He lifts his gaze, and we share a grin until, over his shoulder, I see Paloma on her way back to the table.

"We're about to have company," I tell him, "so unless you want to be part of an all-new status update, you should go get your project."

He nods, adding a curled antenna to his dragonfly doodle. He caps his pen and stands, trailing his hand along my shoulders as he leaves the table.

"Well?" Paloma says, plopping down on her stool.

"You guys were right," I tell her as she lifts plastic from her clay. "Not casual."

She smiles, smug. "Girl, I've been sharing space with you guys for too long not to know as much."

Rendezvous

When the semester began,

the glaze closet was utilitarian, dim, dusty.

Now it's a wonderland of temptation.

A nudge to her foot, a nod of his
    head, a playful wink.

All she has to do is catch his eye.

He gets up first, strutting a casual path,

giving their teacher an innocent smile on his way.

He might as well link his hands behind
    his back and whistle a tune,

she thinks, holding back a laugh as
    she gets up to join him.

It's never more than a few minutes.

The way he engages her senses,

the intensity with which she wants him

—even when she has him—

leaves her breathless.

He's worth the risk of getting caught.

He takes her hands and kisses her mouth.

He lights her like a torch.
She leads him backward, until they're
    hidden by the partially closed door,
then ignites a fire in him.
He brushes her hair back and says...
 "I think I could do this forever. "

DIMINISHING SAND

Sixteen Years Old, Virginia

I pictured my last summer with Beck as grains of sand falling through funneled glass.

In late June, my parents and I went to Rehoboth Beach with the Byrnes, where we rented a house on the shore. Beck and I spent our days playing in the waves with his sisters, and our nights walking the beach. We ate peanut butter and honey sandwiches under the midday sun, freshly caught crab legs for dinner, and locally churned ice cream for dessert. We returned to Rosebell bronzed and happy.

One day in early July, we got up super early and drove to Williamsburg. We were at the front of the line when Busch Gardens opened. We rode our favorite roller coasters, petted the Clydesdales, and treated ourselves to bratwurst and funnel cake. We stayed until the park closed. In the 4Runner on the way home, I clung to Beck's hand and started to worry about diminishing time.

As summer flew by, we worked to finish checking items from our Things to Do in DC—Before Beck Leaves for CVU list. We strolled down Embassy Row, ate Ted's Tarts—a freshly baked version of a Pop Tart—at Ted's Bulletin, and hiked Theodore Roosevelt Island. We took Norah and Mae to parks all over town. We played board games with our parents. We hit up parties with Raj, Stephen, Wyatt, and Macy. We went to fancy dinners and marathoned movies in our pajamas.

And then, on a humid Saturday in August, we ran out of time.

I drove to the Byrnes' to say goodbye. Connor's truck was backed into the driveway and loaded with cardboard boxes, a couple of suitcases, and several plastic totes. I knew what was in each, because I'd spent the last week helping Beck pack. It was all there: his clothing, his sneakers, his tension bands, and a pull-up bar that hooks over a doorway. There were fresh bath towels and new bedding selected by Bernie because her son didn't give a shit about what his comforter looked like. He'd picked a dozen novels to bring along, favorites I doubted he'd find time to reread. There were notebooks, pens, a graphing calculator. A new laptop. Framed photos of his family, of him and me. It was all folded, wrapped, and packed, a whole life tucked into the bed of a truck.

I had to avert my eyes. The sight of Beck's possessions ready to travel more than a hundred miles southwest, where they'd be unloaded into a dorm room, where they'd stay—*with Beck*—made me want to cry my face off.

Instead I went into the house. I could hear Connor, Bernie,

269

and the twins in the kitchen, going on about road trip snacks. All five of the Byrnes were making the drive to Charlottesville, Beck and his dad in the truck, and Bernie and the girls in her Subaru. The 4Runner would stay behind because, according to Beck, parking on campus was a bitch. I'd been invited on the trip, and while I wanted to go, Beck's family was struggling with his move as much as I was. I didn't feel right taking from their goodbye. Also, I was pretty sure that if I set foot in Beck's dorm, I'd have to be dragged out kicking and screaming.

As Norah bellowed about raisins and Mae fought for Goldfish Crackers and their parents did a half-hearted job of mediating, I made my way down to the basement.

Beck was sitting on his bed, phone in hand.

"I was just about to text you," he said, grinning up at me. "We're about to head out."

I burst into tears.

He sprang up and pulled me into his arms. "Shit, Amelia. I don't want you to be sad."

I let him hold me until I'd cried myself hoarse. Then I stepped back, using the strap of my tank to swipe mascara trails from beneath my eyes. I pulled in a breath and got myself together because I would not send him to Charlottesville thinking he'd left me in shambles.

"I'm okay," I said. "I'm fine. I'm *perfect*."

"Liar."

"I am, Beck. Really. I'm so excited that you're off to live your dream."

"*Our* dream." He pressed a kiss to the top of my head. "And in case I haven't made this clear, I'm gonna miss you every single second I'm away."

"Beck!" Connor called from upstairs. "Time to hit the road!"

Outside, Bernie blotted her eyes as she buckled the twins into their booster seats. Connor, reliably unsentimental, was tossing his keys in the air.

When she'd finished, Bernie left Norah and Mae in the idling SUV, then came over to sling an arm around me, the other around Beck. She was still crying.

"Jesus, Mom," Beck said. "You're gonna see me in a couple hours."

"You'll understand one day, when you're watching your babies spread their wings."

Beck's gaze connected with mine. I was imagining it too: him and me in a few decades, standing in a driveway much like the Byrnes', sending a fledgling of our own out of the nest. I bit my lip, trying hard to tough out what I was sure would be the very worst day of my year.

Beck said, "Let's not drag Lia through this any longer."

His mom nodded, then gave me the tightest hug. "We'll get through it, girlie."

"I know. Drive safe."

She squeezed my shoulder before climbing into the Subaru. Connor was already in the truck, engine rumbling. Beck pulled me into his arms; I hugged him like I might not get another chance, hoping with everything in me that our time apart would fly by.

271

When we separated, he sniffed and said, "Shit just got real."

"Beckett," I said. "Don't go getting soft on me."

"I'd never. I'll see you soon?"

"Really soon."

Then he was in the truck with his dad, rolling down the driveway and out of my world.

FRAUD

Seventeen Years Old, Tennessee

Saturday afternoon, my parents go on a date, their first in ages.

"Movie, then dinner," Dad tells me, tying his Sambas. "Sure you don't want to come?"

"Very sure," I say. Even if they hadn't chosen a rom-com and a bistro filled with tables for two, there's no way I'd tag along as their third wheel.

And anyway, I've got a date of my own.

Mom comes skipping down the stairs. She's wearing a floral dress, white Vejas, and a distressed denim jacket she borrowed from my closet. With her sandy hair blown out, she looks fresh and happy.

"Good lord, Cam," she says, eyeing Dad's ancient shoes. "You're wearing those?"

He looks to me. "You like these, don't you, Millie?"

"Love 'em," I say, and peek at the clock. If they don't scoot soon, I'll be late.

"Next PCS," Mom says, "those things are going in the donations pile."

"They'd better not!" Dad says, playing aghast.

She gives a grandiose shrug. "Moves are hectic. Things get misplaced."

"All my fraternity T-shirts," he laments, as if he lost real, valuable treasure. "Gone."

"There, there," I say, patting his shoulder, ushering him toward the door. "You guys will miss your movie if you don't get going. Have fun!"

From the porch, I watch as they get into the Volvo. Dad says something to Mom. She smiles, dipping her head, so it must've been complimentary, and probably cringe. They drive off looking the way they used to before we left Virginia, before Beck passed, before life became muddled with complications.

I swallow back the sour taste of culpability.

They wouldn't be so lighthearted if they knew the secrets I'm guarding.

I fill Major's food and water bowls, shrug on a hoodie, and smooth balm over my lips. Then I head for the basketball court.

Isaiah's there, along with Trevor and Molly. They're swapping wild shots, goofing around. When Trevor sinks a distant three-pointer, Molly prances over and kisses his cheek. That's when Isaiah spots me and his face, seconds ago vexed by Trevor's lucky shot, transforms. He jogs over, takes my hand, and twirls me around.

274

"Okay, why do you look hot in gym clothes?" he says.

I laugh. I'm wearing charcoal running tights and black Nikes with a light blue hoodie. I pull its zipper down to show him what's beneath: the East River High basketball T-shirt I bought from the student store. "I figure if I'm going to be with a basketball badass, I ought to look the part."

His palm finds my cheek, and his mouth meets mine. We kiss, a greeting that fills me with warmth. As it ends, his hand skates over my jaw and down my neck, until his fingers find the neckline of my T-shirt. In an undertone, he says, "I love it."

A flurry of emotion ripples through me. It's the first time he's used that word. It was just an offhanded remark about a shirt, though he could've tossed out a dozen other verbs. His choice, this moment, seems pivotal, like one I'll turn over before I fall asleep tonight, and wake up remembering tomorrow morning.

Is it possible he's falling in love? When our eyes meet, his dance. When he speaks to me, his voice is honeyed. When we touch, his body unwinds, the way I imagine it does as he sinks into bed at the end of a long day. Isn't that love? Comfort realized in another person?

Sometimes I think I might be falling in love too.

But when that notion enters my head, *fraud* follows closely behind, and I worry I'm doing him a disservice, offering him a fraction of a whole.

I'm not sure I'm capable of loving anyone the way I loved Beck.

I lift onto my toes and kiss him again. He answers, pulling me in. My heart dips, then pitches skyward.

Love.

Maybe…possibly. What if?

"Isaiah!" Trevor hollers. "Are we playin' or not?"

Isaiah pulls back, rolling his eyes. "We're playing."

We hang out on the court awhile, the boys running spirited scrimmages, tossing the ball to Molly and me when we're paying enough attention to receive it. After narrowly missing a shot, Molly runs at Trevor, leaping onto his back. He catches her legs, laughing.

"You promised we could get frozen yogurt when we're done here," she tells him. "Which should be right about…"

"Now," Trev says. He looks to Isaiah and me. "Y'all want to come?"

"You guys go ahead," he says.

Watching as they make their way down the block, I ask Isaiah, "Not a fro-yo fan?"

"It's fine. I'd rather have cookies though."

"Me too." I check the time. My parents' movie is probably letting out, which means they're on their way to dinner, which means I've got more than an hour before they get home. "Want to go to Buttercup Bakery? We can walk to my house and get my car."

He tucks the ball under his arm and takes my hand and off we go.

We're approaching my driveway when a silver sedan turns the corner up ahead. I don't pay it any attention; I'm so enchanted by Isaiah's laughter and the heat of his palm. It slows in front of us. Even still, it takes me second.

It's Mom's Volvo. She's in the passenger seat, and Dad's behind the wheel.

My heart free-falls.

Dad stops adjacent to where Isaiah and I stand.

He lowers the window.

He raises his sunglasses, eyes steely.

Mom gapes.

I drop Isaiah's hand.

"Lia," Dad says.

Vapidly I say, "I thought you were going to dinner?"

"We did," Mom says, looking between Isaiah and me.

I slide a step away.

"The movie was sold out, so we ate early." Dad clears his throat. "Are you going to introduce us to...your friend?"

I glance at Isaiah, whose face is shuttered.

"Isaiah," I croak. "My parents. Cam and Hannah."

"Colonel and Mrs. Graham," Dad corrects, and I might throw up. Never—*never*—has he suggested that my friends should address them so formally. The first time Paloma, Meagan, and Soph came over, he was casual and friendly, and Beck never called my parents anything but their first names.

"Nice to meet you," Isaiah says. "Lia and I were just—"

"Hanging out at the park," I butt in. "And Isaiah was walking me home."

His gaze swings to mine. I was expecting confusion or concern, maybe anger. His actual expression, bleakly vacant, is much worse.

277

"Sure," Isaiah says, coolly composed. He gestures toward the house. "And now we're here—*you're* here—so I'll take off." He shifts to face me, looking just over my head, the hand that used to hold mine squeezing in and out of an anxious fist.

I think I could do this forever, he said the other day.

Today he says, tepidly, "Lia, it's been real."

And then he continues down the sidewalk, basketball beneath his arm, alone.

WOUNDED

Seventeen Years Old, Tennessee

Isaiah's retreating silhouette does terrible things to my heart. It's worse when I think about what comes next. He'll call Marjorie for a ride. He'll take to the safety of his room. He'll feel like shit.

Because of me.

I cross the lawn to the front door, where I duck into the house. Major gallops into the foyer, bursting with love and snuffles. I sidestep him, heading for the dining room, where I park myself at the table and glare at our current puzzle, an arrangement of supple green succulents, while I wait for my parents.

I expect a fight.

I *want* a fight.

I've slotted three edge pieces into place before they come through the door.

Dad's agitated.

Mom won't look at me.

They drop keys, phones, and wallets on the counter.

Dad says, "Lia, we're not mad."

I don't believe him.

My friends were right. I should've told my parents about Isaiah. It would've been hard, but this—hurting Isaiah, my parents' shock—is much worse.

"We're...surprised," Dad goes on. "And confused."

Mom inhales a shaky breath. "Who is he?"

I don't like the way they're standing over me. I wish they'd sit. I wish they'd treat me like an equal.

"I know him from school," I tell them. "He's in my Ceramics class."

"Is he—" Mom's voice breaks, and she pauses, struggling to collect herself. "You were holding his hand."

I've no idea what to say—yeah, I was.

Is that so terrible?

Part of me is relieved to have been found out. Part of me wishes I could've kept Isaiah to myself indefinitely. Part of me wants to burn, burn, burn, until I'm a pile of ash to be swept away by a wayward breeze.

Who are my parents to interrogate me about walking down the sidewalk with a boy? I was fifteen the first time they saw me and Beck kiss, and they were elated. For months, they've preached about healing, moving forward, blazing my own trail. Now that they're witnessing me doing exactly those things, they're acting like raging hypocrites.

Mom hovers near the hutch, where she's proudly displayed the coil pot I finished last month; it leans like the Tower of Pisa. Dad sits down at the table. He folds his hands, leaning in as if I'm a junior soldier under his counsel.

"Is it serious between you and this boy?"

For the duration of a breath, I consider lying. I can't do it, though—not to Isaiah, not after the way I minimized his importance outside.

"It's not *not* serious."

"Why is now the first we're learning of him?"

"Because of this," I say with enough sharpness to unhinge both his jaw and Mom's. "Because you're looking at me like I've done something horrific—like I've renounced my fate. I knew it would go exactly this way."

"Lia—" Mom starts, but I cut her off.

"I'm not doing anything wrong. I'm just…I'm trying to give life another chance. But if you think there's no guilt when I'm with Isaiah, you're deluded. If you think I've stopped missing Beck, you're wrong. If you think I'm only capable of loving once, well, maybe you don't know me at all."

Dad's eyes are bright with tears.

Mom's clasps her hands, prayerlike, her expression creased with unhappiness. "We just worry it might be too soon."

"It's not up to you," I snap. "You lost your right to an opinion five minutes ago, in the front yard. The way you treated Isaiah… *God.* I'm humiliated. I can't even imagine how he feels."

Mom steps forward. "Lovey, I'm sorry. *We're* sorry."

Dad nods. "We'll fix this. The next time we see him, we'll make it right."

I flashback to how wounded Isaiah looked on the sidewalk.

I'm not so sure there'll be a next time.

My parents hurt him, but the worst of it's on me.

I let him walk away.

FREE FALL

Seventeen Years Old, Tennessee

I wait until Sunday afternoon to text Isaiah. It's a bullshit What are you up to? because I have no idea how to repair the bridge I demolished yesterday.

He's usually quick to respond, but nearly thirty minutes pass before I get his answer: Nothing.

Crestfallen, I send Paloma a lengthy message with a synopsis of yesterday's enormous screwup. While Meagan and Soph exist in a bubble of sugar-sweet happiness, Paloma and Liam bicker plenty. They challenge each other on topics large and small, but their loyalty runs deep. If anyone's capable of giving advice on how to mend the rift I created, it's Paloma.

She calls immediately. "Girl, you've got to talk to him in person."

"What if he doesn't want anything to do with me?"

"Then he's not who we thought he was."

"Paloma," I say around the stone of worry lodged in my throat. "What if I broke us?"

Her answer is delivered with compassion that only compounds my guilt. "Then I'll help you pick up the pieces."

Monday at school, my stomach's queasy. My schedule doesn't merge with Isaiah's until last period, and by the time Ceramics rolls around, I'm practically vibrating with anxiety. He saunters into Ms. Robbins's garage as the period starts, quashing any chance I had at conversation before the bell.

Paloma gives me a sympathetic shrug.

Ms. Robbins reminds us of approaching due dates, then sets us loose to work.

"I think I'll throw a pot," Paloma says, popping up from her stool. She looks at me and tips her chin in Isaiah's direction before heading for the wheels.

He gets up, too, but before he can step away, I clasp his hand in mine.

"Will you help me pick out a glaze for my project?"

His dark eyes are suspicious—he knows I'm full of shit—but he follows me anyway. I swing the glaze closet's door shut just enough, the way we've done every other time we've come in here together, then turn to face him.

His apathetic air scares me.

"I messed up," I tell him, launching into the dialogue I've been rehearsing since Saturday night. "I acted like you don't matter, and that was so wrong and so the opposite of the way I feel. This is new territory, introducing a boy to my parents.

284

It'd be weird under the best circumstances, but my situation—*our* situation—it's complicated. I'm trying to figure it out, and I'll probably screw up again, but I'm learning. I'm trying. And I swear, Isaiah, I will never treat you like shit again."

His expression is indecipherable.

He says, "Have you been stressing about this all weekend?"

"I—yes. I was hoping we could talk yesterday, but you seemed checked out."

"I was." He focuses on me with such intensity, I have to fight the impulse to look away. "It was fucked, the way you acted."

"I know."

"I'm not gonna pretend to understand."

"I don't expect you to."

"I appreciate your apology, though."

"I meant it."

"I know. So…this is it? Our first fight?"

I think, maybe, there's humor in his voice.

"I guess," I say, hazarding a smile. "How about it's our last too."

He shuffles forward, resting his cheek on the crown of my head, and I sigh, letting go of the anxiety that's been building since Saturday. Over the last few weeks, I've become swept up in him. If he decides to walk away—if I continue to push him away—I'm done for. I'll be airborne without a parachute, free-falling toward an unforgiving Earth.

"Don't give up on me," I whisper into the cotton of his sweatshirt.

He kisses me, an abbreviated kiss, a kiss with an undercurrent of longing. He draws back slightly, as if distance is a need more than a want. Then he skims his palms up my arms, grounding me in the moment as he says, "Lia, I couldn't, even if I wanted to."

WINDFALL

Sixteen Years Old, Virginia

October, junior year, my parents let me visit Charlottesville with Connor, Bernie, and the twins. They'd been reluctant, at first. I was sixteen, their only child, occasionally naive, blah, blah, blah. I'm pretty sure visions of keg stands danced in their heads—the sort of rabble-rousing they got up to in college, *ahem*. I sold the trip more as a CVU visit than a loosely supervised weekend with my boyfriend, which wasn't an outright fabrication.

Autumn had proved itself even more challenging than I'd been prepared for. I was busy in Rosebell, studying my ass off, serving as Key Club's junior class director and French Club's vice president, and hanging out with Macy, who'd become a secondary best friend in Beck's absence. He was swamped, trying to get his freshman-year feet under him. His academic schedule was grueling, his athletic schedule even more so. When he wasn't in class, he was at the library or the gym or with his roommate, James, whose schedule must've been significantly less grueling because he seemed to fit partying into every day that ended in y.

Sometimes when we spoke, Beck sounded grouchy and overtaxed. Sometimes I picked fights to snare his attention. On the hardest days, I let myself wonder if we'd been wrong to try and make it work.

We left Rosebell Friday afternoon, after I'd finished school and Connor had finished work. All the way to CVU, sitting in the third row of Bernie's Subaru while the twins watched movies on iPads in the middle, I simmered in excited anticipation. I'd gotten only one weekend with Beck since he left for college, when he'd hitched a ride home for his birthday. I wanted my time at CVU to be like those days had been: blissful.

I was pretty sure it would be. Connor, Bernie, and the twins would meet us at Saturday's Eagles football game, and we'd see campus and get food with them, but they were sleeping at a hotel. As far as my parents knew, I was bunking in Beck's building, but with James's girlfriend, Trish, on the third-floor women's hall, far from any penises. In truth, James would spend the weekend with Trish, and I would stay with Beck.

He was waiting for us outside.

His sisters scrambled out of the SUV, running down the sidewalk for hugs. Bernie and Connor followed. I lingered, stretching my legs as I watched Beck embrace his mom, then his dad. While Norah and Mae made a game of chasing each other around the nearby lawn and their parents attempted to rein them in so they didn't crash into students hustling back to their dorms, I walked into Beck's waiting arms. He buried his face in my hair, inhaling the way he did when we danced that first time at formal. Like he was trying to memorize the moment down to its finest details.

All my worrying ceased to matter.

Beck and I were together again.

Connor and Bernie took us to dinner at a local pizza parlor. Beck fielded their CVU-centric questions and helped his sisters with the dot-to-dots printed on their menus. Beneath the table, his hand found my knee, then migrated a slow path toward my hip. The longer we sat in that booth, the faster my heart beat. When Connor suggested a dessert pizza, I nearly bottle-rocketed through the ceiling.

The Byrnes dropped us back on campus before heading to their hotel. As soon as Beck and I stepped into the empty elevator, we were kissing, and not with delicacy. After so much time apart, after so much time with his family, decorum had left the dormitory.

With my back against the scuffed wall, Beck murmuring kisses along my throat, I caught my breath long enough to whisper, "Tonight, okay?"

He lifted his head to look at me. Voice raspy, he said, "You sure?"

I raked my fingers through his hair. "Very."

With a ding, the elevator doors yawned open.

He smiled, grabbed the handle of my suitcase, and took my hand. We walked down the hallway, my stomach fluttering all the way to his room. He fumbled with his key, then flung the door open. I'd seen enough of his living space on FaceTime that the tiny room with its narrow beds and unreasonably big TV wasn't much of a surprise.

Finding James rifling through a drawer was.

Beck begrudgingly introduced us, though we'd made lots of small talk on calls over the last couple of months. James grinned while stuffing sweats and deodorant into a duffel. He must've sensed his roommate's edginess, though, because he said, "On my way out, bro. Had to grab a few things before heading to Trish's."

Beck glowered. "You're not supposed to be anywhere near this room for the duration of the weekend. *Hurry up.*"

"I am, I am! Just trying to avoid interruptions later."

I swallowed my laughter and perched on Beck's desk, tidied, I think, with my visit in mind. He leaned in to mutter, exasperated, "This fucking guy."

"Lia," James said, zipping his bag, "it's been a pleasure."

"Likewise."

He shot Beck a waggish smile. Then to me he said, very seriously, "I hope pleasure is a trend that will continue for you tonight."

Beck snatched a pair of rolled socks from James's desk, which was far less tidy, and fired them at his retreating back. James ducked out the door, snickering.

Beck showed me where to store my suitcase, then walked me to the hall's communal bathroom and stood guard while I washed my face and brushed my teeth. Back at his room, he left me to change, returning to the bathroom to shower.

Wearing the pajamas I'd bought especially for my visit—little black shorts with a matching tank trimmed in lace; my mom would have *died* if she'd seen the set—I explored Beck's space. His bedspread was gray linen, thick and soft. On his desk sat his laptop, a couple of textbooks and notebooks, a US Army cup filled with pens and pencils, a framed photo of Norah and Mae dressed as Rapunzel and a dinosaur, respectively, and a framed photo of him and me at the Tidal Basin. The mini fridge was stocked with bottled water and caffeinated sodas, and the shelves were lined with protein powders and energy bars. James had hung a bunch of sports posters on the wall over his bed—New York Mets, New York Giants, New York Knicks—but Beck had gone with a tapestry in black-and-white.

He came through the door dressed in sweats and one of the many CVU T-shirts he'd acquired since he'd committed. His hair was wet, curling where it touched the back of his neck, and he brought with him a familiar scent, one I'd come to associate with him and my happiest moments.

His hand was on the doorknob, the door still ajar, when his eyes settled on me. He looked momentarily lost, like he wasn't sure he'd stepped into the right room, then his expression

291

morphed into something like disbelief, as if a girl on his bed was a windfall too great to comprehend.

"You okay over there?" I asked.

He gave his head a shake. "I think so."

"Would you mind closing the door?"

His face cracked into a grin. He shoved the door shut, then twisted the lock.

"Doesn't James have a key?"

"If James shows his face in this room before Sunday night…" he said, stalking toward me. "I'll kill him."

I laughed. "I'll help."

Scooting back on the bed, I made room. He curved around me, a parenthesis to my comma. Into the space between us, he said, "You've been good to me these last few months. I know I've been a shit boyfriend, but school is hard and throwing is hard and being away from you is the fucking worst. Things are gonna get easier, though. Better. You know that, right?"

"I do. And you're not a shit boyfriend, Beckett. You're my very favorite person."

He smiled, then kissed me with reverence I felt in my soul.

I looped my arms around his neck as his hands roamed. Soon my pretty pajamas fell away. His sweats followed. He pulled a condom from his desk drawer because, even though we'd talked about birth control and I trusted the pills I'd been prescribed, he was the sort of person to be doubly careful.

And then it was happening, Beck and me, together in the only way we'd never been.

I'd read enough pragmatic magazine articles, enough spicy blog posts, enough heartfelt romance novels to have a relatively holistic view of sex. Macy had given me that startlingly uncensored rundown of her first time with Wyatt. I'd seen movies like *American Pie* and *Lady Bird* and *The Girl Next Door*. I knew to manage my expectations, to anticipate fumbling and awkwardness and discomfort, to let go of any notions of fireworks. But being with Beck was more than warnings, advice, and mechanics. It was the way his eyes sought mine, the way he checked in, the way he murmured his love. He laced his fingers through mine. He kissed my temples, my collarbones, my mouth. And then there *were* fireworks, because Beck was mindful and determined, and never did anything halfway.

Later, we lay in his bed, listening to the sounds of the dorm: muffled music, slammed doors, the occasional holler. With his arms around me, his breath falling evenly on my shoulder, I turned over what he'd admitted earlier: it was hard for him to be away from me. His honesty was reassuring, as was the awareness that my challenges were his challenges. Our attempt at making a relationship work over distance and time *was* hard. He could be clueless, and I could be self-centered, and the both of us made assumptions and, occasionally, failed to see reason.

Still, I'd never loved him more.

I snuggled into his chest and chose him all over again.

WORSE FOR THE WEAR

Seventeen Years Old, Tennessee

Is it cool if I swing by?" Isaiah asks, the strain in his voice apparent even through the phone.

It's midweek and nearly midnight. I've been finishing homework in my room, fighting drowsiness, but now I'm wide awake.

No one calls this late with *good* news.

I quickly consider my options. Mom and Dad went to bed a while ago, but I'm not sure they're asleep yet. While they've sworn to make things right with Isaiah the next time they have a chance, I doubt they'll want him visiting at this hour. Major's sacked out on my bed, but if he hears an unfamiliar voice in the house, he'll be up and barking.

"I'll meet you outside in a couple minutes," I tell Isaiah.

I'm wearing flannel pajama pants and a tank. I push my feet into a pair of slippers, then pull a sweatshirt from the pile on my closet shelf. I've worn this Ole Miss crewneck so many times its sleeves are pilly, but it's warm and sentimental. Whipping a brush through my hair, I check my reflection in the mirror propped on my desk: I've looked better.

As I'm straightening, a photo of Beck catches my eye. I took it his senior year. He's fresh from a track and field meet, cheeks rosy from exertion. He's grinning, having just thrown a personal record. I feel the blow of sadness I'm accustomed to, but instead of ramping up, it fades, then dissipates.

How many days has it been since he passed?

I'm not sure anymore.

Someday you'll stop counting the days he's been gone.

I press a hand to my heart.

It's there, safe beneath my rib cage, beating rhythmically. But why isn't it aching?

It won't always be this hard, Meagan told me back in November.

I tiptoe out of my room and down the stairs. I escape through the back slider, then go around the house to the driveway. From down the block, headlights cut through the dark. Marjorie's Suburban. My slippers slap the concrete as I hurry down the sidewalk.

When I reach the SUV, Isaiah leans over to push open the passenger door. His team lost by a basket tonight. The game was hosted by a wealthy private school south of Nashville, a game which, if won, would have rocketed ERHS into the district playoffs. I can only guess that his midnight visit has to do with the defeat and the end of the season.

"Your parents are really gonna hate me if they catch you sneaking out because I asked," he says as I climb into the Suburban, glad for the heat.

There are charcoal smudges beneath his eyes and a shadow of stubble on his jaw. I reach over the console to touch his cheek, sandpaper against my palm. "They'll never know. I'm sorry about the game."

Shrugging, he says, "Doesn't matter."

"No?"

"I mean, it does, but there's something else." He sighs, pitter-pattering his fingertips against the steering wheel. "Marjorie and I had a conversation earlier, after Naya went to bed. Court's scheduled for Friday, and this is gonna be it. There's no reason to drag her case out any longer. She's gonna go home."

"Oh, Isaiah. God, I'm so sorry."

From almost every angle, this is good news: a reunion. The best outcome for Naya and her mom. But Isaiah's been her big brother for more than a year. It'll crush him, saying goodbye.

"I'm glad for them," he says, and though his voice falters, I believe him. "I don't know why this feels like a surprise. The goal's always been for her to go back to her mom. The caseworker's totally supportive, and so's Marjorie—even though watching Naya go is gonna break her heart."

"This is… I'm not sure what to say."

He shakes his head, eyes downcast. "I'm really gonna miss her."

"I know. But what's to keep you from visiting?"

296

"Her mom. There's a stigma that comes with having your kid pulled out of your house, a stranger looking after her while you get your life together. I wouldn't be surprised if Gloria didn't want me coming around, reminding her and Naya of everything that went wrong. I wouldn't blame her for wanting a fresh start."

I hate this for him. Another loss. I lay my hand on his arm. "This fucking sucks."

He laughs, a rocks-over-water sound that pings my heart. "Thanks for coming out. Marjorie and I had a good cry earlier, and that was something. But being with you... I've never had a person, you know?"

A valve opens in my chest, setting loose warmth that travels to the tips of my ears, fingers, and toes. I know what he means: a person you think of first, when something goes exactly right or horrendously wrong. A person who makes you feel like life might be okay, even when you're standing in the middle of a shitstorm.

I had a person. When I lost him, I refused to believe that I could find another.

Instead, new people found me.

Paloma, Meagan, and Sophia.

Isaiah.

"I'm happy to be your person," I whisper.

He smiles forlornly, reaching over to comb his fingers through my hair. "Someday I hope you'll let me be yours."

SCULPTED FROM WAX

Seventeen Years Old, Tennessee

When I get home Thursday afternoon, after an hour spent sipping cocoa and eating pastries at Buttercup Bakery with the girls, I find Dad in the front yard, running the mower over the grass. Inside, Mom's a whirlwind of energy: tidying the living room, folding laundry, packing dog food into Ziploc bags, and prepping meals that will be easy to microwave.

They're flying to Virginia tomorrow. Major is off to spend a long weekend with Dad's Deputy Commander, who's been offering to dog sit since she met our pup last autumn. I'll be on my own Friday night to Tuesday afternoon and, frankly, I can't wait.

As darkness falls, I find my parents in their room to see about dinner. Dad's finished the lawn and is packing a carry-on. Mom might as well be prepping for a weeks-long transatlantic voyage with her clothing, toiletries, and shoes organized into piles throughout the room.

"I'm about to order pizza," Dad says, tucking a pair of black dress shoes into his suitcase. Since he'll be speaking at Connor's ceremony, he'll attend in uniform. He'll stand in front of family, mentors, and peers, and say a million wonderful things about his best friend.

I almost wish I could be there.

Mom's watching me. She pauses folding a pair of slacks to say, "You're allowed to change your mind, lovey. We can still get you a ticket."

"No. Thanks, though."

"You sure?" Dad asks. "We could hit up GMU. See about getting a tour."

Because he thinks I'm waiting to be notified about whether I was accepted.

My face goes warm.

"I wonder if we could find time to drive down to Charlottesville, Cam?" Mom says. "Give Lia another chance to see the campus?"

"We could fit in a day trip," Dad answers charitably.

"I don't need to see CVU again," I say, and for a moment, my parents' expressions shine with newfound hope. I crush it. "I'll be there fall semester. I already sent a deposit."

Dad fumbles the shirt he's holding. "You what?"

This is my chance. They'll be furious, and then they'll leave town for a few days. By the time they come back, they'll have cooled off.

Not that it matters.

What's done is done.

"I didn't apply early action. I applied early decision. When I found out about my acceptance, there was a deadline to commit. So I did."

"But you haven't heard back about your other applications," Mom says, baffled.

I could keep up this part of the lie. They never have to know that I applied to CVU exclusively. Or I could show some integrity. Come clean about the choices that led me to a future at Commonwealth of Virginia University.

A future I'm not even sure I want.

"There aren't other applications. I only applied to CVU."

Dad's face drains of color.

Mom sinks to the bed.

His back is steel-rod straight.

Her hands grip her knees.

Like I've done a terrible thing, getting accepted at my first-choice university.

"Lia," she says. "How could you?"

Dad's face twists in outrage. "I don't know who you are anymore."

He hasn't yelled. She hasn't cried.

They're stony faced, wan with shock.

They look like they've been sculpted from wax.

"Go to your room," Dad says. When I don't move, he looks me hard in the eye and says scathingly, "*Go.*"

300

VANILLA

Sixteen Years Old, Virginia

Over the years, Beck and I argued about the dumbest shit.

Which movie to watch.

What type of pet is superior.

Who was, pound for pound, stronger.

Which Busch Gardens ride is best.

Whether Pluto (outer space) is a planet.

Whether Pluto (Disney) is the same species as Goofy.

When we were little, we nearly came to blows over whose father was most like GI Joe, an argument our parents found infinitely funny.

There were serious arguments too. Arguments that shaped him and me—shaped *us*. Arguments that, in their heaviest moments, felt like monumental battles.

A couple days before he was due to leave CVU for

Thanksgiving break, he called for backup regarding ice cream flavors. He and James were about to have a knock-down-drag-out over which reigned supreme.

"Beck likes Vanilla!" James bellowed. "Did you know that, Lia? Vanilla!"

"It's the only flavor he ever chooses," I said, curling up on my bed. "No hot fudge. No sprinkles. In a cup—not even a cone."

Beck laughed unapologetically and James groaned, as if his roommate's dull flavor preferences pained him physically. "I can't. *Vanilla*. Lia, what's your favorite?"

"She likes Pralines and Cream," Beck said, without missing a beat. "In a waffle cone."

"A respectable choice," James said. "Why's your girl so much more interesting than you?"

"Fuck off," Beck said lightly. And then, to me, "Can you believe the grief he's giving me?"

"Poor baby," I said, burrowing under my comforter, wishing I was there to feed him his boring ice cream, to kiss the whininess from his voice.

"Vanilla!" James hooted. "Why?"

"Because Vanilla's consistently delicious," Beck said in an *obviously* tone. "Why try something new, only to wind up disappointed?"

James started naming ice cream flavors, as if neither Beck nor I had set foot in a Baskin-Robbins. "Mississippi Mud, Bubble Gum, Toasted Coconut..."

I only half listened as they bantered, because I was hung up on what Beck had said: *Why try something new, only to wind up disappointed?*

Was he talking about...me?

A safe, measured choice?

Eventually James gave up and left for a party at one of his fraternity's live-outs. Beck spent a couple minutes telling me about the quiz he'd had that afternoon. He was sure he'd kicked its ass—but the workout that followed had most definitely kicked *his* ass. Then he asked about my day.

Instead of answering, I blurted a question of my own. "Am I your Vanilla?"

He stuttered out a laugh. "My what?"

"Your Vanilla."

"What are you talking about?"

"Beckett. Are you with me because you're scared to try something new?"

He laughed again, though he sounded more annoyed than amused. I imagined him folded onto his bed, dragging a hand over his face as he said, "That's gotta be the most deranged question you've ever asked."

"You're not denying it."

"Because I refuse to dignify it with a response." He huffed. "Are you my Vanilla? Jesus, Lia."

Our conversation had gone from lighthearted to prickly in three ill-conceived seconds.

It was my fault—I knew it was. I'd sparked an argument for no intelligible reason. But it pissed me off that he wouldn't indulge me. That he wouldn't say, *You're the opposite of Vanilla. You're fun and exciting.* And so, I poked again, unable to keep the word vomit from spewing forth. "I'm a safe choice—admit it. You could find yourself a Mint Chocolate Chip girl. But instead of risking your heart, you've settled on me, a girl who doesn't disappoint."

He groaned. "Could you be any more insulting?"

"*You're* insulted?"

"Fuck yes. Is that who I am to you? A coward who settles for just okay because he's too chickenshit to step out of the box?"

"Maybe I don't know who you are," I said combatively.

He gave a deep sigh. "I can't do this tonight. I've got another quiz tomorrow morning and two hours in the gym after that."

"Good to know where I fall on your list of priorities."

"Damn, Lia. You couldn't've waited until this weekend to pick a fight?"

"I'm not picking a fi—!"

The line went dead.

I was up all night, sick with regret.

I'd provoked him. Worse than that, I couldn't pinpoint why. Maybe I'd been feeling neglected, what with everything going on in his CVU bubble. Maybe I'd been lonely, seeking negative attention like a bratty kid. Maybe I'd turned my personal insecurities on him. It's not as if I ever stepped out of the box. Instead of making big choices, hard choices, I relied on a fortune that was older than me.

Maybe I was testing Beck—testing fate.

Whatever the case, I felt terrible.

All morning, I was on edge, fidgety in the empty house. I was already out of school; Rosebell High had a whole week off for Thanksgiving. My dad was on a trip, ten days of TDY in Hawaii. My mom had been working overtime recording reading assessment scores. Macy was spending all sorts of time with Wyatt. Because the morning passed without so much as a text from Beck and I was too embarrassed to reach out, I took myself to lunch.

I left the café feeling full, but not better.

When I got home, a cardboard box was waiting on the porch. It was addressed to me and covered in stickers: *Perishable! Keep frozen!* I lugged it into the kitchen and plucked scissors from the junk drawer. Slicing the packing tape, I noticed the name on the return address, Scoop and Savor, an artisan ice cream shop in Richmond. Inside the box was an insulated cooler stocked with six pints of ice cream. I took them out one by one, stacking them in two towers on the countertop. My smile grew as I read each of the flavors. Lavender Honey, Gooey Chocolate Brownie, Guava Pear with Cashew Praline, Hazelnut Cookies and Cream, Caramel Marshmallow Ribbon with Sea Salt, and...Vanilla Bean.

At the bottom of the box was a piece of cardstock. In neat typeface was a note.

Amelia ~

So what if you're Vanilla? Vanilla's my favorite. I'll always choose you.

~ Beck

I'd started our fight. I'd questioned his devotion. I'd let him go all night thinking I doubted his commitment. I'd made him walk into a quiz and shoulder a workout thinking I was unsure about him, about us.

He'd spent a small fortune overnighting ice cream to my house.

I called him.

The line rang several times before, finally, he picked up.

"Hey," he answered, thick with sleep.

"Hi. I woke you, didn't I?"

"Yeah, but it's okay. What's up?"

"I wanted to tell you I'm sorry. I'm such a pain in the ass, Beck. And you're the best human I know. I love you. Just—so much."

He laughed, groggy sounding. "You got your ice cream?"

"I got my ice cream. Will you share it with me this weekend?"

"Why do you think I got Vanilla Bean?"

I smiled. "You sound really tired. Are you okay?"

"Better, now that you called."

"Go back to sleep. Call me later."

"Okay. I love you, Amelia Graham."

"Love you, too, Beckett Byrne."

UPSTREAM

Seventeen Years Old, Tennessee

I've been instructed to come straight home from school on Friday afternoon, and I'm not happy about it.

Isaiah wasn't in Ceramics, and he hasn't replied to the texts I've sent, and I keep thinking about today's court hearing and Naya. I wish I could make a trip to his house, but my parents, who've said a total of ten words to me since last night's CVU proclamation, have a flight to catch and, apparently, rules to dole out.

"No driving outside town," Dad says, gathering his wallet and keys from the basket on the kitchen counter.

"No friends in the house," Mom puts in.

"No drinking," he contributes.

Her mouth falls open. "Cam, Lia doesn't drink."

He gives her a condemnatory look, nowhere near as trusting as she's chosen to be.

"Check in every morning," he tells me.

"And every night," she adds.

"No boys," he says.

So…I'm grounded, but without supervision.

Fine.

Outside, the sky is blanketed in storm clouds. As my parents head toward the door toting suitcases and carry-ons, the house vibrates with a clap of thunder.

Mom shudders. "If we could postpone this trip," she tells me, "we would."

"You're lucky we're not insisting you come," Dad says, hand on the doorknob.

The only way they'd get me on that plane is by first administering a strong tranquilizer. It's wild, the power they think they hold. Their belief that they can influence where I go to college, who I date, where I spend spring break.

I'm less than a week from eighteen.

"Have fun in Virginia," I mutter, turning for the stairs.

I'm halfway to my room when the front door closes. The dead bolt slots audibly into place. Misgiving tangles around me.

I should've said *goodbye*.

I should've said *I love you*.

It's not as if I don't know what it's like to suddenly lose a loved one.

The day Beck died, Mom came home with almond chicken, fried rice, and egg rolls. She was in a great mood. Thanksgiving was a day away, there was snow in the forecast, and Dad was on his way home from Hawaii. He'd already completed the first of two flights that would have him landing at Reagan early in the morning.

While we ate dinner, I thought of Beck. Hours had passed since I'd called to thank him for the ice cream. It troubled me, the way he'd sounded on the phone: run-down, like he was getting sick. But he'd had a taxing week of classes, and his training schedule was intense. He likely hadn't slept well the night before. I sure hadn't.

I was shoving my worries aside when Mom's phone rang.

That call was surreal, like the moments before you fall asleep, when sounds are muffled, muscles are lax, and eyelids are heavy. I remember the fear that lanced Mom's expression. The way her face drained of color. I remember her dropping into her chair, legs lacking the strength to support her. I remember the tears that pooled in her eyes as she listened to Bernie, whose words were indistinct, whose tone was hysterical.

Mom pressed a hand to her chest and said, "I'll come now. Ten minutes."

Her eyes found mine. She shook her head, stricken, and my chest caved in on itself.

Beck.

As soon as the call ended, she was up, circling the table. She pulled me to my feet and into her arms. "Beck's been taken to the hospital," she told me. "Bernie and Connor need to go to Charlottesville, and they need me to stay with the twins."

"I'll go to Charlottesville too."

"You'll come with me. Norah and Mae need you."

"*Beck* needs me."

"You can't go, Lia. Bernie said—" She covered her mouth, smothering a sob. Through tears, she finished, "It's serious."

If I'd been admitted to the hospital, Beck would've moved mountains to get to me.

I straightened my spine, sure I could change Mom's mind. "All the more reason for me to go. I'll drive myself."

"Absolutely not!"

I flinched, my throat swelling with panic.

She looked into my eyes. "I'm sorry. I'm so sorry, lovey. If I knew more, I'd tell you. If it made sense for you to go to Charlottesville, I'd let you. But I can't have you on the road at this hour, not with all that's going on and snow on the way. Come to the Byrnes' with me. We'll be there for the twins. That's the best thing you can do for Beck."

I was choking on confusion.

I'd spoken to Beck not six hours before.

He'd been fine.

Call me later, I'd said to him.

And to me, he'd said, *I love you, Amelia Graham.*

He died doing the safest possible thing: napping in his fucking bed.

Today, my parents will board a plane, ascend thousands of feet into the air, and rocket toward the East Coast. If there's an accident while they're en route—if they *die*—and our last interaction was drenched in snark, I'll never recover.

310

I'm a half second from running downstairs to apologize, to say what I mean, which is *I'm sorry—I'm sorry about everything,* when I hear a car door slam. Peering through my window, I see Mom in the passenger seat of the Volvo. Dad's loading bags into the trunk. He looks pulverized, as if someone stomped on his heart with heavy boots. He rounds the car, then climbs into the driver's seat.

My stomach clenches with guilt.

Charcoal clouds billow overhead, casting our neighborhood in purple shadows. Lightning fractures the sky; not five seconds later, thunder rumbles.

Dad starts the car, then backs down the drive.

They're off.

To Virginia.

Without me.

Outside, rain pummels River Hollow, but inside, all is eerily still. My family has only been gone a few hours, but I miss the click of Major's claws against the hardwood, the history podcasts Dad's always listening to, and the clanks and clatters of Mom's kitchen tinkering.

She texted after they'd boarded the plane. Thanks to a brief break in the storm, they were moments from takeoff.

I should be with them.

I test the idea out loud. "I could've survived a trip to Virginia,"

I say, tentatively at first. "I could've hugged Bernie, Connor, and the twins. I could've represented at Connor's ceremony. I should've shown up for Beck."

He would've wanted me to. He would've wanted me to do a lot of things: trust my instincts, take chances, follow my dreams.

Instead, I'm drifting.

Even a dead fish can swim downstream, Dad's fond of saying.

I *could* go to Virginia.

And not in theory; I could pack a bag right now. Get in my car, and drive all night. I could be in Rosebell—I check the time— by sunrise tomorrow.

I could battle my way upstream.

The storm is starting to pick up again; God, it would suck if the power went out.

The Magic 8 Ball on my desk catches my eye. I've consulted it enough times to know it'll offer one of twenty answers. Ten assenting, five opposing, and five annoyingly vague. If I ask it the question sprinting circles through my head, chances are decent that I'll get some version of yes. But I don't want a toy to make this decision.

I know what I have to do.

I turn for my closet, eager, now, to get on the road. The air around me cools, like a gust of wind has funneled past. Goose bumps fan out across my arms as I turn to find my window battered by rain, but closed. All is as it should be. Except…my bulletin board. A rectangle of cork has become exposed, negative space left behind by a fallen photograph.

I pick it up and turn it over. My breath catches at the huddle

312

of faces grinning at me. The Byrnes and the Grahams, gathered on my sixteenth birthday—a thousand lifetimes ago. I'm at the center of the group, beaming, wearing a baby-doll dress and a *Sweet Sixteen* sash. Beck's holding my hand, laughing as his sisters twirl blurry circles in the foreground. Our parents act as bookends, Mom and Dad next to me, Connor and Bernie beside him.

The eight of us together, as fate intended.

Except fate erred.

Or, maybe not.

Beck and I shared sixteen amazing years. He taught me to live with compassion. With zeal. He showed me how to find humor in the direst of situations. Thanks to him, I learned to bloom where I'm planted.

He loved me unconditionally.

But fate and forever are not synonymous.

I misinterpreted my mom's long-ago fortune, and that blunder has left me scarred.

Still, every day I'm more okay than the last.

All I can tell you is that your heart will heal.

I trail a finger along Beck's smiling face.

I'm doing the right thing.

SURRENDER

Seventeen Years Old, Tennessee

I drive through sheets of rain with a suitcase in the Jetta's trunk, my nerves frayed, hoping Isaiah will be home. I have to see him before I leave.

Marjorie answers the door, fighting for a smile. "Oh, you're getting drenched," she says, waving me inside. "Isaiah didn't say he was expecting you."

"He's not," I admit. "I hope it's okay that I dropped by."

"Of course." Her eyes are red, puffy, and she's got a tissue tucked into her sleeve, the way my grandma does before turning on a sad movie. "Today was a tough one," she tells me. "He'll be glad to see you. Go on up."

Upstairs, I find Isaiah's door closed. I knock lightly.

"Yeah?" he calls in a jagged voice.

"Hey. It's me."

It's only a second before the door swings open.

He leads me to the bed, where I sit beside him. He folds forward, elbows to knees, face to hands, and heaves a sigh that sounds leaden. I'm rain-damp, but I pull him close. He breathes through his sorrow, thin inhales and shuddering exhales. We sit on his bed, sheltered by the walls of his home, until the storm sweeps eastward and the tension in his body eases. He sighs again, placidly this time because, I'm starting to realize, he trusts me to walk him through hard shit.

Straightening, he drags a hand over his face. When his eyes meet mine, he says, "Hi," like I've only just arrived.

I glide my fingers along his forehead, his jaw, his heated cheek, wishing for an elixir or a charm, something to relieve his hurt. Now more than ever, I understand the meaning of the word *bittersweet*. Naya's move home is an ideal outcome for her and her mom, while simultaneously an acerbic blow to her interim brother.

"I want to say something profound," I tell him, "except...I'm not sure it'd help."

"It wouldn't. Jesus, it sucked to see her go."

"You're such a good brother."

He gives me a desolate look. "Not anymore."

"Yes," I say firmly. "Don't do that. Don't dismiss the influence you had on her, or the effect she's had on you. Losing someone doesn't erase the imprint they've made on your heart."

He nods, closing his eyes.

I think he understands; it's not an empty sentiment.

But it's getting late. I've got a ten-hour drive ahead of me, and a storm to overtake.

315

"I'm leaving," I say.

His eyes snap open.

"For a few days," I hurry to clarify. "Virginia. It's something I've got to do, and if I don't get on the road now, I'll chicken out."

"Wait—you're driving? Alone?"

"I'll be okay."

"Lia... Your parents are cool with this?"

"They don't know. They're already on their way to Dulles. I told them I didn't want to go, and now I've changed my mind. I just... I don't fully understand it myself, but if I don't go, I'll regret it. I know I will."

He tilts his head, regarding me with disapproval and sympathy in equal measures. It's clear he believes I have no business setting out on a solo road trip in the middle of the night, but his empathy is palpable.

"I get that you're chasing closure," he says. "Believe me—I do. But closure is, like, six hundred miles from here. That's too far to drive on your own. What if you get tired?"

"I'll guzzle Mountain Dew," I say, shrugging. I haven't really had time to consider the what-ifs.

"What if you get lost?"

"Impossible. GPS."

"What if you get a flat tire?"

"I'll change it. My dad taught me how."

His mouth lifts in a smile—he wasn't expecting that. Still, he's not finished. "I hate the idea of you going so far by yourself. There're a thousand things that could go wrong."

My conviction's beginning to waver. I want to go to Virginia—I *need* to go to Virginia—but I won't leave Isaiah to worry. I won't put the burden of my welfare on him.

Please don't ask me to stay, I think.

He says my name, beseechingly, and I brace myself.

"Let me come with you."

BEFORE & AFTER

Seventeen Years Old, Tennessee

Not ten minutes pass before we're loading Isaiah's bag into the Jetta's trunk.

Marjorie sees us off from the driveway, partially obscured by an umbrella.

She wasn't thrilled about the idea of Isaiah leaving town, but she heard him out. Then she went to the kitchen to pack a bag with snacks and bottles of water. She hugged him in the foyer, tucking a folded bundle of cash into his jacket pocket.

"Just in case," she said, kissing his cheek, then mine.

I drive the first leg. Isaiah's quiet, gazing out the window as the blustery night flies by. I don't have the energy to carry a conversation. I keep thinking about the last time I traveled this road, east-to-west. How despondent I'd been, but how sure I was of my next steps. Now the reverse is true: I'm optimistic— genuinely happy, a lot of the time—but my future presents like a black hole: vast, mysterious, and terrifying. And so music fills the quiet, thanks to a playlist Paloma curated after I texted her about my impromptu trip and apologized for missing out on meeting Liam during the first few days of his visit.

Just past Knoxville, we stop for gas. The air is briskly cold and uncomfortably damp. There are some shady characters loitering around the pumps. I run inside to pee, then pick up packages of gummy worms and wintergreen gum. Swiping my debit card at the register, I glance out the window and spot Isaiah leaning on the trunk of my car, arms crossed against the wind, waiting as the Jetta's tank fills. His dark hair's tousled, and his jacket is unzipped, baring the ERHS basketball sweatshirt he wears beneath. He must sense me watching because he lifts his chin to peer into the fluorescently lit gas station. Our eyes meet and, despite his day's events, he smiles.

He's an exemplary human. A lionhearted hero.

My heart swells.

It takes a second but then…

… a word to label the emotion: *love.*

Pocketing our snacks, I hurry outside, rounding my car to where he stands. He gives me an inquisitive look before I barrel into him, sneaking my arms inside his jacket to circle around him. He laughs, wrapping me into a burrito hug, keeping me close even after the gas pump clicks to signal a full tank.

I spent my whole life loving Beck. It was involuntarily, like the way I breathe. The way I blink. With Isaiah, it's different. My feelings are considered and conscious, but no less special.

My heart's leaving before to make a faith-testing leap into after.

"All good?" he asks, soft against my ear.

I nod, reluctantly pulling away.

He gets behind the wheel, letting me recline in the passenger seat. I pass him gummies as he navigates I-40, then I-80.

"You doing okay?" I ask as one song fades into the next.

"Yeah. Glad to be with you."

"But…everything else?"

He shrugs. "It's a hurdle. I'll clear it."

"You're a badass, you know that, right?"

He flashes me a smile, then turns his attention back to the road. He drives with his hands at ten and two, the way my dad showed me. As soon as he took the wheel, he turned the music down. He's vigilant, maybe because of the weather, maybe because he doesn't drive every day, maybe because he cares about his cargo. Whatever the case, I've never felt safer.

"You should sleep," he says near Kingsport.

"I have too much energy to sleep."

"This trip…pretty big deal, huh?"

Back in his room, I explained about Connor's retirement as he threw clothes and shoes and a travel toothbrush into a duffel. He didn't ask a lot of questions, but I got the sense he understood that my journey is about more than applauding a family friend who's making a career change.

"When we moved last summer," I say, "it was sudden. I mean, it wasn't—I'd known for months that we were going to

Tennessee—but when I look back, I was living in Virginia and then I was in the car with my parents, going that way," I say, hitching my thumb in the direction opposite the one we're traveling. "I skipped out on major goodbyes. Left a lot of things unsaid. Burned some bridges, probably," I admit, thinking of Macy. "I had myself convinced that I was doing the right thing, cutting ties quickly and cleanly. Making it simple for everyone. But I've started to realize that I left the way I did because that's what was easiest for me. I hadn't even thought of anyone else."

"Hindsight's a real bitch."

"Yeah," I say with a melancholy sigh. "She's been riding my ass a lot lately."

"Because you get stuck in your head, reliving the good, obsessing over the bad. You and I are alike that way. The first time we kissed? It was all I could think about for weeks."

I pull up the hood of my sweatshirt to hide my blush. "Do I want to know whether that qualified as good or bad?"

He reaches for my hand. "Good, Lia. Really fucking good."

I feel like a traitor giving voice to this question, but I have to ask, "Have you ever been *so sure* about a decision, and then, out of nowhere, you start to wonder if you're making the biggest mistake of your life?"

"You're not sure you want to go to CVU," Isaiah says, like he's spent the last few minutes swimming through my head. "And... what? You don't want to disappoint your parents?"

I laugh dryly. "My parents would be thrilled if I ditched CVU."

"Then what's keeping you locked in?"

321

"Well, I applied early decision."

"So? They're not gonna throw you in jail because you don't show up to freshman orientation."

"Still. There are consequences."

"Yeah, and there are consequences to living out a future you don't want. What else?"

I swallow, my throat dry. "Beck."

He lets go of my hand to grip the steering wheel. Because the rain's picked up? Or because he doesn't want to touch me while I speak of my first love?

The night Beck passed, Mom and I stayed at the Byrnes' with Norah and Mae, who were asleep when we arrived.

Just after midnight, Connor called to tell us he was gone. That's when I slipped into a scary sort of shock, something akin to being buried alive.

Darkness, aloneness, hopelessness.

Mom offered comfort in all the ways she could, but I was inconsolable.

I ended up going down to Beck's room. The lights were off, and I left them that way. My eyes adjusted quickly. The duvet was smooth. The desk was clear. The nightstand had been dusted. The air smelled of Tide, of him.

I fell onto the bed, pressing my face into his pillow. I tugged the duvet up to cover my head. My whole body hurt, but the pain was most excruciating in the cavern behind my ribs. Desperate, I tried to imagine that he was with me, breathing into my hair, whispering that he loved me, wanted me, couldn't fathom a world without me. I cried silently, that torturous, convulsive crying that leads to clenched muscles and pounding headaches. Finally, close to dawn, I exhausted myself, sinking into a nightmarish sleep that ended abruptly, with the sound of footsteps descending the stairs.

I shot to sitting, rubbing my eyes, clearing my throat.

Anguish sat heavy on my chest.

The light sneaking through the drawn shades signaled morning, though I wanted to crawl back under the covers and sink into my suffering.

Little hands banged on the door.

Norah and Mae.

Detangling myself from the sheets, I made my feet carry me across the room. On the other side of the door, I found two identical faces framed in strawberry-blond curls. They were wearing matching pajamas, bearing twin smiles. I swallowed hard, thinking about how their expressions would fall when they learned about their brother.

"Here you are," Norah said, as if they'd been looking for me.

"Why is your mommy asleep on the couch?" Mae asked.

I molded my features into a mask of calm. "She must be tired."

"Why does your voice sound like that?" Norah asked.

I cleared the scratchiness from my throat. "Maybe I'm catching a cold."

Mae lifted a skeptical eyebrow. "You're not supposed to be in Beck's room with the door closed."

I walked back to the bed and sat on the rumpled duvet. "That's only if Beck's with me."

"Did you sleep in here?" Norah asked.

"I did, yeah. I'm not supposed to do that, either, I know, but what if we all lay down together for a little while?"

Mae frowned. "Beck doesn't like when we come into his room when he's not home."

I whispered, "I don't think he'd mind."

They looked at one another, communicating in the special, silent way they often do, then clambered onto the bed. They curled up on either side of me, and I combed my fingers through their curls, tears streaming down my face.

I, too, wanted to fall asleep and never wake up.

"Beck went to CVU," I tell Isaiah over the sound of rain and windshield wipers. "He asked me to join him after I graduated. Charlottesville was going to be the beginning of our life together. Even after he died, I thought CVU was where I was meant to be. I thought I owed it to him to carry out our plan, even though it hadn't always been *my* plan. I realize now...that girl who applied to CVU, and *only* CVU? She was chasing a ghost."

He's quiet, pensively absorbing my confession. Uncomfortable in the silence, I study his profile: smooth forehead, imperfect nose, full mouth, strong chin.

A warrior's face.

Finally he replies, using carefully chosen, thoughtfully delivered words. "Maybe you're not chasing a ghost. Maybe you're chasing the person you were when you were with him."

That Lia—the Lia of before—is gone. Dead and buried, like her first love, her best friend.

324

"Maybe," I say, noncommittal.

"What if you don't go to CVU?"

"Then I don't go to college."

I say this as if it's the most epic of fails.

"Okay," Isaiah says, like, *Who cares?* "So you skip college next semester. Next year, even. Let's say you take a gap year. What would you do with it?"

"I've honestly never thought about it."

He glances over at me, eyes sparking in the meager light. "Maybe it's time you start."

In Lieu of College

1. volunteer
2. backpack abroad (intimidating!)
3. vocational school (for what vocation?)
4. trade school (for what? cosmetology?)
5. an internship
6. work retail
7. au pair (okay, maybe?)
8. write...something
9. apprenticeship (different than an internship?)
10. realtor license (lucrative, college degree not required!)
11. tutor
12. enlist (what would Dad say?)
13. dole out fortunes (*laugh sob*)

U-TURN

Seventeen Years Old, Virginia

I awaken to the sound of my name.

Opening my eyes, I peer through the Jetta's bug-spattered windshield. My car's running but parked, warm air blowing through the vents. I straighten creakily, closing my journal, which landed upside down across my lap when sleep took over.

Isaiah's brought us to a parking garage, backing into a space so the yawning exit, twenty or so yards away, is visible. Outside, the dawn sky is clear.

"Where are we?" I ask, hitching my hair into a ponytail.

"Promise not to be mad?"

"No," I say, wondering at his expression, a little smug and a lot hopeful.

Understanding dawns suddenly, making me to feel like I've been flung into a cold pool.

Commonwealth of Virginia University.

Isaiah pit-stopped at CVU.

"We can leave," he says, voice laced with worry now. "You were sleeping when I got off the highway, and you looked like an actual angel, and I couldn't make myself wake you. I just thought that if you could walk the campus, get a feel for this place now, today, maybe you'd be able to figure out what you want."

I fix my gaze on the garage's exit.

I don't know what to say; I'm not even sure I can look at him.

Wordlessly, I get out of the car. I stretch my legs, my spine, my arms high over my head. And then I walk out of the garage.

We're parked near the bookstore, I quickly discover. The sidewalk is quiet and the air is dewy, and while I'm no longer disoriented, I'm at a loss.

I'm in Charlottesville.

Now what?

Go for a walk, Amelia.

I'm standing in the middle of campus. The football stadium lies southwest, the medical facilities southeast. Most of the classroom buildings and lecture halls are north. If I make a right, I'll run into the Academic Plaza, with its marble rotunda and picturesque lawn. If I go left, I'll arrive at Beck's former dorm.

Right it is.

I pass a couple residence halls and the admissions building

before I reach the Academic Plaza. It's quiet thanks to the early hour. Standing at the lawn's edge, I soak in CVU's hub: clean sidewalks, lush grass, brick buildings, blue-and-red pennants hanging from lampposts. There's an irrefutably erudite spirit about this campus, which I love.

Last time I was here, Beck took me on a tour, filling the time before we were due to meet his family at the stadium. We'd stopped here to sit in the grass, crowded with students and families and alumni who'd come to town for the game.

"Two more years," he said, slinging his arm around my shoulders.

I leaned into him. "I can't wait."

Back then, I was so sure of the future I wanted: afternoons in the library, weekends eating pizza and going to parties, nights curled up with Beck in his too-small dorm room bed.

Eighteen months later, I'm living a life I never would've imagined.

I don't know who I am without you, I told him the morning after he graduated.

I still don't.

But I'm starting to appreciate this new version of myself: Lia, independent of Beck.

I'm starting to believe that she'll be okay.

I think of James, who transferred to Virginia Tech for his sophomore year.

I understand, now, why he couldn't stay here.

Birds chirp, engines rumble, students trickle onto sidewalks.

329

CVU is waking up, and so am I.

I leave the lawn to claim a bench. I've only been sitting a few minutes when Isaiah joins me. He holds out a sleeved paper cup. "Mocha?"

"Thank you," I say, accepting the coffee. "Where's yours?"

"Finished it in the café. I wanted to give you some time."

I take a sip. It's piping hot and extra chocolatey, exactly the way I would've ordered it.

When I lower the cup, he asks, "Do you need more?"

"Coffee?"

"Time," he says, smiling.

I shake my head; I've had just enough.

He looks out at the grass, brows drawn. He's left a canyon of space between us. It can't be fun for him, watching me mourn an impossible future. What motivated him to drive through the night, delivering me to Charlottesville? Why's he buying me mochas and sitting beside me at a college he has no desire to attend?

I just know this: I'm grateful to have him by my side.

"The last time I was here," I tell him, "I was with Beck. I came to visit the fall of his freshman year, about a month before he passed. When I went back to Rosebell, there wasn't a doubt in my mind that CVU was where I wanted to go to college."

"Seems like a great school," he says.

"It is. But I don't think it's the right school for me."

His gaze meets mine. "No?"

"I couldn't admit it to myself until this morning, but with

Beck gone, CVU's become this…this *burden*. He wouldn't've wanted me to enroll feeling the way I do." I let go of a dry laugh. "Now that I've come to my senses, though, it's too late to make a U-turn."

Isaiah shakes his head. "It's never too late."

"I did what you suggested. Last night in the car. Thought about what I'd do if CVU was off the table."

"And…?"

"There are a lot of options, actually."

He stands, tugging me up too. "Tell me about them while we find breakfast."

UNCONDITIONAL

Seventeen Years Old, Virginia

The trip from Charlottesville to Northern Virginia passes in a flash.

I drive, insisting Isaiah get some sleep. He tips the passenger seat back and closes his eyes, but I'm not sure if he's nodded off. Regardless, I've got music for company, another cycle of Paloma's playlist and one Macy and I used to listen to, when our friendship thrived.

In Fredericksburg, I stop again for gas, leaving Isaiah in the car while I run into the station for a pair of Mountain Dews. Standing in line, I take out my phone to tackle the correspondences I've been dreading.

First, I check in with my parents, a quick Everything good? sent to the thread the three of us share. I get a thumbs-up emoji from Dad, followed by a picture from Mom: Norah and Mae at the Byrnes' kitchen table, surrounded by crayons, glue, and glitter, grinning as they hold up colorful works-in-progress.

They're adorable—I can't wait to see them.

Draining the last of my courage, I tap out another text, a message I've been mentally drafting since Isaiah and I got on the road last night.

Hey, Mace. I'm the worst for reaching out now, when I need something, but... I need something. I'm on my way to NoVa with a friend, and I'm hoping we might crash at your apartment for a few nights, if you and Wyatt are cool with company. No worries if not. I can figure out something else. But I miss you, and I'd love to see you. Let me know, okay?

I read over my words, feeling like an asshole, calling on this girl I abandoned after so much time has passed, but I have no one else to turn to. When I decided to make this trip, I figured I'd have to buck up and stay with the Byrnes. When Isaiah asked to come, though, I knew I'd need to make other arrangements. I could book a hotel—I have a credit card for emergencies—but, God, I'd feel gross making my parents pay to put Isaiah and me up.

I'm finishing at the register when my phone vibrates. My heart squeezes as I pull it from my pocket: Stay as long as you need, babe.

Macy includes her address, an apartment complex close to George Mason University.

I breathe a sigh of relief.

333

She and Wyatt have a doormat, which strikes me as very grown up. It says *Come back with a warrant*, but still—a doormat. A plant, some sort of palm, flourishes in a pot beneath the doorbell. I try to picture these friends of mine tending to it, but the Macy and Wyatt I know are high school kids. She liked drinking fruity booze, wearing bell-bottoms, and playing violin. He loved few things more than to get a roomful of people laughing. The Macy and Wyatt who live here are college students who pay bills and grocery shop and maybe even have a linen closet. They're living happily ever after.

It's the sort of fantasy I used to spin about Beck and me.

Music filters through the door: Haim, Macy's favorite.

Nostalgia hits hard.

Isaiah clears his throat. "Should we ring the bell?"

"Yes," I say, making no move to do so.

He gives me a consoling smile, then pushes the button.

The music cuts out.

Footsteps approach.

My heart hammers my ribs.

Junior year, I went back to school two weeks after Thanksgiving. Sixteen days after we lost Beck. My parents wanted me to stay home until after Christmas. They practically begged me to take more time. But it didn't matter if I went back in December or January or May, or decades into the future. School would be terrible.

I survived the first half of that first day without incident. There were a lot of piteous looks. A few brave souls shared condolences. Each of my teachers let me know that I shouldn't stress about catching up. All of that was tolerable because I'd expected it.

What I hadn't expected was the memorial that had been created in the foyer of Rosebell High's gym. Someone—an administrator or counselor, probably—had blown up Beck's senior portrait. It sat on an easel, ringed by flowers and stuffed animals and track and field paraphernalia. Battery-powered candles flickered, and stacks of cards and letters extended to the locker rooms, where I'd been headed when I happened on the display.

The lobby cleared out while I stood there, staring at my boyfriend's face: his army-green eyes, his vivacious smile, his copper-penny hair. The bell rang. I was late to PE, and I didn't care. As my gaze traveled the mementos that'd been left, I knelt in the foyer, alone in my grief—

—until a voice called my name.

Macy.

We hadn't spoken since the funeral. She'd texted and she'd called. She'd stopped by the week before, the day after I smuggled Beck's nudie magazines out of his house. I'd told my mom I couldn't handle company, but she'd tried to convince me otherwise, until I sat up in bed and screamed at her to leave me alone. Her eyes filled with tears. She sent Macy away, then did as I'd asked. I'd burrowed under my covers for the remainder of the afternoon.

I must've looked as broken as I felt because Macy rushed forward, stooping down beside me. She gestured at the memorial. "People have been bringing things since we heard. Wyatt and I should've warned you." She put her arm around my shoulders. "I'm so sorry."

I didn't want her to be sorry.

I wanted her to make me laugh.

I wanted her to give me shit.

I wanted her to bring Beck back, to restore life as I'd known it.

Her pity made me feel worse.

I pulled away, rising to my feet. "Mace, I can't do this."

Her expression twisted with confusion.

I didn't want to hear about Wyatt. I couldn't bear the reminder of what she had and what I'd lost. My jealousy was unreasonable and unfair, but it burned hot. "Being around you," I said. "It's too hard. Too much like before. It makes me want to believe that everything's fine. That any second my phone will ring, and it'll be him and I just...I can't."

"Lia, I'm trying to help."

"You can't, though. There's nothing you can do to fix this—fix me."

"I don't want to *fix* you."

"Yes, you do. And you're trying too hard."

She nodded, but I could see that she didn't understand. "I'm sorry," she said again. "I'll give you space. Text me tomorrow. Or next week. Whenever. I'm here for you. Wyatt is too. We always will be."

We.

My stomach somersaulted, my mouth filling with resentment.

"No," I said firmly. "I need you out of my life. You and Wyatt."

She startled with disbelief. "Lia—"

I turned away.

I walked away.

She lost Beck too, but instead of being a comfort, a *friend*, I cast her out of my life.

I feel feverish now, the way I did that day in the gym foyer. Isaiah must notice how my cheeks burn scarlet because he reaches for my hand. He gives a quick, supportive squeeze. He lets go as the door swings open.

Macy.

She's let her hair grow past her shoulders, and she's sporting a tiny silver hoop in her nose, but she's still rocking her thick-framed glasses and her gap-toothed grin.

"Mace, hey."

She springs forward to hug me, laughing as she says, "Long time no see!" She hugs Isaiah too, and if she's surprised that the friend I mentioned is a boy, she doesn't let on. Leading us into the apartment, she says, "Wyatt will be home soon."

She shows us around an eclectically furnished living room, a tiny kitchen with a table for two, and the main bedroom, with mismatched nightstands and throw pillows slipcovered in faux fur. The guest room is tiny, housing only a futon, but still—I can't believe these friends of mine have a guest room. Isaiah and I drop our bags in the corner, then return to the

337

living room where Macy, a most charming hostess, serves a charcuterie board.

I grin as she sets cheddar and pepper jack, a wedge of Brie, a variety of crackers, and bunches of grapes on the coffee table. "Mace, you didn't have to go to any trouble."

"Sure, I did. That's a long-ass drive you just finished. Now, have some cheese."

Isaiah doesn't have to be told twice. While Macy fills me in on her classes—she's majoring in Communications—he builds cheese and cracker sandwiches, passing one over every so often. I devour them, trying not to sprinkle crumbs onto the sofa.

It's not long before Wyatt comes in with a joyful shout, embracing me like not a day has passed since he last saw me. He helps Isaiah polish off the food, launching a conversation about DC's sports teams. I don't know why I'm surprised by the way they're hitting it off; Wyatt's lively and Isaiah's affable, so of course they'll become friends. I smile, listening to them deep-dive into the talents and weaknesses of the Washington Wizards versus the Memphis Grizzlies.

Macy catches my eye, and nods toward the kitchen.

I follow her.

"I'm so glad you're here," she tells me after we've rounded the corner. "You have no idea how much I've missed you."

I come right out and say it, the apology I should've offered before I moved away. "I'm sorry, Macy. For everything. The way I treated you…the things I said that day at school. It was bullshit.

338

All of it. I wouldn't have blamed you if you never wanted to see me again."

"You were grieving. We all were."

"Yeah. But I left you to manage on your own."

"There's no right way to heal," she says graciously. "Trust me—I screwed up plenty along the way. Wyatt really struggled. He still does, sometimes. Beck was incomparable. A shining freaking star. Losing him...if it's been awful for me, I can't imagine how soul sucking it's been for you."

I nod, grasping her hand. "If I had to do it over, though, I'd be a better friend to you."

"I know," she says, and then she grins. "How about you make it up to me by sharing every single detail of the time we've been apart? Starting with how you came to know that hottie sitting in my living room."

DIZZYING

Seventeen Years Old, Virginia

Late Saturday night, after poke bowls with Macy and Wyatt and a hot shower that does little to loosen the kinks I earned after ten hours on the road, I push the door to the guest room open to find Isaiah. He snagged a shower right before me, and now he's sitting at the end of the futon in basketball shorts and a wrinkled T-shirt.

He looks me over, and his mouth turns up in a smile.

"I wasn't expecting company when I packed," I say, suddenly self-conscious of my ribbed tank and baggy sweats.

"What would you have brought if you'd known I was gonna tag along?"

I glance down at my pajamas. I shrug. "Probably this."

His smile stretches wide. "Good."

I turn to set my toiletry bag in my suitcase, then root in it aimlessly, too nervous to turn back around. I've spent the night with only one boy, and I analyzed and planned for and envisioned sleeping with Beck for literal years before I actually climbed into his bed. Tonight, Isaiah and me and a futon dressed in paisley sheets, is far less considered.

Behind me, the floor creaks.

Footsteps pad across the carpet.

Barely touching his chest to my back, he reaches for my hands, guiding them away from my suitcase. He runs his palms lightly up my arms. I begin to relax as he kneads the stiffness from my neck, my shoulders, my wrists, my fingers. I close my eyes and settle against his sternum, apprehensive to blissed in a matter of minutes. When his arms encircle me in a hug, I let go of a sigh. I could melt into the floor and, simultaneously, float skyward. Instead, I find myself thinking about how wretched this day must have been for him. Fresh off losing Naya, he's stepped into the pain of my past—and the life I used to share with someone else.

With a tug on my hand, he urges me to face him, and then, sleepy-soft, says, "I don't mind crashing on the floor. Or out on the couch."

"No. I'll be okay."

"You sure?"

I try hard to filter my needs and my hopes from the storm of emotions in my head. Unconvincingly I say, "I think so."

"I'll keep to my side of the bed if that's what you want."

I peer up at him, sweeping the contours of his face, the crooked line of his nose, the uncertainty of his smile. Our eye contact lingers.

His soul will offer yours a second match.

And then my needs and hopes coalesce, fusing into a clear vision. Isaiah and I, starting a fresh page. Isaiah and I, penning a romance all our own.

His hands glide up my back, and our breaths synchronize.

I walk to the futon and pull back the covers, then sit down.

"I want you to stay, Isaiah, and I don't want you to keep to your side of the bed."

We whisper late into the night.

He tells me about the cities he'll explore next year. The landmarks he'll visit. The streets he'll travel: Highway 1, Route 66, the Great River Road.

"You could come," he says, drawing me close.

I think about the au pair agency I read about online last night while he was driving. I recall the exhilaration I felt, considering the different locations I might choose. Germany, or South Africa, or Australia—Australia! I could go for a whole year. I could hang out with kids while making money and exploring the country of my dreams.

It sounds perfect.

But so does a year on the road with Isaiah.

"Think about it," he murmurs. "It'd be an adventure. An adventure all our own."

OFF THE RAILS

Seventeen Years Old, Virginia

Isaiah, Macy, Wyatt, and I spend Sunday watching movies and devouring bags of buttery microwave popcorn. We order pizza for dinner, then Wyatt and Isaiah fire up the Xbox and start a game of Madden NFL. Macy leaves for a study group, so I text Paloma to ask about Liam's arrival in River Hollow. She replies quickly, telling me they're the happiest couple there ever was, and I'm so glad for her. Then, reluctantly, I check in with my parents, sending bold lies about staying close to home and eating well.

I fear the moment we collide at tomorrow's ceremony, the moment they come to realize I'm full of shit.

Isaiah and I get in bed late, especially considering my early wake-up. I'm looking forward to more of what happened last night, and we're getting there when he leans back to ask, "What time do we need to leave tomorrow?"

For Mount Vernon, he means.

For Connor's retirement ceremony.

He thinks…he thinks he's coming with me?

"*I* need to leave by 7:15."

We're sharing his pillow, our faces a breath apart. His bewilderment is plain. "You don't want me there with you?"

I hurry to smooth the hurt from his face. "It's not that. I didn't think you'd want to come. Wouldn't it be weird?"

He pulls away, swinging his legs around to sit up. "I don't know, Lia. Would it?"

"My parents will be there."

"And they don't like me."

"They don't know you," I clarify.

He makes a fed-up noise.

I sit, too, straightening my top, smoothing my hair, trying to formulate a sound argument, one that won't intensify his hurt.

The best I can do, is "Beck's parents will be there too."

"No kidding."

I lean forward, resting my palm on his back. "I want you to get to know my mom and dad. And I want you to meet Bernie and Connor."

"Do you though?"

"Isaiah, yes. I just—tomorrow's not the right time."

"There's not really a better time. We're going home Tuesday. After graduation, I'm gone for a year. Who knows where you'll be."

I pull my hand away and whisper, "I don't know what you want me to say."

He turns, his gaze colliding with mine. "I want you to say that you're over him. Maybe I'm a dick, asking that of you, but Jesus—if you're not, what're we doing? I want you to say that I matter. Say that you care. Say that we'll move forward, together. I want you to call this what it is."

"What?" I ask. "What is it?"

"You know. You *know* I'm in love with you. But you won't acknowledge it—won't let yourself feel it. You keep me at arm's length so your conscience doesn't go off the rails."

"That's not fair."

"Yeah," he says miserably. "No shit."

I grit my teeth, so full of frustration I've lost the capacity to speak. How dare he put it out there—*I'm in love with you*—then insult me with his very next breath? How dare he heap pressure onto me, only to finish with a flippant *no shit*? How dare he make me feel cherished, and at the same time incandescent with rage?

I imagine it happening: the painstakingly constructed puzzle of our relationship shoved over a ledge, only to land with a devastating crash, pieces scattering, image unrecognizable.

I love him too, in a way that overwhelms me, in a way that makes me feel like I'm one kiss from losing myself all over again.

I let myself get swept away by my love for Beck. He never asked me to change, to sacrifice; he didn't have to. I gave myself over. I abandoned my goals and forgot my dreams willingly— gladly. Maybe it would've been worth it; if Beck and I had grown old together, I might never have had a second thought. But I know, now, all too well, that to yield to another relationship,

345

another boy—even a boy as selfless and kind as Isaiah—would be to undo eighteen months of healing, of rediscovering *me*.

"Remember what you promised last week during Ceramics?" he says, his voice rough with emotion.

I told him I'd never treat him like shit again.

But that's not what I'm doing.

By keeping my feelings quiet, I'm being gentle with him. By maintaining distance, I'm treating him with consideration. By going to Connor's ceremony alone, I'm sparing him stress, and discomfort, and hurt feelings.

I'm trying to do the right thing, for him and for me. But to attempt an explanation... I worry it'll look like I'm grappling. Making excuses. Dodging vulnerability.

He lays back down, toward the edge of the bed, unsatisfied with my silence.

I curl onto my side, swamped by sadness.

There's no way I can bring him to Mount Vernon.

A THREAD

LIA: Isaiah hates me.

PALOMA: No way.

LIA: I messed up. I hurt him.

MEAGAN: So fix it.

LIA: I don't know how. He doesn't think I'm over Beck.

SOPHIA: Aww. 😦 Where is he?

LIA: In bed.

PALOMA: Where are you?

LIA: In bed.

SOPHIA: The same bed?

MEAGAN: Obvs, Soph.

LIA: He's sleeping. We argued. He said harsh things. True things. I said the wrong things. What should I do?

PALOMA: Wake him. Say what you feel.

SOPHIA: Don't wake him. Let him sleep it off.

MEAGAN: Wake him. Seduce him into forgiveness.

LIA: Knew I could count on you for a laugh, Megs.

MEAGAN: But seriously. Talk tomorrow, after the ceremony. He'll have cooled off, and you'll have accomplished a hard thing. It'll go better.

PALOMA: Meagan, coming in hot with killer advice.

SOPHIA: One of the millions of reasons I love her.

PALOMA: Same, honestly.

MEAGAN: Lia? Proof of life?

LIA: I'm here. What if I don't go to college?

SOPHIA: Like, ever?

LIA: I don't know. Maybe a gap year?

PALOMA: Yessssss.

MEAGAN: Do it.

SOPHIA: But what about CVU?

LIA: I've changed my mind.

SOPHIA: Do Austin Peay with Megs and me. Start spring semester.

PALOMA: No—take a full year! How would you spend it?

LIA: Isaiah asked me to road trip with him. See the country.

SOPHIA: *swoon*

MEAGAN: Are you into that idea?

LIA: Very. But I've got ideas of my own.

PALOMA: Like?

LIA: An au pair program...in Australia.

MEAGAN: Bitchin'.

SOPHIA: Okay. That would be so cool.

PALOMA: Could we visit?

LIA: Obviously.

SOPHIA: But what about Isaiah? The road trip?

LIA: Virginia might be the end of us.

PALOMA: Nope.

SOPHIA: No way. That doesn't mean you can't pass on his trip though.

MEAGAN: Yeah. Take a year for you. Figure your shit out.

PALOMA: You two will survive it.

LIA: You think?

PALOMA: I know. You and Isaiah are goals.

LIA: Speaking of goals, things are still good with Liam?

PALOMA: Very good. He's no longer waitlisted.

LIA: What?! He's going to be a Trojan?!

PALOMA: Just like me. <3

MEAGAN: Lovesick.

PALOMA: Hey now!

MEAGAN: No worries—I am too.

SOPHIA: Aww!

LIA: I miss you guys.

SOPHIA: We miss you!

PALOMA: We'll see you Wednesday for your birthday! Buttercup Bakery?

LIA: Definitely.

MEAGAN: Let us know how tomorrow goes.

PALOMA: We're here for you, girl.

SOARING

Seventeen Years Old, Virginia

After a night of fitful sleep, my alarm blares before sunrise.

Connor's ceremony. Eight o'clock. George Washington's Mount Vernon.

I power through a shower, then dress in a burgundy sweater-dress, argyle tights, and camel boots before blowing out my hair and securing it in a neat pony. Then I rush through a makeup job that I'm hoping will make me appear more rested than I feel.

I'm gathering my keys, phone, and bag in the kitchen when Isaiah appears, standing bleary-eyed in the entryway.

"When will you be back?" he asks.

"Like, eleven?" I move closer, running a hand through his disheveled hair. I'm not angry the way I was last night. After texting with my friends, I got to thinking...Isaiah doesn't want to crash Connor's retirement ceremony; he just wants me to want him there.

I smooth my dress and ask, quietly, "Are you okay?"

He shakes his head. "I'm...I don't know. Struggling? But today's about you and your family and his family. I'm not gonna fuck it up."

He's never said Beck's name aloud. I'm not sure how I feel about that.

"I'll text when I'm on my way back."

"Yeah." Eyes downcast, he says, "Drive safe."

"Isaiah."

He lifts his chin, gaze cool, jaw set. "Do what you came to do. We'll talk later."

The air gleams with a dawn chill, but the sky is clear and the sun dazzles in the east. A day fit for celebrating.

I navigate to the highway, where I'm roadblocked by a jam of cars. Antsy, I weave in and out of lanes, trying to gain ground, but as soon as I've found a flow, brake lights explode in front of me. The clock ticks closer toward eight and then, appallingly, beyond.

When I park at the estate, I'm a knot of stress. It's been years since I was last at Mount Vernon, and by the time I make my way to the Visitor's Center and hurry around the Upper Garden and toward the Bowling Green, a large lawn in front of the stately main house, the ceremony is underway.

My dad stands before a few dozen people, distinguished in

his dress uniform, speaking about Connor's selfless and noble service. I hang by a grouping of trees in the back, near enough that I can hear, but not so close that my arrival interrupts. While I listen, I find Bernie and the twins in the front row, as well as her mother and both of Connor's parents. My mom's on Bernie's opposite side, her hair like spun gold in the morning light.

I could cry, looking at these people I love so much.

Dad closes his remarks, finishing with, "It's an honor to have served this great nation with you, Connor, but my truest privilege over the last quarter century has been your friendship."

My chest fills with gratitude. For so long, the Byrnes have been knit together with the Grahams. How fortunate we are, to have each other.

If Beck were here, I'd take his hand.

Before it's Connor's turn to speak, he accepts an abundance of medals and certificates, his grin somehow both dignified and mischievous, so much like his son's once was.

Oh, my heart.

He clears his throat before launching into a highlight reel of his military career. He speaks of his parents, his earliest enthusiasts. He speaks of Bernie, his great love. He speaks of the Grahams, his chosen family. He speaks of his daughters, harbingers of happiness.

He speaks of Beck.

"My oldest child, my son, is no longer with us. That's still an unbearable reality to reckon with. His passing is, in large part, why I've chosen to leave Army life behind. My family needs me—all of me." He pauses, letting his sorrow dissipate as he draws a shaky breath. "I've also become too old and too creaky to max out push-ups on the PT test."

There's a smattering of laughter. Like their auburn hair, Beck and his dad share a flair for levity, a knack for comedic timing. Thank God for that, because I've been teetering on tears since I stepped onto George Washington's lawn.

"I thank you for coming today," Connor continues, "whether you battled the Beltway or flew across the county. Your enduring support confirms my decision to retire. Your smiling faces give me comfort, and bring me a hell of a lot of happiness. It's funny: When you've trudged through deep pain, the joys that follow are all the greater."

A hollow screech echoes across the historic estate.

Everyone looks up as an eagle glides overhead, the white feathers of its head stark against the cobalt sky.

It calls again, dipping low, showing off, exuding credence.

A shiver dances across my skin.

Beck is with us.

He always will be.

I drop my gaze back to the ceremony to find that Connor's face has changed. He looks astounded—except he's not watching the eagle anymore. He's staring right at me. It must take him a moment to make sense of what he's seeing, to register my presence as more than a trick of the light. His face breaks into a smile.

Bernie turns to find the source of her husband's surprise.

When she spots me, her mouth falls open.

So does my mom's.

My dad lifts a hand to shade his eyes, peering through the sunshine to where I stand.

In perfect unison, the twins squeal, "Lia!" and before Bernie can snag their little hands, they're scampering through the grass and into my open arms.

Norah and Mae stay by my side as their daddy's ceremony comes to an official end.

The eagle lingers, swooping and soaring in the sky.

Connor has guests to receive, but Mom, Dad, and Bernie hurry to where the twins and I wait. Bernie wraps me in a hug before nudging me into Mom's arms. She holds me tightly, smoothing a hand over my hair, and then it's Dad's turn.

"You were supposed to stay close to home," he says. For a second I think he's mad, but when he pulls back, his eyes are full of fondness.

"How did you…?" Mom asks.

"I drove, Friday night. I left after your flight took off. I just—I couldn't miss this."

I broke rules. I lied. Our dynamic has never been messier. But I'm hoping for grace.

Mom loops an arm around my shoulders. "I'm so glad you're here."

"Me too," Dad says.

"Where are you staying?" Bernie asks as the twins run circles around us.

"Near GMU, with Macy and Wyatt."

Dad ruffles my hair. "I can't believe you drove all the way here by yourself."

I swallow, hoping his goodwill endures my next bit of news. "Actually, Isaiah came with me."

If he's unhappy, he doesn't let on. I look at Bernie, trying to discern whether she recognizes the name, whether Mom told her about the new person in my life. I find pain in her expression, but acceptance too. She reaches for me, and I lean into her, wishing I hadn't spent the last year and a half avoiding her hugs.

"I'm glad you haven't been alone," she whispers.

Bernie's never given me anything but the truth.

"You're not upset?"

"Girlie, no. I expected you to move on eventually. What you and Beck had was extraordinary. Your next love will be too."

I nod, teary all over again.

She smiles. "All I want is for you to be happy. So would Beck. He'd want you to live, Lia. He'd want you to love."

The eagle calls out, a resonant *caw* slicing through the tranquil morning.

We watch it ascend over the estate, wings spread wide, beak aimed toward the Potomac.

We watch it disappear into the dazzle of the spring sun.

CHANGE OF HEART

Seventeen Years Old, Virginia

Bernie and Connor host a brunch reception after the ceremony at a nearby restaurant called Café Americana. They've reserved a private room, starring a buffet of quiches, pastries, chafing dishes full of eggs, breakfast meats, and platters overflowing with fruit. I follow my parents through the line, filling my plate with pineapple, bacon, and a glazed Danish, then join them at an empty table. Bernie, Connor, and the twins sit nearby, with Nana, Bernie's mother, and Grandpa and Grandma Byrne.

Dad gives me enough time to finish a piece of bacon before saying, "What's—" he clears his throat "—Isaiah up to this morning?"

I poke a chunk of pineapple with my fork. "He's waiting for me at Macy and Wyatt's."

Mom smiles. "It was good of him to drive all this way with you."

"I think so, too," Dad says. "I'm glad you decided to come. Having you at the ceremony made Beck's absence easier to bear—for Mom and me, but especially for the Byrnes. It wouldn't've been right, the both of you missing."

It's true. Watching that eagle fly over Mount Vernon affirmed that I'd made the right decision, returning to Virginia. Witnessing the Byrnes' joy at my arrival, I wish I would've visited them sooner, but I'm proud of myself for coming when it counted the most. "I wanted Connor and Bernie to know how much I care," I tell my parents. "I wanted Mae and Norah to know how much I love them."

"They do," Mom says.

"I love you too," I say. "I've been the worst about showing lately, but I do."

She leans in to hug me, smelling of jasmine and comfort. She holds on a few extra moments before straightening, dabbing away a tear with her napkin.

Dad says, "When we get home, we hope Isaiah will come by the house. Supporting you in making this trip...he must be a good kid. A good friend. We want to get to know him."

"Okay," I say, although after last night, I'm not sure Isaiah's going to want to have anything to do with me, let alone make nice with my parents.

Today, though, I can spark change. I can start to repair my relationships. I can reroute my course. I meet Mom's eyes, then Dad's. "I have something else to talk to you about... I don't want to go to CVU anymore."

Dad releases a breath that sounds like relief.

Mom asks, "Why the change of heart?"

"Isaiah and I stopped in Charlottesville on our way here. Being there without Beck...it wasn't what it once was. It never will be. I just wish I hadn't applied early decision. I screwed up so bad—my whole future, probably."

"No, lovey," Mom says. "This is not a mistake that's unfixable."

Dad nods. "We'll contact CVU. Help you explain the situation."

"But the deposit."

He grimaces. "I'd rather lose the money than leave you on that campus knowing you won't be happy. Don't worry about the deposit, Millie. Focus on what comes next. After graduation. After this summer."

"Not college," I say. Watching his face fall, seeing Mom's eyes go round, I add, "Not yet. I need to figure some stuff out, just be me for a while. I need an adventure."

They look at one another. Education is important. College has always been assumed. They might tell me I have to go, which would lead to more conflict.

Or they might support me. They might trust me to set out on a path of my own.

When they look back to me, I find approval in their eyes.

"What kind of adventure?" Dad asks, and my heart overflows with love.

"I'm not sure yet. All I know is that I want to do more. See more. *Be* more."

358

"I can get on board with that," Mom says.

Dad smiles judiciously. "I'm not opposed."

"Opposed to what?" Connor asks, coming over to thump Dad on the shoulder. Bernie joins us too, taking the chair next to Mom, leaving the twins to finish brunch with their grandparents.

"Lia's going on an adventure," Mom tells them. "After graduation."

"Oh, a gap year!" Bernie says. "I wish we could have done one, Hannah. Imagine the trouble we would've gotten into!"

Connor snorts. Dad laughs, rolling his eyes.

"Too late now," Mom says, grinning. "We'll have to live vicariously through our girl."

"Yes! Then CVU—so exciting!"

"About CVU," I say, hoping Connor and Bernie will be as understanding as my parents have been. "I just…I can't. Not without Beck."

Connor tweaks my ponytail. "You've gotta do what's right for you, kiddo."

"Absolutely," Bernie says. "We're in your corner no matter where you end up—so long as it's not Mississippi State."

Dad laughs. "She knows better."

They fall into reminiscing about their Ole Miss days, as they so often do.

I sit back in my chair feeling, for the first time in many, many months, excited about the future before me.

THE MALL

Seventeen Years Old, Washington DC

After brunch, I take Isaiah to DC.

Because he's traveled all this way and should see what our nation's capital has to offer.

Because if I can survive a walk around The Mall, I can survive anything.

Because I owe him an explanation.

I owe him an apology.

We ride the Metro and, after disembarking at L'Enfant Plaza, walk to the Tidal Basin. The day has warmed, and the cherry trees wear baby-pink buds. We navigate the busy paths, cruising around the water and past the Jefferson Memorial, where my throat tightens.

I breathe through the worst of it, and soldier on.

We check out the FDR Memorial, one of my dad's favorites, before moving on to the Martin Luther King, Jr. Memorial. Isaiah takes it in, reverent. He's been quiet—I know he's not over what happened last night—but I'm grateful to him for indulging me in this touristy walk. I can't imagine making my first trip back to The Mall with anyone but him.

Somberly, we approach the Lincoln Memorial.

I can do it: I can climb the stairs, all the way to the top.

I'm okay—I know I am.

A few steps up, though, I'm suddenly not okay.

I stop, turning to face the Reflecting Pool, drawing a wheezy breath.

I fucking adore you, Beck told me before we kissed and claimed our fate.

I startle when Isaiah touches my shoulder.

"You good?"

I nod though, no. I'm most definitely *not* good.

"Want to keep going?"

"You can," I say.

"Without you?"

The last thing I want is for him to continue on his own, but my body is rebelling.

Lungs: sluggish.

Muscles: trembling.

Vision: spotty.

I nod again, disappointed in myself. *Pissed* at myself. I sink down to sit on a cold, hard step, and track Isaiah's progress. He gets halfway to the statue before pausing to peer over his shoulder. Our eyes meet. He lifts his hand in a subdued wave. I smile encouragingly, inhaling full breaths now.

He pivots and ascends.

My attention catches on a family of four, a pair of fathers holding hands, and two children, a boy and a girl who look to be close in age, one a little taller than the other. They're romping around by the water and the stockier of their dads keeps trying to wrangle them, but they're full of energy, giggling. They play the way Beck and I used to: freely, jubilantly.

And then, low in my ear: *Go, Amelia. Play. Love. Live.*

I make myself a promise...

I will embrace my new fate.

Rising, I turn to search for Isaiah, except he's disappeared beneath the overhang of the memorial.

I don't even think about it—I dash up the stairs, dodging tourists, focused singularly on making it to the top. When I do, I'm exhilarated, my newfound fortitude solid as the marble beneath my feet.

Isaiah's one of many surrounding Lincoln's statue, gazing up at his chiseled face. I walk toward him with brisk, confident steps until I collide with his back and thread my arms beneath his. I feel him startle, but as soon as I clasp my hands into a hug, fitting my cheek in the hollow between his shoulder blades, he exhales, ribs contracting, lungs emptying, before turning to gather me against his chest. I feel the vibration of his heart through his sweatshirt and jacket. Mine's pounding too. We stand together a long time, silently piecing our puzzle back together.

When at last he draws back to look at me, he says, "What changed?"

"I finally made peace with what I want."

He smiles, then leads me into the sunshine and down the steps.

Hand in hand, we continue around the Reflecting Pool, stopping when we reach the Washington Monument, where we find a patch of grass and sit to look back the way we came.

He was right: I've been careful—with my heart and his.

I've been reluctant to trust, both myself and him.

Instead of treasuring the past, I've let it control me.

"I'm sorry about last night," he says before I have a chance to share my revelations. "I had no right asking to go to the ceremony with you. I shouldn't have given you shit about it, but I was jealous. Which is fucked, I know. How can I be resentful of a guy who's not around to compete?"

"It's not a competition, though. It never has been."

"Jesus, I know. He—*Beck*—will always be a part of your story, and last night I wasn't respectful of that. I don't blame you for being mad."

"I'm not. Not anymore. I need you to understand, though… I'll never be over him. He was my childhood. My best friend. My first love."

"I get it. And I'm starting to realize… It's him I have to thank for who you are today."

I smile. "He would've liked you."

He turns the ring on my finger in a slow circle. "I'm not sure about that."

"I am. After he died, I thought I'd lost my chance at happiness.

How could I find joy in a world without Beck? He would have liked you because you showed me that my heart's capacity to love is infinite. It has room to keep memories of him, and room for new memories with you."

His eyes flicker with hope. "What're you saying?"

I weave my fingers through his. "I'm saying that somewhere along the way, I fell in love with you."

He grins. "It was that first day for me."

I laugh. "When I sobbed all over your shirt, then accosted you while you waited for your ride? You should've run fast and far."

"Then I wouldn't be here, with a girl who makes the future feel a hell of a lot less scary. I was serious the other day, Lia. My road trip could be *our* road trip."

I shake my head. "I can't. As much as I want to go with you, I need to spend next year living for me."

"You're gonna end up on the other side of the world, aren't you?"

I smile, nudging his shoulder with mine. "Hopefully."

He opens my hand, then uses his forefinger to draw a heart on my palm. He scoots my sleeve to my elbow before tracing a path of hearts up my arm. When he runs out of room, he says, softly, "What about when the year's done? When our adventures are over?"

"Then we start a new adventure. Together."

He leans in to touch my jaw, grazing his thumb along my lower lip before his mouth presses a kiss to the same place.

"Together," he whispers.

FORETOLD

Epilogue: One Year Before

A few months after Beck died, I got it in my head that I needed to consult a clairvoyant.

When she was seventeen, my mom had her future foretold, a fortune that became a compass, prophesying her life's most significant events. I was sure a reading of my own would give me the direction I'd lacked since losing Beck—since losing my fate.

Scouring the Internet, I found a psychic reader in Arlington, a woman named Jasmine who, in her website's headshot, looked safe enough. I booked an appointment for a cold afternoon in early March. The drive took forever and, by the time I stood at the storefront with *Jasmine's Readings* painted on its window, a brisk wind stinging my cheeks, I was a tightly coiled spring.

Bells tinkled as I pushed open the door. Stepping into the small lobby, I wondered if my mom had been so nervous before her long-ago reading.

An interior door swept open, and a woman stepped through. In the movies, psychics always have robes, bangle bracelets, and whimsically braided hair, but she looked like she was headed to the grocery store in khakis, a cable-knit sweater, and brown boots. Her face was lightly made up, and her brown hair was loose. She looked me up and down before offering a smile.

"Lia Graham?"

I nodded, then blurted, "You don't look like a psychic."

Her smile became bemused. "You don't look like someone who needs a reading."

"Is that a casual observation or a professional conclusion?"

She lifted a brow. "Would you like to come back to my office?"

I followed her into a space that wasn't unlike my grief counselor's: desk, sofa, crowded bookshelf, vining plants. No star charts, shells, or bones. No incense or tarot cards.

She gestured to the sofa. I sat.

She relaxed into the chair opposite it and said, "Well, Lia. What is it that you're interested in learning?"

I hesitated, then stumbled over a response. "I guess—I just—I need to know what I'm supposed to do. You know...with my life?"

She looked at me, unspeaking, for a long time. I'd expected a certain level of uneasiness, but I felt utterly exposed, and deeply uncomfortable, like she was rifling around in my cache of secrets. I didn't avert my gaze, though. It seemed important to remain vulnerable.

In a businesslike tone, she said, "You've experienced a loss."

"Is it that obvious?"

She gave a tight smile. "You're...astray. You won't always be."

"Promise?" I asked, a weak attempt at humor.

Crisply, she said, "The loss was recent."

"It's been ninety-nine days."

"He was important to you. Your lives were entwined."

My eyes burned as my vision blurred. In a small voice, I said, "It still feels that way."

"You weren't expecting his death."

"No."

"And now...your soul misses its mirror."

The woman I spoke of—your soul's mirror—will mother your daughter's fated.

A bone-deep shiver rattled through me.

Clamping my hands together, I dammed my tears.

My sorrow must've been palpable, though, because she said, in a voice gentler than anything I'd heard from her yet, "I'm very sorry."

I nodded, afraid speech would steal my composure.

"My impression is that you're seeking specifics," she went on. "You asked what you're supposed to do with your life and...I don't know. You'll face choices—difficult choices made more so because you have a unique understanding of the fragility of our existence. Sometimes you'll make the wrong choice. Sometimes you'll choose exactly right, but the outcome won't be what you expect. Regardless, the choices are all yours."

I shifted on the sofa, frustration building. "But you're supposed to tell me my future."

367

You're supposed to help me, I thought despairingly.

She leaned in, resting her elbows on her knees. "I'm a guide, not a choreographer. All I can tell you is that your heart will heal. Someday you'll stop counting the days he's been gone. Someday you'll laugh without second-guessing whether you're allowed to feel joy. Someday you'll think of him and instead of feeling like you can't breathe, can't *exist*, you'll warm in the glow of his memory."

I shook my head, unable to imagine the scenarios she described.

"Someday," she said with the sincerity of a promise, "you'll love again. You'll cherish that love because you know the fickleness of forever."

She stood. Reluctantly, I did too. I followed her into the lobby, irritated at having wasted my time, furious to be without a fortune.

I wanted fate.

I wanted magic.

I wanted hope.

In the foyer, she startled me with a hug, one as prolonged and discomfiting as the look she gave me when I sat down in her office. There, in her warm embrace, my body began to sense what my brain lacked the wherewithal to register: a shift, a current of electricity traveling a closed circuit between the two of us. My skin cooled, goose bumps rising on my forearms, the hairs on the back of my neck standing on end.

She spoke in a tone soft but sure, her voice urgent in my ear. "He'll appear when you least expect it, long limbs and ebony hair, scarred on the surface and deep within, nose crooked as a woodland trail. In you, he'll find a confidant. In your heart, faith will regain its footing. He'll embrace you as I am now and if you let him...his soul will offer yours a second match."

When she pulled away, her eyes were distant, her mouth a solemn line. She pushed the door open and waved me out into the cold.

My heart, for weeks still and dark, flickered, then flared.

A new future, promised to me.

A Geographical History of Amelia Graham

Ages: 0, 1, 2
  Duty Station: Fort Drum
    Location: Evans Mills, New York
      (Location of the Byrnes: Fort Riley,
        Junction City, Kansas)

Ages: 3, 4, 5
  Duty Station: Fort Bragg
    Location: Spring Lake, North Carolina
      (Location of the Byrnes: Fort Bragg,
        Spring Lake, North Carolina)

Ages: 6, 7
  Duty Station: Fort Leavenworth
    Location: Leavenworth, Kansas
      (Location of the Byrnes: Fort
        Stewart, Hinesville, Georgia)

Ages: 8, 9, 10
  Duty Station: Joint Base Lewis-McChord
    Location: Lacey, Washington

(Location of the Byrnes: Joint Base Lewis-McChord, Lacey, Washington)

Ages: 11, 12, 13
 Duty Station: Fort Carson
   Location: Colorado Springs, Colorado
     (Location of the Byrnes: Fort Jackson, Columbia, South Carolina)

Ages: 14, 15, 16
 Duty Station: Pentagon
   Location: Rosebell, Virginia
     (Location of the Byrnes: Fort Belvoir, Rosebell, Virginia)

Ages: 17
 Duty Station: Fort Campbell
   Location: River Hollow, Tennessee
     (Location of the Byrnes: Fort Belvoir, Rosebell, Virginia)

ACKNOWLEDGMENTS

From start to finish, I've never experienced such joy working on a book. I'm indebted to each and every person who had a hand in the completion of *Everything I Promised You*.

I feel so fortunate to call myself a Sourcebooks author. Annette Pollert-Morgan, thank you for your expertise, thoughtfulness, and enthusiasm. Thank you for caring about Lia, Beck, and Isaiah as much as I do, and for asking all the right questions. Working with you has been a dream! To those who had a role in the acquisition of this book, and to those who helped make it shine, including Kay Birkner, Jenny Lopez, Thea Voutiritsas, Sarah Brody, Stephanie Rocha, Neha Patel, and Kerri Resnick, thank you for your time, talent, and creativity. Thanks, too, to Karen Masnica, Rebecca Atkinson, and Delaney Heisterkamp in marketing and publicity. Finally, Dominique Raccah, you are an inspiration.

I'm enormously grateful to my agent, Pam Gruber, whose guidance I lucked into so serendipitously. Your feedback, patience, and championing have helped me become a better (and happier!) writer. A heartfelt thanks to the whole team at High Line Literary Collective. Additionally, so much appreciation to Heather Baror-Shapiro at Baror International, Inc. for her incredible foreign representation.

Alison Miller and Elodie Nowodazkij, my first readers and my writer besties, thank you for your critiques, commiseration, and celebrations. Temre Beltz, Jessica Patrick, and Christina June, thanks so much for your friendship and continued support. Thanks, too, to the community of Monterey-area writers—Liz Parker in particular—who made drafting this story much less lonely.

Everything I Promised You is a deeply personal book, both in its portrayal of military families and its depiction of a teenager who's grown up in the foster care system. I've been an Army spouse even longer than I've been a writer, and my appreciation for service members and their families is boundless. Cheers to the friends we've made at our many duty stations. To the military brats who've befriended *my* military brats—I aspire to your level of kindness and resiliency. Liz, Donna, and Virginia, our angels in child welfare, you have my infinite gratitude.

Mom and Dad, thank you for giving me the childhood that went on to inspire the warm family dynamics in this story. Bev and Phil, you are an exemplary military couple; thank you for your outpouring of love. And heaps of appreciation to my brothers, Mike and Zach; my siblings-in-law, Jena, Michele, Danielle, Andy, Sam, and Kacie; my incredibly supportive aunts, uncles, and cousins; and all of my nieces and nephews.

Claire, you were the very first teenager to read this story; your adoration of its characters was exactly the encouragement I needed. Thank you for your compliments and criticisms, and for being my OG fan. Lizzie, your awe at seeing Mama's books in libraries is the very best motivation. I can't wait for you to read this one someday! Love you so much, girlies!

Matt, you are an exceptional provider, nurturer, humorist, and best friend. The sacrifices you make for our family are never unnoticed, and always appreciated. Thank you for starring in my love story.

ABOUT THE AUTHOR

Katy Upperman is a graduate of Washington State University, a former elementary school teacher, an Army spouse, and an insatiable reader. As well as *Everything I Promised You*, her novels for young adults include *Kissing Max Holden, How the Light Gets In*, and *The Impossibility of Us*, which won the 2019 YAVA Award for Excellence in YA Literature by a Virginia author. When she's not writing, Katy can be found baking batches of chocolate chip cookies or exploring California's beaches with her husband and two daughters.

sourcebooks fire

Home of the hottest trends in YA!

Visit us online and
sign up for our newsletter at
FIREreads.com

. . . .

Follow
@sourcebooksfire
online